THE
A'ZYON
WARRIOR

THE A'ZYON WARRIOR

THE ARMOURED BUTTERFLY BOOK ONE

TRUDY ADAMS

Ambassador International
GREENVILLE, SOUTH CAROLINA & BELFAST, NORTHERN IRELAND

www.ambassador-international.com

The A'zyon Warrior
The Armoured Butterfly, Book One

©2020 by Trudy Adams

ISBN: 978-1-62020-679-9
eISBN: 978-1-62020-715-4
Library of Congress Control Number: 2020941738

Scripture taken from the New King James Version®. Copyright © 1982 by Thomas Nelson. Used by permission. All rights reserved.

Cover Design by Megan McCullough
Interior Typesetting by Hannah Nichols
Ebook Conversion by Anna Riebe Raats

AMBASSADOR INTERNATIONAL
Emerald House
411 University Ridge, Suite B14
Greenville, SC 29601, USA
www.ambassador-international.com

AMBASSADOR BOOKS
The Mount
2 Woodstock Link
Belfast, BT6 8DD, Northern Ireland, UK
www.ambassadormedia.co.uk

The colophon is a trademark of Ambassador, a Christian publishing company.

To Stephanie

With thanks to the following people for helping me to refine this story over time: Mum and Dad, Belinda Shaw, Ken and Margaret Smith, June Gray, Kylie Kelly, Fae Lund-Colon and Lucy Myers.

Cazarma

Sapphire Lake

Rydmarien River

Rydmarden

Hyandya

Hazmere Desert

Red Mountain

Ellaway

The Red River

Jazmarda

The Keeper's Mountains

Keep

Valley of Kest

Eturbelec

Kest River

Katurba

Jawren River

Saltran

Red Bay

The Hewn Mountains

Rorinhall

Kingdoms of the West

The Rhea Lands

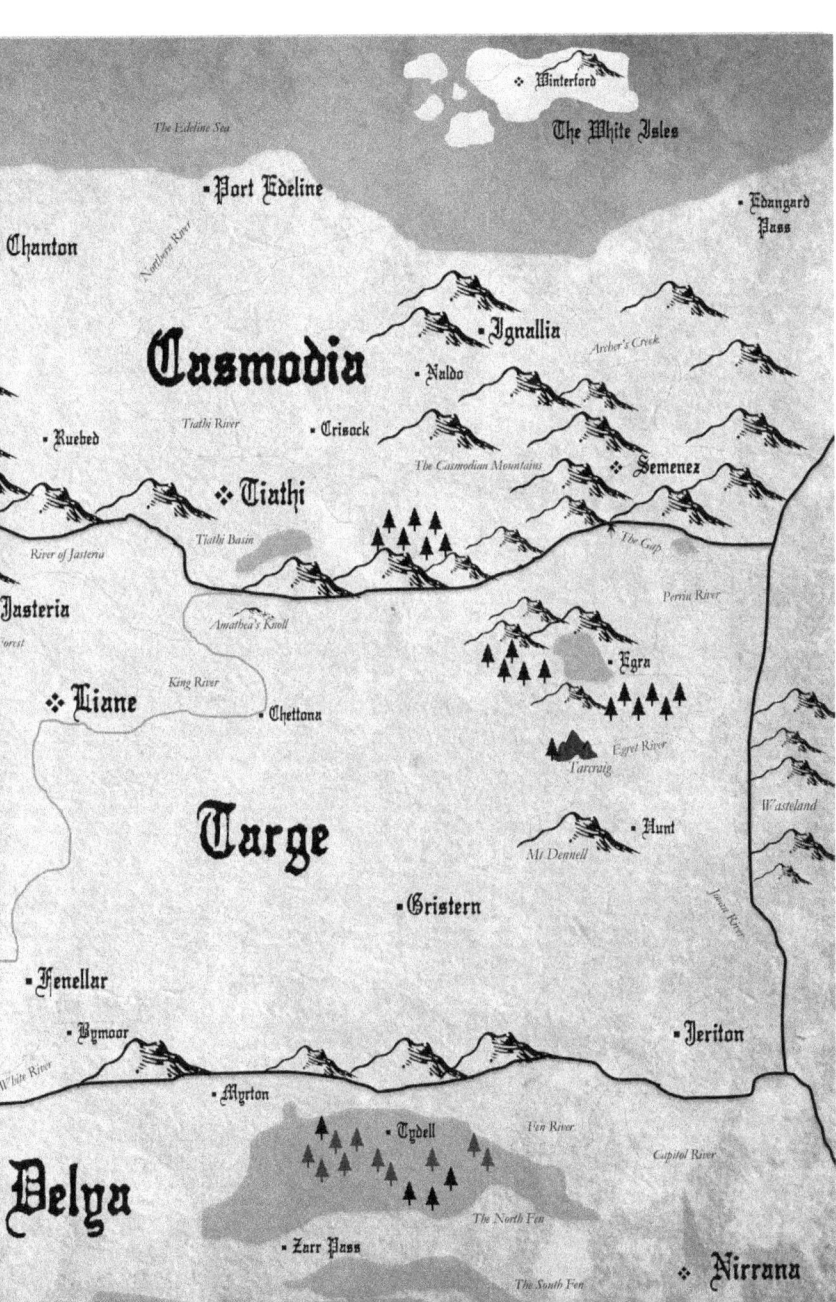

CHARACTER PRONUNCIATIONS

Adaliah—*A-dar-le-ah*

Elryane—*El-rye-an*

Darj—*Darge*

Zavad—*Za-vard*

Naclen—*Na-clen*

Amaz—*A-marz*

Jenethea—*Jen-ee-thee-a*

Elhian—*El-high-an*

Edangard—*Ed-an-guard*

Cades—*Kay-dees*

Jag Warhin—*War-hin*

Hae—*Hay*

Parrian—*Pa-ree-an*

Hazaka—*Har-zack-a*

Cazine—*Ca-zeen*

Though an army may encamp against me,
My heart shall not fear.

Psalm 27:3

1
THE VALLEY OF KEST

The first thing that stirred me was the stag's wet nose pressing against my cheek. The second was a branch taking hold of my clothing and scratching my collarbone. I opened my eyes and found myself floating on my back in a wide, shallow river. A wave of cold water washed over my face and slipped into my lungs. I spat it back out, coughing and gasping for breath until my insides were burning and tired.

Where am I?

I pulled myself up so I was sitting on the riverbed with my legs and bare feet stretched out in front of me. My black hair clung to my forehead and neck in strands that I clumsily pushed away. Taking deep breaths, I saw my rippled reflection in the water and was met with bloodshot eyes and a pale face.

What happened?

I ripped my clothes away from the imprisoning branch that was reaching across the river. The cool water swelled over my legs in waves as I watched the stag walk away and disappear behind some thick bramble. I turned my calloused hands over in front of me—they were almost blue. A tall mountain range followed one side of the river. The highest peak was tipped with red, like a sword point dipped in blood. The mountains looked old and it felt like they were gazing at me. Somehow, I sensed they should be familiar, but they weren't.

Nothing was.

I tried to stand and follow the stag, but my waterlogged and frozen legs gave way beneath me. I fell and cut my hand on a sharp rock. The blood ran into the water. I gritted my teeth and covered the wound with my other hand, now feeling both drowsy and confused. 'Where am I?' I asked aloud, my voice shaky. I searched my mind for an answer, but it was as empty as a cloudless sky.

Nature did not echo back an answer to my question either, and I was too cold to try again. I floated my body on the water while I felt for smoother rocks beneath with my good hand. The current was strong, and I had to grip the rocks tightly to pull myself against it and towards the shore.

My fingers dug into the muddy bank. I dragged myself up and lay down on a patch of grass. The sun was painfully blinding; I draped an arm across my eyes. My body insisted that I sleep, and I didn't have the strength to fight it. While the day faded around me, I drifted in and out of consciousness. As the sun disappeared, so, too, did any warmth. I began to shiver and felt close to vomiting more than once. I put a hand on my stomach, trying to settle the nausea. When I woke later, the wound on my hand was still weeping. I tore a rag off my already worn clothes and wrapped it around the cut twice and held it until the bleeding stopped.

It wasn't until the full moon rose that my head cleared enough to think. I gripped my stomach and carefully pulled myself upright. I gazed at my surroundings again, unsure of the valley's beauty. I spotted a purple light somewhere in the trees, but it disappeared so quickly I thought perhaps I had imagined it.

I closed my eyes and tried to remember what had happened to me. I searched my mind again for an image, a thought . . . a memory . . . but nothing came to me.

I couldn't remember anything, not even my own name. I knew that I should have one. I knew that other people existed and that they had names, but I couldn't remember mine. Tears dripped down my cheeks, and my hands started shaking.

I crawled to the base of a large beech tree where small autumn leaves had fallen in the wind, making it a soft place to rest. I eased myself onto the leaves. My back felt swollen and sore across my shoulder blades. My wrists looked raw with faded bruises and old cuts around them like bands, and my legs were aching as if I had run for hours.

I noticed a long and narrow sword thrust into the trunk above my head, the sort that would cut through the air swiftly. The name 'Bagred' was engraved into the blade and there were streaks of dried blood on the steel.

This is not a place of rest.

This is a place of war.

I flinched at a noise behind me. I held my breath and listened. I heard it again—a footstep crunching on grass. A dark figure was crouched by the water further down the riverbank, staring back at me. I scrambled to my feet.

'Stop!' the man shouted. He unsheathed a sword and ran towards me. 'How . . . how are you alive?' He lifted his sword and glanced back over his shoulder. 'She's over here!' He gripped his weapon with both hands and looked at me as if I were something between a ghost and a dangerous animal.

I staggered back against the tree. 'Who are you?' I asked. He was wearing a blue tunic with a pattern of white curls across his chest, but it was the blade in his hand that kept my attention.

'T-there's no need to fight,' he said, ignoring my question. 'It's her!' he called over his shoulder again. 'We're over here!'

Someone in the distance yelled back.

'Fight? What do you mean? Why would—'

He raised his sword and struck at me, but I instinctively stepped out of the way and the blade landed in the dirt.

'Please—' I held up my palms in a desperate attempt to protect myself, but the man struck at me again.

I ducked under his arm and ran towards the river, stumbling through the water in the moonlight and limping across the grass on the other side as fast as I could. The man's footsteps were heavy, determined, and always just behind me. Every part of me hurt, but the vicious look in his eyes when I glanced back and his fierce intent to kill kept me going. I ran onwards, tripping over tufts of grass and dead branches until we entered an autumn forest.

I searched for a place to hide. I felt too weak to go on, but I couldn't escape the man's sight.

'We're over here!' he called again.

'Keep after her!' a second voice shouted.

I looked back; there were now three men chasing me.

'Don't let her get away!'

I turned and ran over a small hill. I slipped down the other side but, when I regained my footing, I saw a campfire ahead. Three more men were asleep around it. Hearing my pursuers running down the hill behind me, I hurried towards the campfire. 'Help! I need help!'

I drew closer and saw that the three men were wearing the same blue tunic with white curls. They lurched to their feet at my call and unsheathed their swords. I came to a sudden stop, swaying on my feet.

'How did you survive?' one of them demanded. He struck at me, but I took an unsteady step out of the way.

The other soldiers caught up and all six of them pointed their blades at me. There was fear in their eyes—desperation—as if they were confronted with a beast and could not let it escape. They kept their distance.

I didn't understand. *Who am I?*

I saw their horses tethered to a tree. They were watching us with a calmness that suggested they were used to battle.

The men glanced at each other. 'You grab her,' one said to another.

'No. You report directly to Jag. You should do it.'

I lowered myself to the ground until I was resting on one knee, my legs aching again. I put a hand on the dirt as if to steady myself.

'Look, she's just a child!' a third man said.

I slowly drew a handful of dirt into my palm.

The third man walked towards me. 'Come on. The fight's over.'

I waited until he took one more step. Then, I stood and threw the dirt into his face.

He cried out and raised a hand to his eyes, stumbling backwards. The others fell back in a panic, almost losing their footing and their blades. Only one lunged for me with his hand, but he was far too out of reach. I took my chance and ran for the horses.

I mounted the nearest one and dug my heels into his side while the men shouted behind me. The black horse lifted his head and neighed, violently snapping his tether. He lurched forward and sped down a leafy path. The soldiers yelled after us.

'Run, Bagred,' I said to the horse. The name from the blade in the tree seemed to suit him. I pressed my heels into his sides again and clung to the reins.

2

CAPTURED

I ducked under tree branches as I rode, recoiling at every hooting owl and shuffling leaf as I glanced over my shoulder like a frightened deer. I was terrified that the men pursuing me would appear at any moment. I imagined their figures lurking amongst the trees at every step, watching me.

Hunting me.

I couldn't make sense of what had just happened. I couldn't remember what I'd done to cause such a violent reaction. I didn't know where I was going, but I didn't slow down either. I needed to put as much distance as possible between me and my pursuers.

Why couldn't I remember my life? My parents, my childhood, my name? If I knew where I belonged, I could return there. If I knew who my friends were, I could ask for help. But I knew nothing.

The sun was just rising above the horizon when the yellow forest ended. The tree line stopped, and suddenly I was faced with boundless plains. I'd been afraid amongst the tall trees, but now I felt exposed. I stopped at the edge of the forest. My stomach was grumbling, but I had no idea where to get food. I didn't have any weapons for hunting, and there were no provisions in the saddlebag apart from a bit of tobacco and some tea leaves. I didn't have any water, but even if I did, I couldn't have lit a fire to boil tea; the smoke would have given me away.

I have to keep going.

I peered at the sun ahead of me, reasoning that I'd been riding east from the moment I'd mounted Bagred. I turned him to the south so the sun wasn't piercing my eyes.

Surely there's a town close by. Surely I will find help there.

An hour or two passed as the sun rose higher into the bowl-like sky. My stomach rumbled and my mouth felt parched. I was starting to feel faint. I chewed on some of the dry tea leaves, but they were bitter and unsatisfying. I could feel them sticking to my teeth and tried to scratch them off.

Bagred took advantage of my waning energy and slowed to a lazy trot, taking sporadic chomps at attractive clumps of grass. I envied his full belly. I let him wander for a while but regretted it when I heard his hooves click on gravel.

I'd been riding with my eyes half closed, but now I was alert again. We'd reached a road. A long line of people stretched ahead of me. My heart began to race.

What if they want to kill me, too?

But they weren't my pursuers. They were a dishevelled mob, walking towards me like a herd of livestock. There were women and children and a few older men. They looked like me, with blue eyes, raven hair and pale skin. I was still too confused and scared to speak to them, to find out where they were going and why. A few grubby children smiled at me as they passed. A tiny girl was crying, and her mother was trying to comfort her, but she was holding back tears herself. I found myself unable to move as they walked by. I could feel their sadness and knew even then that some of it was mine.

I could hear shouting at the end of the line, and saw more men in blue tunics, hounding the people. One had a whip. I drew in a sharp breath and thought about my next move. I couldn't be seen. These men seemed to know me, even if I didn't. I kicked Bagred and rode him off the path, but I was too late.

'It's her!'

'Grab her!'

My shoulders tensed when I heard the sound of horses cantering behind me. I saw two soldiers. One I recognised from before. The other was bald and tattooed.

I quickly dug my heels into Bagred again, forcing him into a gallop, but the soldiers came up on either side of me. I leaned forward as the bald man reached out to grab me, trying to evade his hand. He missed at first, but then he pulled out a chain and threw it towards me. It wrapped around my waist unforgivingly. The man pulled on the chain; I came off Bagred's back and hit the ground with an agonising thud.

I rolled in the sandy soil. I couldn't feel pain but was conscious of a red dampness forming around my waist. When I stopped moving, I felt breathless and broken. The soldier grabbed me and pulled me to my feet. The pain shot through my body, and I wished I were dead.

'How are you alive?' the bald man yelled in my face. He let me fall to the ground again, kicked me, and smiled when I whimpered. He began to laugh. 'I see the warrior child died in the river after all. If this shell is all that's left, then the king will be pleased.'

'I don't understand. What warrior? What king?' I stared at the soldier's well-used boots as he dug them into the ground. I could smell the dirty leather at first, but then dust filled my nose.

'You don't remember? That's even better. But there is one name you should not forget and that is mine.' He gripped my hair at the top of my head and pulled me up by it. I gritted my teeth, refusing to give him the satisfaction of making another sound. 'I am Jag Warhin. I defeated you once, and I will take pleasure in doing it again.'

I lifted my gaze but when I saw the coldness in his eyes, I quickly looked away. I could feel him staring at me and hoped he wouldn't notice the tears filling my eyes or the way I was drawing blood from my wounded hand with the anxious grip of the other.

He grabbed my elbow, tied my hands together, and lifted me onto his horse.

The other soldier mounted Bagred. He dug his sharp spurs into his sides, and the horse whinnied in pain.

'Bagred!'

Jag turned and unsheathed his sword, pressing its point into my chest until it drew blood. 'Don't you dare speak that name or any other. They're all dead. You, girl, are alone.'

3
ELHIAN

It was dawn the next day when we arrived at a large city protected by stonewalls as tall as pine trees. A large gate reinforced with iron bars began to open, and a man on the wall said in a loud voice, 'It's Jag.' His eyes widened when he saw me. 'He's with her. The girl!'

The city was deserted apart from the blue-clad soldiers. A torn green flag adorned with twelve gold stars lay in a muddy puddle. A few campfires burned in the streets and were surrounded by more soldiers who stopped and gaped at me. I shifted uneasily. My tattered and bloodied clothes hardly reached my thighs.

It took a good part of the morning to travel through the city to the palace where the king I had heard Jag speak of was 'staying', as if the palace did not quite belong to him.

Men opened tall gates when we arrived: golden vines weaved across the iron bars and formed a flower in the middle. Beyond that was a courtyard, the heart of the palace. In the centre there stood a beautifully carved statue of a winged horse on its hind legs. A crowned man sat on top with his sword raised high and his face tilted upwards. Behind him was a younger man doing the same. The entire structure was gilded, and as we drew closer, I saw the words 'King Phylip and Prince Jovan' engraved in the base. I wondered who they were and what it meant. Their faces seemed so honest, as if they would risk their lives to protect their kingdom. I hoped they would protect me.

The palace itself shouted power and wealth—the extravagant height, the cream stone blocks that seemed to shimmer, the marble balconies . . . Ahead, long curved steps edged with gold rose to the front doors. On the roof was a tall flagpole capped with a golden dove, but there was no ensign blowing in the wind.

I didn't get to go inside. I was taken instead to the nearby barracks and cast into a dank, underground cell. A prison guard gave me water but no food. He locked me in with my arms chained to the ceiling and left me all alone.

The darkness was unbearably thick and felt like it was closing in on me. My chest tightened until I could hardly breathe, my strained gasps the only sound in the prison. My mind started playing games with me, envisioning creatures and eyes in the darkness and imagining movements and sounds until I felt like I was on the brink of insanity.

With no way to keep myself warm, my body began to quake with the cold. I slipped in and out of consciousness again. My wrists felt raw, but there was nothing I could do to take the weight off of them. When the door opened after an immeasurably long time, I could no longer even lift my head.

'Girl,' a man said with a voice that sounded like it had never spoken a nice word, 'the king wishes to see you.'

He released me from my chains, and I fell on the ground. I could sense him waiting for me to get up, but I couldn't. My legs refused to obey. The man groaned and threw me over his shoulder. He carried me out of the cell, through the barracks and into the palace. We came to the door of the throne room and he set me down on my feet. 'Kneel in front of the king,' he commanded as he opened the door and shoved me in.

My hands still bound, I stumbled up a stretch of golden-edged carpet until I came to the foot of the stairs that led to the throne. There I fell to my knees, but not out of respect. I felt tiny in the grand room. Its tall green walls seemed to take years to reach the flamboyant, golden ceiling. Ahead of me was an empty throne: an elegant crown and an *A* were embroidered onto the backrest in golden thread.

The king was standing at the bottom of the steps just before the throne. He didn't see me at first. He had his hands around the neck of another prisoner, a young man whose arms were tied behind his back. The king was holding the man's face to the stone floor. My stomach lurched. My neck would have snapped like a fowl's.

'Where is your sovereign?' the king asked.

The prisoner's bare back was covered in blood and stripes and his hair had been pulled out in chunks. He sobbed but said nothing.

The king banged the prisoner's head against the stone; I winced as I heard the thud. 'Where is the Targian queen?'

The man remained silent. He looked at me with blood trickling down the side of his face.

The king stood and spat at him. Then, he made a gesture with his hand.

Two archers took aim and released their shot.

I choked as the young man slumped on the ground and blood pooled around him. The king kicked the body and gave a satisfied nod.

Then, he saw me.

He took a seat on the throne, resting his feet on another torn, green flag. 'I heard you were alive.' He gripped the armrests with thin, wrinkly fingers.

I watched as the dead prisoner was taken away, certain I'd be next.

The king gave a smug smile. 'Tell me your name, child.'

'I don't . . . remember . . .'

'You don't remember who you are? Or whom you serve?'

Meeting his eyes, I recognised the same inhuman coldness there that I'd seen in Jag, an emptiness that I found both frightening and pitiable. 'I don't remember anything.'

'Do you know where you are? Where your queen is? Who I am?'

'All I know is that you are a king.'

'A king?' He scoffed. 'My girl, let me remind you of a few things. I am Cades Edangard, King of Casmodia and conqueror of Targe. Here Queen Alexia was overthrown one month ago, at which point she . . . well, she disappeared.' He grimaced. 'This is my son, the prince.' He pointed to a boy with a blue stone in his sword, a boy staring at me with intent. He seemed different than his father, but the king went on before I could define how. 'And you are no peasant, daughter of the Keeper of Kest.'

A hum of concerned interest spread through the people in the room, and the king raised his voice so that it bounced off the walls. 'You were supposed to be dead in Kest River. I will kill you myself before everyone at first light!' He stood and slashed the *A* on the throne, revealing the stuffing within the chair. He stormed out of the room followed by the prince and his party.

A soldier dragged me back to my cell. My stomach growled and I winced as it began to cramp, desperate for food.

I tried to remember something, anything. My life depended on it. *What is the Keeper of Kest? Why does everyone want me dead?*

My hands were shaking in their manacles.

'Adaliah?' a young male voice called in the darkness. I sensed he was talking to me, but I couldn't reply. I heard the door open and footsteps walk towards me. A moment later I was set free of my chains. The boy caught me and laid me on the ground. I lay there, unable to move while he took off his cloak, rolled it up and put it under my head. 'Here, drink this.' He placed a vial of water on my chapped lips. I managed a few sips and felt it trickle deep inside my body. 'Can you eat?' He fed me some dates before I could answer. I chewed slowly, relishing their rich flavour.

'I'm going to take you into the palace where we will decide what to do next.'

I sat up to see who my rescuer was. 'You are the prince.'

He pursed his lips together like he'd tasted something sour. 'If being a prince means torturing the innocent, killing women, creating war in peaceful cities, and burning anyone who resists, then I am no such thing, nor will I support a king who does so even if he is my father.' He spoke sternly and I bit my lip, not about to argue with him. 'If you can walk, come with me, Adaliah.'

'Is that my name?'

He paused with a pained look. 'Yes, and I am Elhian Edangard. Do you remember?' His eyes searched my face.

I pondered on the name but shook my head. *Nothing.*

He helped me to my feet and guided me past another cell where two others stood in silence. I could feel them watching me and wondered what they had done to find themselves trapped as well.

'Look Xander,' one of them said in a rough voice, 'I told you she was still alive.' It was the first time someone didn't seem disappointed to know it.

'I never doubted it, Raggin,' the second said.

Elhian turned and peered at them. I wondered if he was going to rescue them, too, but he frowned and put a hand on my arm. Leaving the two prisoners behind, he led me through several dark passages. 'I sent one of my men ahead of my visit to stand down the prison guards for an hour,' he said. 'I told him I wanted to make a private visit without any listening ears. Thankfully I still have some power . . . for now.'

We came to a path that gave us entry into the palace. 'Does any of this look familiar to you?' the prince asked as we quietly stepped into a warm gallery filled with fine portraits. 'You lived here for some time.'

'I did?' My heart sank. *Why don't I remember it then?* 'Whatever your father did to me has stolen my past.'

'I'm truly sorry for your pain, more so than you can know. Here.' He stopped outside an exquisitely carved wooden door. 'These chambers belonged to your queen's son.'

'Who is this queen?'

Elhian paused in his step before glancing over his shoulder and quickly taking me to a large portrait further down the hall. It was a painting of a beautiful woman wearing an elegant green dress and a crown made of interweaving threads of gold and silver. It was covered in jewels and had stars raised up around the rim. The woman's blue eyes suggested fearlessness.

'May I present Her Majesty, Alexia Joanna Grace Elryane, the Queen of Targe.' Elhian said this as if the queen was in the room and we were meeting for the first time. 'She is the only heir of King Amaz, the mother of little Crown Prince Jeri, much loved of her people . . . and overthrown by a brute. Cades . . . ' Elhian turned his face away from the portrait. 'He murdered her beloved husband. He died in her arms, one month ago now.'

'How old is she?'

'Twenty-three. Just six years older than you.'

We moved back towards the bedroom door. 'Where is Cades from?'

'Casmodia, in the snowy north. We are in Liane. This is the capital city of Targe.'

Elhian opened the door and led me into the room. At the centre was a large bed lavish with pillows and quilts of every shade of green. There were paintings of ancient monarchs on the walls, intricate tapestries that each told a story of their own, and a hearth alight with flames. Elhian moved a cushioned chaise in front of the fire and invited me to use it.

'I've already heated some water for a bath. I'll prepare it now.' He disappeared behind fabric partitions. The panels were embroidered with pictures of the yellow forest I had ridden through just two days before. It seemed far more peaceful in thread than in reality.

I could hear Elhian pouring the water behind them. He reappeared a few minutes later and told me it was ready. 'You will feel better if you are clean,' he said, 'and it will make it easier for me to treat your wounds. You must be gone by morning, so we need to build your strength up as much as possible.'

'Gone? Where?'

'Anywhere but here.'

The idea of going anywhere made me realise how exhausted I felt.

There's nothing to say I should trust him. Perhaps I should run away while he's asleep.

But where would I go? I'd only get lost in the city and shot with an arrow like that man in the throne room.

The prince might keep me alive a bit longer.

I walked behind the partitions, undressed and immersed myself in the warm water. The cuts stung when the water touched them, but I could feel some of the tension in my muscles beginning to ease and slowly breathed out. I washed the blood away from my waist.

I heard Elhian throwing more logs on the fire. 'You could go to Kest and lose yourself amongst the crowd of Targian exiles,' he said. 'I think that's what you were trying to do before.'

'Kest?'

'It's a valley and river to the west of here.'

One place I do know.

'I was trying to get there before?'

Is that why I woke up there?

'Yes.' He hesitated as if waiting for me to remember but went on when I said nothing. 'After the Battle of the Yellow Forest, just over a month ago, you were captured. I was in Casmodia at the time and wasn't told you had been imprisoned.'

'Here in Liane?'

'Yes. Cades told me you were dead.' Elhian sighed and, when he continued, his voice had a weary edge to it. 'But you defied him with an escape and his men chased you all the way to Kest River. They told Cades they killed you there, and yet, here you are. Adaliah, your father was the Keeper of Kest, so going back to Kest may help you remember your past. But . . . I just don't think it's safe. Not yet. Cades obviously has men there. I say go east, as far as you can.'

'Why are you helping me?'

'Because I won't let Cades kill another young woman merely to satisfy his own blood lust.'

I sensed he wasn't telling me the whole truth, but my head was already spinning.

'I have some clothes for you when you're ready and a balm for the wounds on your waist.' He hung the clothes over the top of the partition. 'I'll get you something to eat. You must be hungry.' He left.

I soaked in the water for another few minutes before emerging and drying myself. I found the balm on a chair and applied it to the rash-like wound around my middle. It immediately relieved the stinging. Of the clothes he had laid out for me, I chose a simple linen dress and eased it on over my cuts. I stood near the fire and combed my hair, water spattering into the flames at the end of each stroke.

Elhian returned with a platter of cold meats, date rolls, and sliced fruit, which he placed on a wooden table near the fire. 'You look much better already.' He indicated with a wave of his hand for me to take a seat.

I picked at the fruit and studied his face. It was tanned but held more worries than seemed right for his age. If I was seventeen, he was only a year or two older. He narrowed his dark brown eyes as he looked over my injuries with care and patience. I watched his hands as they wrapped a clean bandage around my cut palm. They were strong and made him seem in control and certain about what he was doing. I longed for certainty as well, but I knew nothing about him except that he left me feeling a little less frightened.

Elhian tied the bandage off while I leaned into the chaise and closed my eyes. I felt like I could sleep for days.

'Why don't you sleep on the bed?' he asked with a nod towards it. 'I'll wake you when it's time to go.'

The bed was warm and comfortable, and I was exhausted. But an hour passed, and I couldn't sleep. I watched Elhian from across the room and wondered if it were truly safe to close my eyes while he was nearby. He was unarmed and seemed to be sleeping soundly on the chaise, but I knew he could kill me in an instant. As a prince, he'd be well trained in combat and politics, and he seemed both fit and intelligent. Why had he been kind to me?

Sleep overwhelmed me in the end, but it was haunted. I was trapped in a small dark room again, like the cell. Cold black bricks surrounded me. I couldn't find a way out and was running out of air. I started to scream. The sound bounced off the walls, my own fear echoing around me. There was no light, no way to distinguish up from down.

I fell to the floor with a scream.

'Adaliah?'

I heard Elhian's whisper somewhere in the back of my mind. 'Adaliah!' I felt him shake me by the shoulders, felt him sprinkle some water on my forehead.

I opened my eyes, saw him, and moved back.

'Adaliah, it's me, Elhian. It was just a dream.'

I drew away from his touch. 'How do I know I can trust you?' I asked, tears filling my eyes. 'How do I know I am who you say I am? Why is everyone trying to kill me? I don't know what to do! I don't know if there is a queen and if this was her home, and most of all, I'm scared I won't live to find out!' I crawled back onto the bed, shaking, sweating, and losing control of my breathing.

Elhian sat on the edge of the bed just as Jag burst in.

'Is everything all right, Your Highness?' He saw the prince with me and smirked. 'Oh . . . Sorry to interrupt. Excuse me.' He bowed and turned to go.

Elhian waited until he closed the door again. 'Adaliah, there's so much I wanted to tell you, but he will go to my father, who will be suspicious.' He rose to his feet, took my hand, and helped me up. 'I can't imagine what you're going through, but I don't have time to convince you to trust me.'

He turned at the sound of footsteps in the passageway, grabbed his cloak and wrapped it around my shoulders. He picked up his sword and opened a door at the other end of the chambers.

The footsteps drew closer.

'In here,' Elhian said. 'Quickly.'

I slipped into the dark tunnel-like passage and let Elhian take the lead. He guided me to the palace courtyard. We kept close to the wall and moved unseen towards the stables. There, Elhian took a burning torch from the stable door and used it to find Bagred.

'He will keep you out of trouble better than he did last time.'

'I hope so.'

Elhian saddled the horse. 'Go east until you come almost to the border of Targe. Find the village of Hunt and ask for a man called Lezan. He should be able to help you. You must find your queen.'

'How can I find the queen when I don't even remember her?' I mounted Bagred and gripped the reins.

'You will find her. Use my sword.' Elhian concealed it under my saddlebags. 'Faith will keep you on the right path.' He pulled a bag of coins out of his pocket, reached up and gave it to me, squeezing my hand.

'Go!'

4
LEAVING LIANE

There were soldiers everywhere. I slowed Bagred to a walk, stayed in the shadows, and edged my way to the eastern gate street by street. I had already heard my name shouted more than once and knew a search party was looking for me. I placed a hand on my chest and could feel my heart beating hard and fast.

I rode around a few more corners and the tall city walls appeared in front of me. I saw the eastern gate to my left as well as five soldiers chatting and laughing as they guarded it. I looked both ways and noticed a smaller door in the wall up from the gate. I dismounted and walked towards it, leading Bagred. I tried to open it, but it was locked. I tried to force it. The handle slipped from my hand and sounded a loud tap.

The men stopped laughing.

'Hey, it's her!'

'Grab her!'

'Don't let her get away!'

'Wait!' I raised my palms when they unsheathed their swords.

Bagred tossed his head and tried to back up. The handle of Elhian's sword was sticking out from under the saddlebags. I pulled it out just in time to block a strike.

The blue stone in it glowed mildly, as if a small flame had ignited inside it, but it was the sound of the two swords clashing that ignited

a memory in my mind—an image of trying to escape, of a dark space
... Chaos, like the dream.

I blinked and forced myself to refocus. I intuitively pushed against
the sword, making the soldier step back. I swung the blade around me
to establish a boundary. Two soldiers charged forward, but I disarmed
one with a swift blow and sliced the arm of the other.

I bent down and grabbed the blade of the disarmed soldier. Now
with a sword in each hand, I crossed them back over my shoulders to
block a strike from behind. I turned to face the attacker and brought
the swords down against him, cutting across his chest and another's.

Perhaps this is why they're afraid of me.

I wasn't even sure what I was doing. My body was responding by
itself. I tried not to think. All I could hear was the blur of footsteps
dancing about me, the breaths of the soldiers in the still night. All I
wanted was to get out.

I turned to confront the fifth and final soldier. He lunged at me,
but I sidestepped him and kicked at his knees. He lost his balance, and
I took the opportunity to kick the sword out of his hand. Then, I hit
his head with Elhian's sword handle.

He slumped to the ground at my feet, unconscious and bleeding.

I took a deep breath. All five were conquered. I dropped the spare
sword, retook Bagred's reins and hurried out of the main gate, trying
not to think about what I'd just done and what it might mean.

5
HUNT

I rode all night and only came to a small village at daybreak. By then, I was slumping over in the saddle, barely awake. The streets were quiet and the houses mostly closed-up, but I was able to buy some nuts, salted meat, and bread from a shy merchant standing outside the town's church. I used four of the coins Elhian had given me.

'Which way is Hunt?' I asked.

The merchant pointed towards the east and said something about 'the mountain', but that meant little to me. I led Bagred out of the village and, for five days, carefully avoided all paths and settlements while riding towards the rising sun. I was still ever watchful of my surroundings, paranoid about being pursued, but also afraid that I would never find Hunt or the queen whom Elhian seemed to think was so important. The plains were thankfully void of soldiers and people in general—safe, but also lonely.

I rationed my supplies meticulously but was often hungry and lightheaded. I ran out of food altogether on the morning of the sixth day and went without anything to eat at all until I glimpsed a small village tucked in between a collection of low, undulating hills. By then my stomach was aching and I no longer cared if Casmodian soldiers were waiting for me in the town, but it, too, seemed to be mostly deserted. The only food I could find for sale was in the tavern and, since I was there, I decided to rent a room. I was exhausted from the constant riding and open-air living, and tired of being hungry. I decided to indulge and ordered a hot meal to be sent up to my room. I ate the meat stew and then collapsed into a straw bed, where I slept without moving until morning.

I bought more food supplies from the publican and rode back into the plains. The unyielding autumn winds covered my tracks with dust, but they also made riding uncomfortable and tiring. After nine days, I only stopped travelling altogether when I came to a small brook and realised it was the same one I had seen the day before.

'I'm lost,' I said.

Trying to decide what to do, I dismounted, stood in the shadow of a lone mountain and practised with Elhian's sword. I swung it one way and another, finding it easy to rotate with my wrist. I felt empowered by my skill—it seemed to be the only thing left that I could do—but, remembering the face of the soldier who had fallen at my feet, it frightened me as well.

I couldn't deny that Elhian's instructions had been simple: Go east. Use the sword. Find Lezan and Queen Alexia of Targe in Hunt.

'But where is Hunt?' I asked my black horse, who was grazing nearby. I switched sword hands and turned. 'I probably would have known once.' The sword cut through the air as I raised it above my head and brought it down again. 'But now I have no idea about anything, including the prince. I'm alone.'

I heard the words come out of my mouth and dropped the sword. Did I still have parents? Elhian mentioned my father—where was he? Did I have any family at all? Were they looking for me? Or was I an orphan girl whom no one cared about? I sat on the grass and hugged my knees.

I placed Elhian's sword across my lap and studied the intricate craftsmanship that decorated it. Two curls were engraved into the blade, and they interweaved and passed over each other until they reached the tip of the sword.

The grip contained the blue stone, just below the cross-guard, and was also heavily decorated with smaller curls. Upon closer inspection, I saw a small word engraved just below the stone.

Faith.

I turned the sword over. *Fear* was engraved on the other side.

I remembered what Elhian had said.

Faith will keep you on the right path.

I didn't know what he meant or why the words were engraved on the Casmodian sword.

I thrust the sword into the ground, preparing to stand up. Once I was on my feet, I realised the stone in the sword was glowing a little. I bent down and tapped it with my finger on the *Faith* side. Without warning, a great light shone out of it like a blue ray of sunshine. I gasped and stood back. At first the beam shone directly upwards, but then it moved until it was parallel with the earth. It was shining towards the southeast, towards the lone mountain.

'That must be the way I need to go, Bagred,' I muttered in amazement. 'That must be the mountain the merchant mentioned.'

Bagred remained unconcerned. The beam faded and the stone returned to normal. I sheathed the blade, climbed up into the saddle, pulled Bagred away from his lunch and rode towards the mountain.

I was relieved to have some purpose again. Whenever I lingered, so did the fear.

I soon found a well-used path and picked up the pace until we began to ascend. A sign by the road told me I was at Mount Dennell. The path travelled over the mountain's shoulder and was covered with orange, yellow, and red leaves that fluttered at Bagred's feet as we passed through. By the time we reached the highest point of the shoulder, it had grown dark with both night and forthcoming rain. I pulled my cloak around myself when it began to shower and tried to decide whether to make camp or press on.

Judging by how long it had taken to come as far as we had, I estimated it was still at least a half-day's ride to Hunt. Bagred was tired, but I wasn't sure about enduring another night without shelter. The drops of water began to soak through my clothes and slither down my neck. I decided to keep moving but, when I came to a spot out of the woods where I could see the countryside dotted with trees and farms below me, I hesitated.

In the distance there was a village on fire and a haze of smoke. Hunt was burning. I could see the flames as well as a long line of survivors leaving town. I stared at them, trying to understand what had happened and why. I felt cold and alone again, oppressed by a darkness I couldn't explain.

It was then I heard the voices behind me. I dismounted, led Bagred off the path and tethered him to a branch. I drew Elhian's sword and hid myself behind a thick tree. I could see who belonged to the voices by then—three men, now identifiable to me by their blue uniforms as Casmodian soldiers. After all those days of travelling, they were the first people I had seen outside of a village. They were walking down the path towards me and stopped where I had been only a few moments before.

'King Cades is separating the men and women,' a familiar voice said. 'Most of the men will go into Casmodia with the others, leaving the women vulnerable in Kest. We'll put them to work soon enough and use them to inhabit Kest.'

I peeked around the tree. It was Jag and two others. I hoped one would be the prince but knew when they started talking that he wasn't with them.

'What is being done about Alexia Elryane?' a man asked Jag.

Jag's laugh was more of a distorted grumble this time. It made me shiver. 'What does it matter? She's stripped of everything—powerless!'

'Yes . . . When will Cades send Elhian to take the south of Targe?'

'He's more likely to do that himself. Elhian doesn't have the authority needed to take a kingdom. At least, not that I can see.'

'You're suspicious of him,' the third stated.

'It's not my place to make treasonous judgments.'

The rain became heavier and I had to strain to hear what they were saying.

'But, take Adaliah,' Jag went on, making me tense and still. 'He either saved her or had his way with her and fed her to the dogs. He is either undermining his father or supporting him behind closed doors. Either way, something isn't right.'

The others didn't respond, and they made their way down the hill, walking away from Hunt.

I hurried back to Bagred. Did Elhian expect me to be taken in the attack on Hunt? Was I supposed to help save it, or die in it, or be sent to Kest with it?

I pushed my thin wet fringe out of my face and decided to rest for the night instead of going straight to Hunt. I rode to the bottom of the mountain, came to a small rocky overhang and stopped. The area it kept dry was not large—it would keep me out of the rain while I tried to get some rest, but nothing more. I had no pillow, no warmth, but an hour later the rain subsided, and I got some sleep.

It was a cold and uncomfortable night. I was up before the sun fully dawned. By the time Bagred and I passed the farmlands on the outskirts of Hunt, the sun was in full strength.

I took off my damp cloak and walked my horse into the village. There, some of the buildings were still burning. The road was black with ash and there was an awful stench that was explained when I came to the village centre: burnt bodies lay heaped on the ground. Some were strung up on posts. One of them was a small boy.

I could feel the bile creeping up my throat. It was another second before I could look away, but the revulsion of what I had seen was already carved in my mind.

Who would do this?

I forced myself to dismount. I walked into one building that was still standing. Just as I did, part of the back wall fell away, and I could see the street on the other side. I quickly retreated. The dead boy's body caught my attention again. As much as I wanted to, I couldn't ignore him and the others. I searched the surrounding houses for a shovel and found one in what would have been the blacksmith's. I cut the boy down with Elhian's sword and dug a small grave for him right there in the street. After carefully placing his body inside it, I began to fill it with dirt and charcoal. Even though I didn't know him, tears filled my eyes when I covered his face. Like me, his life had been stolen from him, and he was just two or three years old.

'Burying them won't save them,' a frail voice said.

I turned and peered at the old man who had spoken behind me. He walked to me, taking slow steps and relying on an old staff for support. He was black with ash, but his skin was naturally dark as well.

'They deserve to rest in peace,' I said, trying to sound assured. 'Especially one so young.'

'They are already at peace. Cades, however, will find none when he dies.' The man paused by the boy's grave while I leant on the shovel. 'My name is Lezan.'

'Lezan?' I repeated. He held himself in a way that suggested he had been important once, but his clothes were torn, and he coughed like he was seriously ill.

This is the man the prince said could help me?

'I'm—'

'Adaliah, I know. I was expecting you earlier, before . . . before this. I cannot tell you how relieved I was when the prince sent word that you lived.'

'How did he do that?' I asked. 'Without the king knowing?'

'There are a few whose loyalties lie with Prince Elhian and not with Cades, myself included.'

I wasn't sure what to believe and I was too tired to try and understand it all. 'He sent me to find you,' I said, 'though I don't know why. I got lost. He wanted me to find Queen Alexia, but I don't . . . remember.'

'Her Majesty was here,' Lezan said with a faint nod. 'She left with the exiles, hidden in the crowd. She has suffered great loss—first her husband, then Liane, Targe, and now her princeling.'

'What? What happened to him?'

Lezan stared at me with an expression tinged with grief. 'You just buried him. The boy.'

'What?' I walked back over to his grave, an image coming to me of a cheerful boy running through the palace, dressed in white . . . An elegant woman catching him up in her arms, a woman with a crown . . . I frowned, trying to make the memory last to find my place in it, but it wouldn't stay.

'It will come back to you,' Lezan said, 'but now is not the time. You, too, have suffered.'

'If I have, I've forgotten it, just like I've forgotten you, even though you seem to know me.'

'Of course I know you. You are Adaliah. Your name is as familiar as the queen's.'

'Why?'

'You have done great things. Sadly, a rumour spread after your capture that you had died by Cades' hand.' He said this with a melancholy smile. 'It caused many to lose hope and that, of course, was his intention.'

I rubbed my forehead, but my mind refused to do what it was asked.

'It is good that you are free of your past for now,' Lezan said.

'The only reason I'm going to Alexia is because of the past and yet, it's a past I've only been told about. I don't remember anything, and I'm afraid.'

'Then do not go for Alexia's sake, and do not go anywhere until you have had rest and food. Come with me.'

6

THE PATH OF THE DEAD

We slept that night in one of the few untouched farmhouses outside the town walls. Lezan woke me just before dawn. The night was still lingering, and a wisp of cloud hovered low as we left the deserted village and travelled northwest. Before an hour passed, it began to rain again, and the track was soon both muddy and plagued with slippery rocks. I let Lezan ride Bagred while I walked in front and held onto the reins. My horse shook the drops of water out of his mane from time to time, niggling against my grip. He walked with his eyes half closed and was generally disinterested in being laboured on such a day.

After a morning of slow travel, the rain became heavier and, even though I wanted to adhere to Lezan's persistent request for shelter, there was none to be found. Up ahead, I saw a patched blanket spread over a body on the road. I hurried towards it, bent down and pulled the cloth back. Underneath was a dead woman. There was no obvious cause of death, but her face was tinged blue. Another body was lying further down the road: a young man. And then another. They were all pallid with death.

'We should bury them,' I said. There was no practical way to do so but I felt such sorrow and unrest at the sight of them.

'We need to get out of this rain, or we will join them.'

I was holding back tears but, knowing there was some truth in what Lezan said, I continued walking along what I now deemed the

Path of the Dead. I felt like I'd woken up in the wake of frozen innocents. Fear was at my shoulder again, mostly because I didn't understand what was happening. Why had these people died here, cold and alone?

I tried to piece together what I did know. *I'm Targian.* I knew that from my colouring and by the way the Casmodians hated me. *Casmodia and Targe are at war.*

Something bad happened to me. I figured that's why I couldn't remember anything.

The Queen of Targe has lost everything. This didn't bode well for her or her kingdom.

I'm the daughter of the Keeper of Kest. I still had no idea what that meant, just that I had belonged, once. I'd been a part of a family.

I've been trained to fight.

That was it. That was all I knew. Some of my tears escaped but I felt determined to find the queen, as if that would somehow make everything all right, as if my life would make sense again.

I was drenched. My clothes clung to me and water ran down my back. My long black hair was as soaked as Bagred's mane, but I walked on with as much dignity as I could muster.

'Do you think all the people from Hunt are in this rain?' I asked.

'Yes. They will be going to Kest, but the Casmodians may want to go through Egra first.'

'Have I been to Egra?'

'From what I have heard, you visited it with the queen once or twice a year. It was her mother's hometown, a beautiful place known for its crystal-like lake and tall mountains. It was one of the first towns to fall, being so close to the Casmodian border.'

'Where are you from, Lezan?'

Lezan shifted in the saddle before answering. 'I am a Jazmardian. Jazmarda is a kingdom to the far west, beyond Kest. I lived in our beautiful city, Etarbelec. In fact, I was once very prominent there.' He gave a wistful smile. 'But . . . I had some ideas that the others did not like. I travelled in search of answers and met Cades, then Elhian. Now I am working for the prince to stop Cades from becoming a tyrannical emperor. So you see, our stories are not so unalike.'

'I'm not working for the prince.'

'Oh?' Lezan gave another small smile.

Within another half-hour my legs were heavy with mud. We were trudging. Bagred paused every now and then in hope he wouldn't have to go on, but I kept tugging at the bit in his mouth until we came to another body lying in the middle of the road. I bent down beside it and touched the boy's face. He was colourless but, when I held my hand just above his mouth, I felt his breath.

'This one's alive, Lezan!'

The Jazmardian looked forward and frowned. 'Only just.'

'We need to take him with us.'

'It is a lost cause, Adaliah,' Lezan said. My perception of him was not of an unsympathetic man, but of a weary and dejected one. 'You will kill yourself trying to save him, and then he will die anyway.'

'He can't be any more than seven years old. He deserves a chance! Please, Lezan, I need to do this.' I gathered the boy up in my arms.

Lezan relented with a sigh and climbed down from Bagred. The two of us lifted the boy onto the horse's back and Lezan re-mounted behind him. Once I felt sure the boy wouldn't fall, we continued our journey into the afternoon. I turned and checked on the boy from time to time, wondering how such a vulnerable being could find himself abandoned in the rain. Somehow, he reminded me of myself.

Thinking about this, I didn't notice the large rocky hill that had appeared out of the misty clouds until Lezan pointed it out to me. The crag seemed out of place in the otherwise flat plains that surrounded us. It was dotted with wide, ancient trees that grew tall in the most impossible crevices and which were bright with the shades of autumn. Their leaves spiralled downward in the cold wind.

'Tarcraig,' Lezan said. 'If we find them at all, it will be there.'

7
ALEXIA

Lezan and I stopped when the boy began shivering in his sleep. Not wanting to keep moving while he was so fragile and with Tarcraig still in the distance, I did the only thing I could think of: I tied my cloak to Bagred and pulled it to the ground on an angle, where I fastened it with Elhian's sword.

Lezan and I lay the boy down under the rustic shelter as gently as we could, protecting him from the rain. Lezan wanted to light a fire but couldn't find any dry wood, and in the end, I lowered myself beside the boy and tried to warm him in my arms.

'What's Alexia like?' I asked, wanting to take my mind off the cold.

'Oh, she is everything a queen should be. Strong. Beautiful. Deadly with a bow and arrow. A good leader. Impatient, perhaps, but she loves her people. She has suffered much for them.'

'Do the other exiles know she's among them?'

'I hope not. When we arrive, we need to find Darj Ryder.'

'Who?' I could tell by the way Lezan spoke his name that he respected this man, too.

'The general of the Targian army and a great military leader. A great man. He and the late prince consort, Alexia's husband, were very close friends. I believe they grew up together. He is wise for his age and very protective of the queen. He is a friend of yours, so he will be relieved to find you alive.'

As we talked, the boy's breathing began to calm again. We let him rest for another hour, and then put him back on the horse to continue our journey.

By the time the sun began to set again, Tarcraig was directly in front of us. I saw two men sitting on top of the crag—Casmodian scouts—but they didn't notice our small party making its way towards the group of exiles. There were a few tents here and there, large ones that could fit up to ten people. I indulged myself by imagining a soft bed waiting for me in one of them, even though I knew most people would be finding shelter amongst the rocks and caves.

'Pull your hood on,' Lezan said as we passed the first rock. 'You do not want people recognising you and causing a stir.'

'No one recognised me in the villages I visited on the way here, and what does it matter if they do cause a stir? There are few to resist us.'

'You are in no state to fight, and neither are these people.'

I watched a few drenched exiles wandering up ahead. They glanced at me but didn't pay me any attention. Even if I were recognised, I doubted anyone could rally the enthusiasm to care, but I did as Lezan asked.

'Excuse me, child,' Lezan said, drawing a small girl aside. 'Can you bring me Darj Ryder?'

The girl pulled away and disappeared amongst the others before we knew if she'd even heard the question.

We stood in the same spot for a few minutes, searching the dreary faces around us. I was just contemplating speaking to one of them when a rugged, tall man approached us. I hid my face from him but saw the leather armband tied around his right upper arm. He was dirty and wet from the rain but didn't look as cold as I felt.

'Lezan.' He sounded tired. 'Have you followed us all the way here in this weather? You look awful.'

'I had to bring you something, Darj,' Lezan said.

So this is the queen's protector?

'Where is she?' I asked. 'Where is the queen?'

Darj narrowed his eyes at me. 'What do you want with the queen?'

My enthusiasm faded. I felt like I'd stirred a lion. 'Please—' I stepped forward, but my sudden movement alarmed Darj and he raised his hand to detain me. I saw this and ducked, grabbing Elhian's sword at the same time. The stone glowed a little.

'That is a royal sword—Casmodian blue,' Darj said. 'You're a spy!'

I pointed the sword at his chest before my mind registered the fear I felt at his anger. 'I am no such thing. I once served the queen.' I wasn't sure if that were true, but I removed my hood and let him see my face.

'It is Adaliah, Darj.' Lezan spoke under his breath, apparently hoping no one else would overhear.

Darj staggered back, his face contorted with a mixture of surprise and hope. 'Adaliah?' He shook his head with a scowl. 'She's dead. I was there—I saw them take you . . . her away!'

I tried to think, to remember what he was talking about, but Darj was as unfamiliar to me as everything else.

'It is her, I promise you,' Lezan said.

Darj pointed his finger at me, his eyes reddening with unwanted emotion. 'What did the queen's husband call her?'

I tensed, trying to think as I sheathed the sword. How could I explain why I didn't know that, if I ever had? I hadn't even known my own name.

'She has lost her memory,' Lezan said. 'You know what happened to her, what Cades is like—it is not as unbelievable as it sounds. I know you have faced dark and evil times, but Darj, it *is* Adaliah.'

Darj lowered his finger. 'You don't remember anything?'

I shook my head. 'I remember waking up in Kest River and what has happened since, but nothing before that. I didn't even know who I was until someone else informed me, and even now I'm not sure. Prince Elhian asked me to find the queen. We need shelter, at least for this boy. We found him on the road almost dead. Please,' I searched his face for the friend Lezan said I had, 'can you help?'

He stared at me, a tear rolling down his face, and then he slowly embraced me in a way that told me he was not accustomed to affection. He squeezed my upper arm as if to ensure I was real. 'Adaliah . . .' he said fondly. 'Back from the dead. I . . . I can't believe it! Maybe there is hope after all.' He hesitated like he wanted to say more but walked over to Bagred and lifted the boy down instead. 'He's barely alive.'

'Do you know him?' I asked.

'Me? No, I'm not from Hunt. I fled there with the queen and a few others to organise a defence before Cades hit, but we were too late. Her son . . .' He stopped himself and held the boy closer. 'I will take you to see the queen, but don't tell anyone she's among us. She's . . . vulnerable.'

'Was she wounded?' Lezan asked.

'No, but she is dangerously ill.'

Lezan and I followed Darj along a path through the rocks. Everything looked the same, but Darj seemed to know where he was going and, after passing over a small but deep creek, we soon came to a lone, wind-battered tent. The warmth I felt when I followed the men inside surprised me. The mystery was quickly solved—there were two bowls of oil burning inside, keeping the icy chill at bay.

Darj laid the boy down on some furs and replaced his wet clothes with a blanket. 'It's up to him now,' he said, patting his head. 'I don't even have medicine to offer him.'

A handmaiden, whom Darj introduced as Brenna Caylith, was rinsing a cloth in a basin nearby. She stopped mid-motion when she saw me. 'You're alive?'

I couldn't tell by the shocked look on her face whether she was happy about that or not. 'As you see.'

Brenna stepped back and then walked outside altogether, leaving me a little confused, but a groan at the back of the tent distracted me. I walked towards a low bed and found a young woman lying there, tormented with fever. I recognised her from the portrait Elhian had shown me.

The Queen of Targe.

I hadn't thought a lot about what to expect, but I was impressed by how lovely she was, and yet, how sick. Her skin was pale and sweaty, but with her delicately curved face and long dark eyelashes, she was beautiful, elegant, even in her illness. I felt sorry for her and all she had lost. Before, she had just been a name Elhian had given me. Now she was a human being as displaced as me. I knew she was the reigning monarch of Targe but, lying there in front of me, she was also just a young girl, suffering for her kingdom in a way she probably never could have imagined. I couldn't remember anything about her, but I could feel the almost sisterly connection with her straightaway. I grimaced as my mind launched into a rapid attempt to remember. I held her hand, certain that everything was about to come back to me, but my mind stopped burning as suddenly as it had started, and I was left lost.

Alexia was overheating and sleeping fitfully, and her breathing was labourious. I could sense the struggle. 'How long has she been like this?' I asked Brenna, who had just returned to her queen's side.

'Two days now. She fell ill after we left Hunt and has worsened every hour since. We're doing all we can, but I'm not sure she wants to live. Her heart is broken.'

'She must live,' I whispered. 'She just needs rest . . . '

'So do you,' Lezan said, appearing next to me. He pulled me away and helped me take off my wet cloak. I draped it over a rugged chair. 'You should sleep by the fire,' he said. 'The last thing we need is for you to get sick as well.'

I woke late the next morning in the midst of quiet disorder. Darj, Lezan, and Brenna were all standing around the queen. A man dressed in muddy green robes was with them. He prayed while Darj held Alexia's hand and whispered something. Tears were dripping off his chin.

I moved to them to see the queen for myself. She was turning about in her bed, delirious and mumbling. Dark shadows haunted her eyes. I couldn't remember this girl, but I felt like I was on the brink of losing something integral to my being, a key to my past. I also sensed from Darj that to lose the queen would break the kingdom altogether. If Alexia died, so would Targe.

The man, who I presumed to be a priest, finished praying. He nodded at Darj and moved aside. Brenna quietly talked to him while Darj
leant on the edge of Alexia's bed. 'I never thought it would come to
this,' he said to me. 'The Casmodians are insisting we pack up and
leave first thing tomorrow morning, but . . .'

I studied him as I had Elhian. He was a man single-handedly
trying to save his queen and, by extension, his kingdom. I imagined
he was also a man who tried not to live by his feelings but who was
struggling with them now. His eyes hinted at his exhaustion, and I
wondered how many sleepless nights he had already spent keeping
watch over Alexia.

I stroked back her damp hair.

'You care about her, even though you don't remember her, don't
you?' Darj asked.

'Yes. It's like my heart remembers, even if my mind does not.'

I stayed by Alexia until the boy stirred. He had slept for hours, but now
he sat up and looked about in a daze. 'Where am I?'

I smiled, relieved to see him awake. 'It's all right, you're safe. What's
your name?'

'Zavad . . . Erowen.'

'Well Zavad Erowen, you're safe now.' I gave him some fruit and
explained how he had been found.

He told me his family had survived Hunt, but he couldn't remember
how he ended up on the Path of the Dead alone. 'I have many brothers
and sisters. We may have been separated. There were people everywhere
and lots of shouting.'

'We will help you find your family, Zavad,' I said. 'But you need to rest and get better first, all right?' I tucked him in and watched him fall asleep again, his childlike trust giving me a little peace.

I later returned to the queen and felt more and more helpless. 'Do you care about her, too?' I asked Darj, who had still yet to leave Alexia's side.

'She is my queen, but I hope I'm her friend as well. We have already lost so much. To see her son, our prince, grow from a babe into a healthy child, only to die the way he did . . . and so soon after her husband was killed . . . I cannot blame her for not wanting to wake up.' He brushed the back of his hand across her cheek. 'Her body can't take much more of this fever.'

As he spoke, Alexia let out a long breath. Her face relaxed. I leant forward and saw that she was peaceful and quiet.

My face contorted with unexplainable grief as I gripped her hand. *No . . .*

Darj studied the queen and placed a steady finger on her neck. 'Adaliah, wait. She's alive.' Alexia's chest started to rise and fall again in an easier rhythm. He touched the queen's forehead with his palm. 'It's just the fever breaking. She doesn't feel as hot, and she's still breathing.' He let out a sigh of relief and even laughed. 'Adaliah, I think she's going to survive!'

Things began to change after that. Colour came back into her face and she slept better, giving her body a chance to recover from the fight. I stayed by her while the others rested. Darj was the hardest to convince to lie down, but as soon as he did, he collapsed into a deep sleep.

After midnight, Alexia blinked and woke.

'Adaliah,' she said, smiling up at me. It was reassuring to hear her use my name. Her voice was tired but loving. 'I knew you would come and collect me when I died. Please, take me to my family.'

'You have not died, my queen.'

'I must have, to be here with you.'

'I'm not dead, Alexia.'

She frowned. 'What?' She glanced around the tent. 'Where am I? They . . . they told me you died . . . that you were killed by Cades himself.'

'You are in the Targian countryside with exiles from Hunt. I didn't die, and neither have you. But you have been ill these last few days.'

'Ill . . . ' She massaged her forehead, trying to remember. It came back to her all too easily. 'Jeri . . . Jeri died, didn't he?' Her eyes swelled with tears as the memory of her suffering came back. Her breathing quickened. 'No, Adaliah, I can't live when everyone I love has died. It's not supposed to end like this. It cannot end like this!' She propped herself up and, when I tried to touch her, pulled away. She attempted to stand but her body was so weak she fell to the floor.

I took her arm and helped her back onto the bed. 'Please, you must rest. I know you have suffered—'

'Suffered?' Alexia glowered at me. 'I am a monarch without my kingdom, a wife without my husband, a mother without my child. I have nothing left to exist for. Now please, leave me!' Hot tears ran down her face.

Shaken, I stepped away and left the tent, but looked back when I heard Zavad move. Standing just outside, I saw him walking to the queen.

'What's wrong?' he asked.

She flinched when he touched her arm. 'Who are you?'

'My name is Zavad. Adaliah saved me.'

'Did she?'

'Yes. She says she'll help me find my family.'

'What happened to them?'

'I don't know. I just lost them.'

Alexia grimaced. 'Me, too.'

The boy sat down and leant into her. 'I miss them.'

Alexia wrapped an arm around him and permitted him to snuggle into her. Then, she kissed the top of his head, letting her tears dampen his hair.

8
TARCRAIG

The next morning, I was standing outside the tent in the brisk wind with Lezan, Brenna, and Darj when Alexia came out. Darj's face filled with relief when he saw her. She was still pale and holding her stomach like she didn't trust it, but she wrapped a green cloak around her shoulders and walked over to us, Zavad close behind.

'I'm so sorry,' she said, hugging me. 'My grief overtook my joy in finding you alive. It means so much to me to see you again. You're here, and that at least gives me one less to grieve for, my dear cousin.'

'Cousin?' I repeated, stepping back.

'Yes . . .' Alexia furrowed her brows at the blank look on my face. 'What's wrong?' When I failed to speak, Alexia turned to the others for an explanation.

'She has lost her memory,' Lezan said.

'What?' Alexia's mouth dropped as she put a hand on my arm. Her touch eased some of my fears somehow. 'Oh my darling, what happened to you?'

'Someone will explain it to you later,' Darj said. 'For now, we have a plan to execute.'

We left the tent as it was and only took a few essentials with us, including blankets and animal-skin water bottles. The general led our small party along a dirt path between the tall, rounded rocks, keeping us out of sight of any Casmodians. 'We can't leave Tarcraig until Alexia is better—'

'I'm perfectly—'

'You are not,' Darj said. 'You are in a fragile state—'

'I am still the queen,' she said, pausing in her step.

'And I'm still one of your advisors.' Darj saw the stubborn expression on her face and relented. 'Please, just listen to me. We need to wait until the Casmodians leave anyway. If we hide strategically in the caves, we should be able to make our own journey once they're gone.'

'Where to?' I asked.

'I haven't decided yet—'

'And what about Zavad?' Alexia asked, holding the boy's hand as we continued to walk.

'I've made enquiries into his family. I'm sorry, my boy. I haven't been able to find your parents. Some believe they escaped and are hiding somewhere near Egra. Either way, Egra may be a good place to start looking for them.' He patted the boy's shoulder. 'You're an obedient boy. Mind your ways and you can stay with us a while longer.'

We arrived at a half circle of grass bordered by tall rocks. There was nothing there but a hollow tree. 'Now what?' I asked.

Darj walked to the tree trunk and disappeared inside it, as did Brenna. We followed and discovered that the hole in the tree led to a dark but large cavern.

Darj lit a small fire using flint. We could see now that he and Brenna had made preparations—there was food and water, blankets, a few pillows, some tack, two swords, and a small supply of wood. There was also an impressive bow made out of dark wood with a golden grip.

Next to it was an equally decadent quiver full of arrows, each with gold-tipped, green fletching. Lezan told me they had been made especially for the queen, a gift from her father on her fifteenth birthday.

The saddlery brought Bagred to mind. 'Where's my horse?' I asked.

'I let him loose in the plains last night,' Darj said. 'He's a good Targian horse. He won't go far.'

Alexia walked to the middle of the cave, portraying dignity in her stance even though she was white and sweating in the near freezing conditions.

'Why don't you lie down?'

She touched her head as if it were swimming, and I realised she wasn't quite sure which way down was. Before I could help, she moved over to the back wall, placed a clammy hand on the stone, and vomited.

I stepped to her side once she recovered and, with a hand on her arm, guided her back to where Brenna had prepared a bed. 'Come on, lie down,' I said. Once she did, I pulled a fur blanket up around her neck and tucked her in.

She was shivering. 'Do you think the rest of my life will be like this?'

'No. It can only get better from here, I'm sure.'

'Alexia?'

I heard Darj call for her the next morning and watched as he walked toward the opening of the cavern to find her. She was standing outside, not wearing enough clothes to withstand the cold weather. I knew now her stubbornness extended to neglecting her own needs. I also noticed how she ignored his call and didn't look at him when he walked to her side.

'Alexia, it's not safe to be out here yet,' he said. 'There could still be Casmodians around.'

'My people have gone.'

Darj touched her arm. 'You will sit as the queen again, and your people will still love you.'

'Most of the councillors are dead, and some of the lords and ladies. People I trusted . . . people I cared about. My husband . . . my son . . .'

She pulled away from his hand. Relenting, Darj walked back towards me and Lezan, who had arrived by my side in the meantime.

'I could not help but notice the extent of your care for Alexia,' Lezan said to the general with a raised eyebrow.

Darj refrained from scowling, but his hand moved to his sword. 'Do you question my honour?'

'I question your motives.'

Darj narrowed his eyes at the Jazmardian. 'I protect Queen Alexia because I fear she may consider . . .' He hesitated, then straightened his back. 'It is my job to protect the Targian monarchy, even against itself if necessary.'

I gasped. 'She would not give up like that, would she?'

Alexia's face was turned to the sky and her eyes were closed like she was praying.

'Cades has thrown her into a desperate state,' Darj said. 'I'm no longer sure what she'll do.'

'I hate sickness,' Alexia whispered to me as she lay down later that morning. 'I hate feeling restrained, helpless, and a burden. Now I'm all three.'

'You are not a burden,' I said. 'And you're not helpless.'

Darj began to think she might have been poisoned as part of an assassination plot. He asked her numerous times what she'd eaten, forcing her to remember every detail, but all he found out was that she'd hardly eaten at all since Jeri died.

'It is just grief, Darj,' I heard Lezan tell him later, 'and we cannot proceed until she is at least a little better.'

Alexia lay on the cavern floor, drifting in and out of sleep while Brenna provided her with water and kept the fire going in silent service.

I sat beside my cousin, concerned, but also growing restless. I held Elhian's sword in my hands and touched the stone with my finger, wishing it would shine again. 'Alexia?' I asked. 'Can you tell me my story, please?' Longing for answers, it had already taken a lot of strength not to plague her with questions. It was a relief to know I had one family member, one connection to my past, but I needed to know more.

Alexia didn't move at first and I was prepared to let it be, but then she propped herself up a little. 'Where should I start?'

'I don't know . . . What happened to Targe? To me? My parents?'

'It's so strange to think you can't remember any of it.' She searched my eyes and took a deep breath. 'All right. I'm told your mother was a wise, somewhat spirited woman, but she died many years ago with your younger brother in childbirth. As the second born in the royal line, your father—my uncle—was the Keeper of Kest, a tradition in the Targian monarchy. This is a noble task designed to maintain peace between Jazmarda, Casmodia and Targe, three kingdoms with a history of conflict. He was to report to his brother and my father, King Amaz, routinely and immediately if there were any signs of war. He was considered neutral: the

Casmodians respected his position, as did the Jazmardians, and both were aware of his purpose.

'My father died in his bed with me by his side, about three years ago now. I became queen as there was no other heir, and you, Lady Adaliah Clair Elryane, began to spend the summers at my palace. Your father visited frequently.

'As queen, my uncle was required to report to me about his duties. Not long before Cades attacked us, his weekly report failed to reach me three times in a row. You were rightly worried about this, so you led a small party to check on him, myself and Darj included. When we found him, two Casmodian soldiers were holding him hostage and, as soon as they saw us approaching, a third appeared: General Jag Warhin. He impaled your father with his sword.' Alexia closed her eyes at the memory.

'I loved my father,' I said, remembering the feeling but not an image to accompany it.

And I am an orphan. Alone.

'He was all you had, and he was taken right before you. You were severely grieved. You became my fierce protector, I suppose because by then I was your only other living relative, and Cades was on the move. After the death of your father, Cades led an army against a battalion of my strongest men near the Yellow Forest and destroyed most of them. He took the palace, and men attempted to attack us, but you fought them off. I was blind with grief, having just lost my husband. You were blind with anger, and you fought twenty men single-handedly and won. I didn't know whether to be proud or terrified of you.'

'Which did you decide?'

Alexia didn't answer that. 'You saw me out of the palace and away from the Casmodians. It looked like you would be safe, too, but you were taken at the last minute by Jag . . . ' Alexia closed her eyes again. 'Darj and I rode to Chettona first. We were told once we arrived that the great A'zyon Warrior had been killed at the hand of Cades.'

'The A'zyon Warrior?'

'Yes. It's what the soldiers call you. A simple name but an affectionate one, too.'

'But what does it mean?'

She met my eyes. 'It's an ancient Targian word that means "fearless".'

I swallowed. *How could they bestow such a name on me?*

'And?' I could sense Alexia's hesitation.

She sat up properly. 'You were there, in the first battle at the Yellow Forest, when Cades attacked. You fought for me because I could not fight for myself. You didn't lead the army—Darj did—but you led a group of one hundred horsemen that flanked Cades' army, giving Darj the chance to lead a retreat that saved many more lives than would have been the case had you not been there.' Alexia looked away and hugged her knees. 'And I . . . I failed my people by staying in my palace.'

'Don't you dare say that! You were trying to protect your heritage, your child, and your husband—a man I assume you loved very much.'

Alexia's eyes became red and glassy once again. 'I did, Adaliah, much more than I can bear to live without.' A small sob rose in her throat, but she swallowed it. 'And I had the presumption to believe he would live on in Jeri . . . I have failed in all my roles. I do not deserve—'

'Alexia, you are the rightful queen, and your people still love you, I'm sure. We need you now more than ever. You haven't failed. When you are not a queen, wife, or mother, you are a woman. That is all I am. That is all I remember being. You can exist as that first, too, to begin again, and then resurrect as the queen only when you feel able. Right now, you are ill, grieved, and lost.'

'A great pair we make,' Alexia said with a sad smile. 'You without your memory and me without my people and both of us without our family. How can two girls, existing as that alone, be enough?'

The cavern at Tarcraig provided shelter but little warmth. After everyone else had fallen asleep, I watched as Alexia held her hands over the fire. I knew she hadn't been able to get comfortable or to calm her mind. I suspected she thought I was asleep, and, when Lezan woke in need of some water, it became clear he thought the same.

'The sword Adaliah carries . . . ' Lezan began.

I closed my eyes, knowing Alexia would look over at me. I had my head on my left hand, using it at as pillow, but my right held Elhian's sword close to my chest.

'The blue stone is mostly dormant.' Alexia's tone suggested her mind was somewhere else, but the fact that she knew about the stone caught my interest and I listened intently. 'Fear is reigning.'

'And yet it is still as great as yours.'

Alexia has a sword like this, too?

I watched as she turned her hands over in front of the fire. An ember spat at her feet and she kicked it back in. A tear appeared under her eyelash. It glistened in the orange light.

'The fire,' Lezan whispered.

'Yes . . . I appreciate the warmth, but every flame reminds me of my son's death, of his calls to me. The image of it haunts me.'

Lezan didn't say anything at first, and when he did speak it was with tentative care. 'You need Ru'ach on your side, Alexia. You must let him back into your life.'

'I never said he wasn't.'

'No, but I can see the unrest in your eyes. In your pain, you have turned your shoulder to him.'

'Can you blame me? After everything I've been through?'

Lezan peered at her. 'He is the Great Spirit, Alexia, the only being you must ever bow to. He feels your pain,' he added softly. 'He understands better than anyone what you're going through.'

She looked back at the fire, defiant tears dripping down her cheeks.

'Are you still angry with Darj?' Lezan asked.

Darj was moving restlessly in his sleep every few minutes. Lezan had told me earlier that the leather armband he wore was a gift from Alexia's prince consort, who had given it to him as a symbol of his authority over the Targian army. Both arms were brown from dirt and mud and he smelt like he needed a bath. His face was unshaven, giving him a handsome but gruff look. His hair hung over his forehead as if to shield him from the world.

'He is rugged,' Alexia said, 'but a truer man than any I've met, apart from my husband. He is loyal. Distant but kind. I can rely on him more than myself sometimes.'

I noted that she hadn't answered Lezan's question.

'I think about my people, the women and children, being taken to the beautiful Valley of Kest,' Alexia said. 'It is so ironic that such beauty brings such thoughts of pain and separation. The men have been taken to Casmodia as slaves. I know they will refuse to fight for Cades, but at what price?' She looked at Lezan. 'I want to save my people, but how is that possible?'

9
LOSING FENELLAR

'Adaliah, wake up,' Alexia said, gripping my shoulders as I turned in my sleep.

I was stuck between the dream world and real life again. *Father! . . .* I saw him falling down dead, heard my own scream . . . *No!*

Alexia's grip on my shoulders tightened; I could feel it bringing me back.

But the scene in my mind changed. I was standing in a green-walled city and people were racing around me, screaming and running from something. Some of them were being shot down with arrows. There was blood on the cobblestone roads.

'My dear cousin, what did they do to you?' Alexia cupped my face with one hand. 'Zavad, use the cloth on her forehead. Gently now.'

Cold water dripped onto my skin and I blinked, released from the nightmare. 'Alexia?' My breathing was forced, and I was choking on tears.

She pulled me into a sitting position and wrapped an arm around me. 'It was just a dream,' she said. 'You're safe.'

I rested my head on her shoulder, dazed. 'It was so real.'

'What was? What did you see?'

'I don't know exactly . . . My father . . . and a city, a green city, under siege . . . '

When dawn came and I woke for a second time, Alexia and I realised Darj was gone. Brenna and Zavad were still asleep at the back of the cave and Lezan was cooking something over the fire, so Alexia and I stepped outside to find him. It didn't take us long—we saw him just returning, walking towards our half-circle of grass with a prisoner.

It was a Targian. I could identify that by his black hair and iceberg eyes. He was only a youth, and a spirited one at that: he flailed his arms against Darj even though he must have known who he was.

'Settle down boy,' Darj said. 'I only want to talk to you.'

The youth saw Alexia and stopped moving. Darj let him go and he fell to his knees. 'Forgive me, Your Majesty,' he said, lowering his gaze and bowing. 'I did not know you were here.'

'Who are you?' Alexia asked.

'My name is Naclen. I am from Fenellar. It is lost, my queen.'

Alexia's expression was unchanged, but she tensed. 'Come inside.'

We introduced him to Lezan, who served him some stew. Darj and I took some as well. He and I both noticed how Alexia declined her share.

'Where is Fenellar?' I asked.

Naclen gave me a confused look, but Darj indulged me. 'It is Targe's largest city in the southern part of the kingdom. Tall green walls surround it in a perfect square. They're famous for their coat of evergreen moss. Those walls have protected the city for hundreds of years and stand like ancient guardians, both tired and steadfast.'

Like you.

'It is the city you dreamed about, Adaliah,' Alexia added.

The green city. The terror of my nightmare returned, and I shivered, wondering what it was Naclen was going to tell us.

'It has always been a peaceful city,' Alexia said. 'I have a good agricultural trading agreement between Fenellar and Nirrana, the capital of Delya, which is the kingdom that borders us to the south.' She turned to Naclen again. 'Now, what happened?'

Naclen closed his eyes and drew the image into his mind. 'Cades appeared at the north hill at dawn. Fenellar was not peaceful that day, my queen. Our scouts had told us he was coming, so the farms that lay outside the walls were deserted, and I'm sure Cades could hear us shouting in the city, getting ready for battle. Officer Hae—'

'Who?' I asked.

'Cades' next most trusted man, after Jag,' Darj said. 'A fierce fighter.' He added this with a hint of bitterness.

'We saw him ride up to Cades, and then a whole line of cavalry appeared on the hill.'

I imagined them pausing and considering the city coldly, as if deciding how to carve a meal for dinner.

'Four thousand men followed their king and officer down the hill towards us.' Naclen told us he was the second soldier to come out of Fenellar, riding to his place behind his captain, Quion. 'Quion tried to hurry our men into formation. Two and a half thousand were prepared for battle, and with the Casmodian wave almost upon us, Quion ordered us to charge. He turned his horse to lead, but an arrow split his neck.'

Alexia's mouth dropped at this. She glanced at Darj, who shook his head with quiet anger and murmured, 'He was a good captain.'

'And a good friend,' Naclen added.

'So you were leaderless?' Alexia asked.

'Yes. He fell from his horse, dead before the battle had even started. More arrows rained on us; more men fell. How I was not one of them I will never understand. The Casmodians were riding ever closer. As we rode out to meet them, I began to think of them as the army of all evil.

'Without meaning to, I drew near to Cades. I saw him slay several soldiers. His men were brutal, and we fell like scattered children. I managed to kill just three Casmodians before another one knocked me to the ground. I groped the dirt for my sword, but the Casmodian dismounted and kicked it away. He walked towards me with a sword in one hand.

'I looked around for something to defend myself with. Before I found anything, another Targian pounced on the Casmodian's back. The Casmodian flipped the man over his shoulder and onto the ground in front of him. The Targian asked him to wait, but the Casmodian laughed and asked, "For what?" He pulled a dagger out of his belt and . . .' Naclen gently squeezed his throat. 'I don't think I will ever forget the look on his face as he slumped to the ground. I tried to back away but the Casmodian walked to me again. He pressed the point of his sword into my chest. Blood poured down my side and I was paralysed with fear.'

'How did you survive?' Alexia voiced the question we all had.

'The battle finished. They had slaughtered us in half a day. I don't remember much else except being dragged into the city by the same soldier, following Cades and Officer Hae. I heard them talking. "My wife visited Fenellar once," Cades said. "She called it the cornucopia of Targe. I told her I would take it as my prize one day, and she said she regretted having ever married such a greedy brute." Hae asked how he'd responded to that. Cades said he gave her something to truly regret.'

'What did they do to the women and children?' Darj asked.

'Well, his men ran ahead and killed the few Targian soldiers who remained in the streets. He talked about how there were only a few more towns in Targe to take, and something about Jazmarda—'

'Jazmarda?' Lezan asked.

'Yes, but please don't ask me what. I only remember him mentioning it.'

'The women and children?' Darj asked again.

'Hae stood in the street, demanding that the women and children vacate their houses in an hour. One woman ran at him, screaming, "How dare you! How dare you!" Cades took a bow and arrow from a nearby soldier and shot her. She died at Hae's feet.'

He stopped while we all thought about this, picturing the scene. Alexia rubbed her arm. 'He is truly a disgusting man,' she said.

'He told them they weren't there to negotiate. Some people went to gather their things at once while others ran onto the battlefield, searching for their men . . . I could hear their eerie wailing. It filled the night.'

'What happened to you?' I asked, still trying to understand his part in it.

'They took me into the citadel. I didn't know what they wanted with me until the soldier dropped me at Cades' feet. He told me the only reason I had been spared was to tell the world that Targe was now entirely defeated and . . . ' He glanced at Alexia, 'that its queen was broken, most likely dead. They made me promise to spread the word in return for the safety of my sister, who left Fenellar for Liane three years ago. I haven't seen her since and still don't understand how they even know of her existence. Then they talked about you, my lady, as if I wasn't there.'

'Me?' I asked, confused and intrigued at the same time.

'Yes, he and Hae. He said you'd lost something that would ensure you would never be powerful again.'

'Your memory,' Alexia said.

'Ah, that explains a lot,' Naclen said. 'He couldn't understand why you were still alive. He kept asking, "Didn't we torture her enough?" Hae explained that they did everything but run you through with a sword, which they had decided was too quick and clean for the A'zyon Warrior. He said Jag had made sure your heart and breath had stopped. Then, Cades made the comment that "slaughtering the Keeper of Kest on her own land had probably woken something better left asleep".'

Darj, Alexia, Lezan and I all looked at each other, searching each other's faces for ideas. 'The river . . . ' Lezan mumbled.

Before we could ask Lezan what he was thinking, Naclen finished his story by saying that Fenellar's people left the city in a long line, most taking very little. 'The Targian soldiers who had survived with minor injuries were already being herded together, ready to go to Casmodia to be trained as part of Cades' army like the others. Casmodian soldiers spread oil over the dead and cremated them. The smell of burnt flesh poisoned the air and the yellow fields. They'd already turned red with blood, but now they became black with ash.'

Naclen asked Alexia for permission to go to Kest and find his family, his sister in particular. I think he was concerned that Cades would not keep her safe for long. Alexia granted his wish but became silent once he left. She didn't say how she felt about the fall of Fenellar, so I was left to imagine how it would reinforce her sense of failure and overwhelming defeat. I was glad she didn't speak it. I felt if I heard the words coming from her lips, the sound would dry up all hope.

Darj became restless after Naclen's report and by that afternoon, he had packed everything up and was determined to get us moving. I knew then that Darj was a man of action who had been forced to do nothing for too long.

Zavad clung to Alexia's cloak as the six of us weaved between the clusters of rocks in the shade of the old trees, obediently following Darj's lead. The exiles had left many things behind—ragged clothes, abandoned shelters, rotten food, footprints embedded in thick mud, and simple graves made for those who had not survived.

We rounded a corner and came across a tall, black warhorse. Bagred. I ran to him and stroked his neck, relieved that I had not lost him.

'I told you he wouldn't go far,' Darj said, bringing over the saddle. 'He's a good Targian horse.' He lifted the saddle onto Bagred's back and began to tighten the girth.

I turned at the sudden movement behind me. Two Casmodians were crouching up on the rocks, one of them aiming an arrow at me. I had just reached for my sword when an arrow landed in each of their chests. Their bodies fell from the rocks and thudded on the ground.

Stunned, I turned and saw Alexia with her now empty bow in her hand.

'Thanks,' I said, impressed by her swift dual shot. She gave me a nod.

I climbed up the rock face to get a better view.

'What do you see?' Lezan asked once I pulled myself to the top.

I stood to make an evaluation of the land beyond Tarcraig. 'I can see the exiles in the distance,' I called down to them, 'but nothing else out of the ordinary.'

'Where are they headed?' Lezan asked. 'Kest?'

I orientated myself by the sun and, deciding that they were travelling west towards Kest, I relayed this to Lezan and climbed back down. 'Where should we go?' I asked, jumping the last step and landing on the grass. My question had been directed at Darj, but it was Alexia who answered. 'Casmodia.' We looked at her, waiting for an explanation. 'Adaliah,' she said, 'when you were with Elhian . . . did you remember anything? Did he tell you anything?'

'He saved me and gave me both food and an escape, but I didn't remember anything, no. He doesn't seem to support his father. He just told me to go to Hunt to find you and Lezan.'

'Do you know anything of his plans?' Alexia asked.

'No, nothing. You?'

Alexia tapped her finger against her lips. 'He didn't fight against us that day at the Yellow Forest. He wasn't there when we fled Liane. He didn't intervene, but I know he didn't support it, and I believe he will soon make a stand against his father. But there's only one way he can do that, isn't there Lezan?'

Lezan raised his eyebrows, a smile pulling at his lips. 'Yes, he and I talked much about stirring the Jazmardians before we were separated, and I gave him detailed information about my kingdom. I am sure he has gone there.'

'Yes . . . He got his information from you, but before he could move, he had to get a message to us. He knew that by sending Adaliah to find you, his mentor, and then me, his ally, we would find a way to support him. He couldn't move without that certainty. Now, he will go into Jazmarda to rally an army against his father, but even if he succeeds, he will need our help.'

For the first time, Darj began to look a little excited, not only because of Alexia's observation but, as he told me later, because of the glimpse of life in her. 'So what you're saying is the only way we can do that is if we go to Casmodia,' he said, 'to liberate your men and bring them to join Elhian in battle.' Alexia gave him a satisfied nod. Darj smiled. 'Then lead the way, Your Majesty.'

10
THE ORDAINED

We travelled through the Targian countryside for two days, avoiding Casmodian encampments. Zavad rarely spoke but colour returned to his face and he began to walk more and more each day, a testament to his growing health. While I could not say the same for my cousin, she managed to keep up with us. Darj was setting a fast pace with his new found determination to fight back, but I was glad. I developed a belief that the sooner we did something, the sooner I could get my memory back. I longed to stop feeling like a stranger to myself.

'But we have to go around Egra because it will be full of Casmodians,' Darj said after noon on the second day.

'If we don't go into Egra we'll never get supplies and other horses and we'll never make it to Casmodia in time,' Lezan said.

'I'd rather be late than dead. Their archers alone could kill us.'

'Would you rather starve than take a chance?'

'We can catch our own food.'

'What about the women?' Lezan asked.

'Please don't bring us into this,' Alexia said.

The decision of whether or not to go into Egra consumed Darj and Lezan for at least an hour. Alexia passed the time by telling me how we had both regularly visited the royal family's mansion by the lake there. She said King Amaz had been visiting the town on political business when he first met the lord's daughter and Alexia's future mother, Jenethea Perrin. He had also fallen in love with the scenery and built the royal mansion so he could return whenever he needed a retreat. In the end, he died there and, when Alexia returned home to Liane, she returned to be crowned as queen.

'Do you miss your father?' I asked.

'Of course I do.' Alexia struggled to keep her voice even. 'I miss all the men who were in my life. Father would not have let Targe come to this. Cades waited until he was dead before waging this war. He would not have dared to invade while Father was alive.'

'Darj?' I called later. He stopped and waited for me to catch up. 'What if we go into Egra as Casmodians?'

'Three women, two men and a boy is not a likely Casmodian party, especially in these times,' he said. 'Nor do we look like them.'

'Perhaps Brenna and I . . . ' I paused as I prepared my next words carefully. 'Perhaps we could find some soldiers, ask about Zavad's family, and . . . persuade them to give us food and horses.'

'"Persuade" them?' Darj asked, his eyebrows rising. 'I don't think so.'

'So you plan to just walk to the capital of Casmodia?'

'Well, I'm yet to hear a better suggestion. I'm sorry, Zavad.' He patted the boy's knee as he rode Bagred beside us. 'But there's still hope for your family.'

'Where's Queen Alexia?' Zavad asked.

I realised the queen had disappeared. I walked to a small cluster of rocks near the side of the road, the only place she could be concealed.

I found her leaning on a rock and vomiting again. 'You're still not well, are you?' I helped her sit down.

Her face was pale and covered in a faint layer of sweat. 'Please, don't tell the others.' She put a hand over her stomach. Her lips turned in a weak smile. 'Whenever I felt sick in the past, my husband would bring me food in bed, read my favourite book to me, and ensure I was comfortable in every way. I . . . I don't think I can do this without him.' Tears came and she placed a hand over her face, trying to mute her grief.

'Alexia?' Darj called from the road.

She wiped the tears off her cheeks. 'I'm coming!'

I put a hand on her arm, wishing I could say something that would ease her pain. She gave me another small smile and stood.

'Are you all right?' Darj asked when we arrived back at the road.

'I'm fine,' Alexia said. 'I just shouldn't drink so much water.'

I could tell Darj wasn't convinced—he was far too intelligent to be fooled so easily—but before he could reply, something else drew our attention. We stopped and listened to the unusual sound. It wasn't the wind or distant lone crow, the only noises there had been for hours. This was man-made—heavy footsteps, clinking armour. I scanned the grassland to my left and unsheathed my sword. Still carrying Zavad, Bagred stopped next to me and pointed his ears forward.

A contingent of men appeared over a small hill nearby. They were armed and dirty. One of them pointed at Alexia and me and there was suddenly a lot of yelling as they ran towards us. I recognised their barbaric determination to kill—I'd seen it before—but they stayed in formation, remained emotionless, and focused in on their enemy to the point where even Zavad could see that these were no barbarians.

'Get Zavad out of here,' Lezan told Alexia.

She mounted Bagred behind the boy and dug her heels in before I even registered we were about to fight.

I handed Brenna a knife. 'You must protect your queen,' I said, though the words were to give myself courage as well.

'They can't be sure it's us,' Brenna said.

'They will kill us anyway.'

'How many, Darj?' Lezan asked.

'At least forty. No, fifty.'

'Can we defeat fifty?' I asked.

'Perhaps, but not all at once.'

'Look.' Brenna pointed to about ten men leaving the group. 'They're chasing the queen!'

'The queen is a skilled archer and a swift rider,' Darj said. 'She will manage them. Are you ready?'

Darj killed the first man and the second. He flung them to the ground with ruthless force and ran at a third. I saw a sword tip to my left, turned, and ran my blade through the man who had been about to strike me.

I ran at another warrior. We fought, but he kept pushing me back, trying to make me trip. I was stronger than he thought though. I forced him back, disarmed him, and pushed him to the ground. I picked up his sword and threw it in the dirt near Brenna. She saw it but did nothing.

Lezan knocked a man down with his staff but was hit from behind by another. I ran to his aide and impaled the soldier who had felled him. I pulled Lezan to his feet and made sure he was standing steadily before running back towards Darj.

He had killed more than ten soldiers in just a few minutes, but he was surrounded by many more. I saw Alexia riding back towards us, without Zavad. She carried her bow in her hand and there were men still behind her, but not as many or as close. She shot another one as she rode. She yelled something at me, but I couldn't understand what until she was nearer and tried again. 'Drop Elhian's sword! Drop it!'

Without even thinking about it, my grip slackened, and the sword fell to the ground. The Casmodian I had been fighting picked it up. As soon as he wrapped his scarred, brown fingers around the grip, the stone glowed brighter than I had ever seen. A great blue light shot into the sky and fell down around us. It was blinding. I put my hand over my eyes and dropped to my knees. Everything around me seemed to slow. The fighting stopped. All I could hear was Alexia riding closer, Alexia knocking down the man who had the sword. I heard the blade drop to the ground with a clink. The light disappeared, and I slowly opened my eyes.

The men around us had fallen. They were dead. Only those who still followed Alexia—four men—had survived. They bent down on one knee and drew their bows.

Alexia, who had ridden past us, now turned and rode between the archers and us just as they released their arrows. One hit Bagred. He panicked and fell, taking Alexia with him.

Darj ran at the remaining men with swords in both hands, but they turned on their heels and fled back across the plains. Darj yelled something after them, raising his sword threateningly. They didn't look back.

I hurried to my cousin, my quick steps crunching over the rocky path. 'Alexia—'

'I'm fine, but I think I've killed your horse.' She grimaced as she tried to pull her leg out from under Bagred.

I stroked his dark cheek. 'No, he's all right. Just hurt.'

'I cannot believe you put yourself in that position!' Lezan yelled at Alexia. 'Do you have any idea what you risked? Do you realise what could have happened?' He was puffing and red-faced. It surprised me to see him angry.

'What was the alternative? Let you all die?'

'That does not mean it was all right for you to risk everything. If you endanger your life, you endanger your entire royal line as we know it!'

'Do you think I don't know that?' Alexia asked, raising her voice, too. 'Now stop arguing with me and get me out!'

Darj was already trying to coax Bagred to get up despite his injury. The horse was solid, heavy and stubborn, and it took both Lezan's and my help to get him to stand again.

We pulled Alexia to her feet, too. 'My leg feels a bit bruised, but I'm all right,' she said, now calm again. She pointed at a line of blood dribbling down my arm. 'You, however, are wounded.'

'It's nothing.' I hadn't even noticed it, but the blood that stained my clothes hinted at a significant cut. Alexia pulled back my sleeve and revealed the slash on the back of my upper arm. Without saying a word, she broke off some material from her own tattered dress, cleaned the blood away and tied the cloth firmly around the wound.

'Thank you.'

Alexia smiled at me and turned to her maid. 'Brenna, I hid Zavad in a tree over that hill.' She pointed to the one she meant. 'Please go and get him for me.'

'Of course.' Brenna ran off straight away.

Alexia considered the poor horse she'd almost sacrificed and bit her lip like something was wrong. I realised myself there was only one arrow in his back when four had been shot. Two had landed in the dirt nearby, but the fourth . . . Alexia turned to Lezan, but before she could speak, he said to us all, 'I must get to Egra.'

It didn't take much longer for Egra's renowned mountains to come into sight after that. It was only then that I asked Alexia what had happened with the sword.

'No one can touch the swords except for those ordained. Anyone who does so is killed, as are those who fight with them.'

'Am I ordained?' I asked.

'Yes.'

'Are Darj and Lezan and Brenna?'

'No.'

'Then why didn't they die?'

'Because they came under your protection. They were on your side.'

'Who is ordained then?' I asked.

'Elhian and Cades, myself, Hazaka Cazren the King of Jazmarda, the Keeper of Kest and his daughter. Leaders and their heirs. Following your father's death, you inherited his title. You are the Keeper of Kest now.'

I stopped. 'But why me and my father?' When Alexia kept walking, I grabbed her arm and made her face me. 'Why?'

'You truly don't remember any of this?' she asked, searching my eyes. I shook my head. Of course I didn't.

'All right,' she said, and we continued walking along the road. 'Our ancestors believed that Jazmarda, Casmodia and Targe needed to be allied. I think they had long been at war with each other. Three swords were forged as tools of friendship and protection, and each one had a rare stone that came from the land it represented. Elhian's blue stone is unique to the Casmodian Mountains. The swords were meant to represent the pillars our kingdoms should stand on: faith, hope, and love. Faith for Casmodia, hope for Jazmarda, and love for Targe. I believe Targe's sword was the most powerful at first.'

'Why?'

'Because nothing is as strong as love.' She took a deep breath and linked her arm through mine. 'But they were not made wholly good, Adaliah. I wish they had been, but whoever wields one of these swords decides whether to use it for good or evil. They have a choice between faith and fear, hope and despair, love and hate . . . '

'Was there a sword for Kest?'

'Yes. The Valley of Kest has never had people, but it was considered a place in its own right and worthy of its own sword. Its river is an important source of life, so life is what Kest's sword came to represent, an even stronger force than love.'

I nodded. 'If one is not alive, one cannot love.'

'Exactly. The Jazmardian queen, Cazine, prophesied that Kest would become the salvation of the other three kingdoms. So, it needed a caretaker, but whom? A championship was arranged to find who was worthy to take the fourth sword and with it maintain peace between the kingdoms. This was a championship our ancestor Prince Jovan won. The Jazmardians believed this was unfair. Against Cazine's will and without her knowledge, they went to take Kest for themselves the night after the championship. They say only ten Targians defeated them with help from Ru'ach and the living waters of Kest River. They believe they were cursed that night for their disobedience, warmongering, and greed. Jazmarda has not been a powerful kingdom since.'

I could tell by the way Alexia was now looking at me out of the corner of her eye that she was deciding whether or not to share her next piece of information. She continued but seemed to be choosing her words carefully. 'What many don't know is that with this sword came not only the position of the "Keeper of Kest", but a medallion, a large silver coin that would look meaningless to an average person. They called it the Medallion of Courage. This medallion could, under special circumstances, take the power from the swords, but no one knows how exactly. Lezan predicted this would have to happen before the curse on Jazmarda would end.'

'And he was exiled for that?'

'Yes, but also because he believed that, as the descendants of the champion, Targe would be the one to administer the change and return hope to the Jazmardians. Jazmarda is a proud kingdom. They didn't like the thought of needing our help for anything.'

I shook my head as I tried to take it all in. 'Where is this medallion now?'

'Only the Keeper of Kest knows.' Alexia glanced at me but didn't ask me to remember, which I appreciated. 'In any case, Prince Jovan was the king's brother, which is where the tradition of passing the Life Sword onto the second born began.'

I thought about the sculpture in the palace courtyard at Liane—the two men on the winged horse—and how the inscription had read 'King Phylip and Prince Jovan'.

'Were any other kingdoms given a sword?'

'No, only those three kingdoms of the Rhea Lands, and Kest.'

'The Rhea Lands?' I was beginning to realise how much I didn't know, how much I couldn't remember, but Alexia remained patient with me.

'The Rhea Lands is the collective name for the five kingdoms of Casmodia, Targe, Jazmarda, the White Isles and Delya. The White Isles and Delya were not given a sword. I think that's because they had never been at war with the other three kingdoms.'

'Why was the Life Sword passed on to me though? Why am I the Keeper of Kest?'

'Because I am the only child of King Amaz. If I'd had a younger sibling, they would have taken the role. Or, if I ever have two or more children alive together, the second child would soon be ordained in your place, but they would not become the "Keeper of Kest" and leave the palace until they were sixteen.'

'So because you don't have two children, I am ordained?' We had fallen well behind the others by now.

'Yes. You see, to prevent the rise of rebels or false governments, peace would only last as long as the swords remained in the hands of their rightful owners—those ordained. It's a reminder of a monarch's responsibility for the care of their kingdom. A leader decides whether to guide their people into good or evil. Monarchs can borrow each other's swords if needed—that's why it was the best thing Elhian could have given you, but its power will prove much greater when it is returned to his hands. While it will help you, so long as you have it there can be no peace.'

'Is this how peace was lost?'

Alexia tucked a stray lock of hair behind her ear. 'Yes. My sword was stolen from my chambers, giving Cades easy victory when he attacked at the Yellow Forest the next day. I can assure you he won't use any of the swords for good. My sword was to protect love, but he has used it for hate. If he gets the other three swords, I believe he will misuse them, too. Instead of faith, he will bring fear. Instead of hope, despair. Instead of life . . . death. With those qualities, he will have power to kill whom he likes, to dictate which kingdom he likes. But first, he needs your father's sword, your sword, as it is the key.'

'The key to what?'

'His divinity.'

11
POISONED

We continued our travels towards Egra. Darj led our group through a dense forest. There, the air smelt like rotten wood—sharp but fresh. The sun was trying to reach through the branches of old trees, but it hardly touched the wet fern fronds that covered the ground.

Zavad ran here and there collecting mushrooms, bringing them back to Darj for approval before storing them in a saddlebag. When the forest became more of woodland with a floor of golden foliage, Zavad abandoned his quest for mushrooms and ran about kicking up leaves until Egra's walls came into view. A large section of the wall had crumbled to the ground, presumably under the attack of catapults. The city itself seemed empty and desolate, like it, too, had been wounded in battle and left to die. Swords and rusting armour lay on the ground near the main gate, as well as many rotting bodies that hadn't been buried.

'It's like their spirits are still here,' Darj said.

The stench was revolting. I covered my nose and mouth with my hand before kneeling beside an older man lying in mud. A silver necklace in his hand had caught my attention, and I lifted it up for examination.

Zavad saw me holding it. 'That is my mother's,' he said, taking it from me. He looked at the dead man and threw himself at the body. 'Father!' He yelled the word over and over until he began to cry, his little arms trying to reach around the stiff, white neck.

I touched Zavad's shoulder. 'Oh Zavad . . . I'm so sorry.' His body was rigid with grief.

He looked up at me with tears on his cheeks. 'Is he really dead?'

'Yes, Zavad,' I said softly, 'he is.'

Alexia joined us, her face paling as she knelt beside Zavad. She held the boy and rocked him gently as he cried into her shoulder.

Darj searched the field of bodies for a digging implement. The nearest thing he found was a curved piece of wood, which he used to clear out a natural ditch. I helped him lower Zavad's father into it. The body was inflexible and the process an inelegant and numbing one but, once he was in place, we moved his hands over his sword, making him look more at rest.

'Whatever he went through,' Darj said, 'he is at peace now.'

Zavad left Alexia and knelt down next to the grave, looking at his father one last time. Then, he put his mother's necklace on the body. 'You can cover him now.'

The sun fell slowly behind the mountains as we filled the grave back in. I used another piece of wood to mark it out in the field of dead, while Zavad clung to Alexia, fatigue overtaking his tears.

'Adaliah?' Alexia called later. 'Can you put Zavad on Bagred? We need to find a safe shelter in the city. The royal manor will be occupied, but I'm sure the old stone cottage near the road that goes up to the mountains will be neglected. It was even before the war.'

'Of course,' I said but, before I could move, Darj picked the boy up and then offered a hand to help Alexia stand.

She took it and walked over to Lezan. 'How bad is it?' I heard her ask.

'It is quick,' he said. 'There is not much time.'

We followed the back roads through Egra and stayed in the shadows. I walked ahead of the others and found the cottage first. I forced the door open with my foot and brushed away the spider webs that hung just inside. There was a view of the mountains through one of the windows, and through another I could see the royal manor and gardens on the other side of the lake. Further down the road was the Lord's House where Alexia's mother once lived. Now it belonged to Lord Fenton, Alexia's distant cousin on her mother's side.

Darj followed me inside and found a bedroom to lay Zavad down in, while Alexia led Lezan into the main room. There, the cold, stone floor was littered with autumn leaves. Alexia asked Brenna to start a fire with them, and I covered up the windows so the light wouldn't give us away.

The cottage was already feeling warmer when Alexia rolled back Lezan's sleeve and revealed the wound where the missing arrow had scraped him. There was a red streak down his arm and his frail body was shivering. 'Lezan . . .' Alexia began. It seemed it was much worse than she'd imagined. I walked over to get a closer look. 'It's poison,' Alexia explained, 'and moving fast.'

'What?' I knelt beside him. 'But it can't be harmful, otherwise Bagred—'

'Animals are immune,' Lezan said, coughing over his words.

'And you lecture me about taking care of myself,' Alexia said.

'*I* am not the sovereign of a significant realm.'

'What can we do to help?' I asked.

Lezan listed three types of plants to be used in a tonic. 'This is why I wanted to come to Egra. These plants can all be found here near the mountains. The tonic will reverse the effects of the injury.'

'Are you sure?' I asked, sensing he was keeping something from me. Something didn't quite add up.

'Yes, I am sure.'

Still, I asked Darj and Brenna to find the plants instead. I didn't want to leave Lezan's side.

Alexia bound his wound tightly, presumably hoping the bandage would slow the poison.

'Your Majesty . . .' he said in between shallow breaths, 'I have to go.'

'Don't you dare speak of such things,' she said, pulling the bandage tighter. Her slender fingers were gentle but firm.

'And you will have to speak.'

I wondered what he meant, but she ignored him and tied the bandage off.

'Alexia,' Darj called before he left, 'Zavad is asking for you.'

While we waited for Darj and Brenna to return, Alexia tried to coax Zavad to sleep and I stayed by Lezan. He soon had a faint yellow tinge in his face and the poison was spreading both up and down his arms. He told me he could no longer feel his legs.

Darj and Brenna returned with the requested ingredients. Lezan gave me broken instructions as to what to do with the unusual combination of leaves and flowers, and the final result was a brown, muddy concoction that smelt like a horse's stable. He asked me to look in his pocket for a small, empty glass vial, which I found.

'Mix it together, and shake it up,' Lezan said, now only able to move his head.

The sound of Alexia singing to Zavad came in from the next room. It warmed me and made Lezan smile. 'You must take care of your cousin,' he told me as I finished with the tonic. It had turned green. 'She may soon be the most wanted woman in history.'

'Don't speak. Just drink.' I held the vial to his lips.

He moved his head in a vague 'no'. 'It is for you,' he whispered.

My heart began to beat faster. 'No, Lezan, this is for you. It's the tonic we made for you.'

'Adaliah, the remedy for this poison can only be found in the Casmodian Mountains. This is for you. It lacks the last ingredient, but . . . ' He closed his eyes.

'Lezan?' I shook his shoulder, but his body was already limp. Froth appeared between his lips. I shook him again. 'No! I need you!'

I turned at the sound of footsteps. Darj had heard me and rushed into the room. The look on his face was one of disbelief. He picked up Lezan's aged wrist and felt for a pulse, but there was none. He checked to see if he was breathing, but there was no moving air. After resting his hand on his chest, he found no heartbeat.

'He's . . . he's gone.' Darj put a hand on my shoulder, unable to offer justification or words of comfort.

Alexia's lullaby finished, and there was silence.

We buried Lezan at the bottom of the mountains, far from Jazmarda. Darj was tearless, Alexia numb, but I couldn't help but cry. *It's too much.*

'What do we do now?' I asked.

'We remember him,' Darj said, 'and we press on.'

I moved to my cousin and she put an arm around me. 'So much death,' I said.

'I know.' She held me close. 'But when you least expect it, there is also life, and that is what we fight for.'

12
BRENNA

Sometime later, the three of us began the walk back to the cottage along a dark, friendless road.

'How will you stand being the only man amongst three women?' Alexia asked Darj in little more than a whisper.

He smiled at her. 'I feel privileged to be the only one who knows where Targe's two most valuable women are.'

'Where?' Alexia asked with feigned enthusiasm, and both Darj and I laughed. 'I am grateful for all you've done for us,' she said more seriously. 'I hope you know that.'

Darj tried to hide another smile. 'Hush, Your Majesty. You never know who may be out and about.' But he walked a little taller as he spoke.

The cottage came into view and we saw a light shining within. We glanced at each other and hurried back.

Zavad was sleeping and safe, but Brenna was gone and the front door had been left open. Darj searched for her in the surrounding streets while Alexia and I guarded Zavad, but Darj soon came back without having seen her.

'Why would she leave Zavad unaccompanied?' Darj asked as he peered out one of the windows, still trying to locate the maid.

'I don't know,' Alexia said. 'Perhaps she was taken by a soldier?'

'Why would they take her and leave the boy?' I asked.

'You're right,' Darj said. 'She must have left of her own accord.'

'I know what you're thinking, Darj,' Alexia said, 'but I don't think Brenna would do anything to cause us harm. She has come this far when many wouldn't have.'

'That's true,' I said.

'There!' Darj said in a strained whisper, pointing to something out the window. 'She just went around a corner. Come, Adaliah.'

We left Alexia and Zavad at the cottage and followed Brenna towards the centre of the city along a paved road that edged the silver lake. The way Alexia had described it, the streets of Egra were usually busy with people and horses and markets. Now, there was only the lone figure of a young maid, and she was far too conspicuous for my liking. She leant against the small stonewall that separated the road from the lake, like she was waiting for something.

That something came in the form of a man a few minutes later, a man who greeted her with a kiss. He'd walked down from a large, well-lit house further up the road. I couldn't see what he looked like from where he was standing, but the bright moon showed his uniform.

It was blue with a silver curl on his chest.

We continued to make our way around the lake until we got as close to them as possible. We hid behind a cluster of small trees. I watched as Brenna giggled when the man kissed her neck from behind and slipped his hand around her waist.

'Do you remember when you first saw me, Baryan?' She spoke softly, but it was a still night and her words were clear. 'Before the war?'

'Of course. To think I almost said no to accompanying Elhian on his trip to Liane! You were the most beautiful servant I'd ever seen. Even your queen must have been jealous of you.'

'She was too in love with her husband and child and kingdom to notice me.'

'Yes, but with our help she's lost all three.' He muffled a laugh in her dark hair.

'Hmmm . . . But even though I stole Alexia's sword, she and Adaliah still hope to change their fate.'

'And how do they think they will do that?'

Brenna turned and left a light kiss on his lips. 'If I told you that would be treason,' she said with a childlike smile.

'Well, it wouldn't be the first time, would it?'

I wanted to stay and listen, but Darj tugged on my arm and pointed towards the soldiers' house. 'Horses,' he whispered. 'We have to get the queen out of here first thing tomorrow.'

We found a stable behind the building and, when we walked in, we could hear Casmodian men jeering inside the house.

Darj untethered the two horses closest to the door. He mounted the large red stallion he'd chosen for himself—Guntar was the name etched into the saddle—and held the reins of the other horse while I mounted it. They were restless and their hooves clattered on the cobblestone road in a way that sounded like a herd of horses rather than just two. I could see Darj cringing at every step, his muscles taut for the slightest hint of an ambush or shout of realisation from the house. If he was anything like me, his mind was clear and focused, but his heart was betraying him. Mine certainly was. Every part of my being wanted to send the horses into an unrestrained gallop back to the cottage, and it placed an immense strain on my self-control to walk them around the corner like we were nothing more than merchantmen doing business in the coolness of the night.

We turned at the closest corner and heard Brenna's laugh echoing into the sky. I'd never had a proper conversation with her, but she still sounded so different than what I had imagined her to be.

'I thought she was just a willing maid,' Darj whispered. 'Now she's a scheming woman. I can't believe she stole Alexia's sword. She was in one of the palace's most trusted positions, and she used it to start a war.' He said it like he'd been at fault somehow, as if he should have taken her more seriously and stopped her from betraying the queen.

'Go back to the house,' Darj said once we were far enough away. 'I will find some more supplies and join you soon. Don't . . . don't tell her about Brenna. Not yet.'

At the cottage, I joined Alexia as she sat in front of the fire. I explained that Darj was still searching for supplies. She didn't press me for anything further, and we were silent for some time.

I thought a lot about Lezan, and Brenna. I gathered I was to keep her betrayal a secret to protect the queen's faith in the people around her, but was I right to trust everyone as I did? But then, what choice did I have? I hadn't trusted Elhian, but he had sent me in the right direction to find my cousin. I wondered where he was now, what he was doing, if Alexia was right to suspect he was raising an army in Jazmarda, and if they would fight for us. The questions filled my mind, and I began to feel cold and alone.

'What are we going to do, Alexia?' I asked, waking her from her thoughts.

'I've been asking myself the same thing,' she said. 'All I know is we need to get into Casmodia. I need to free my men. I don't know how, but I do know we can't walk in there as Alexia and Adaliah Elryane. We must pose as common Targian women.'

'Yes . . . But . . . ' I wrapped my arms around myself, thinking of Zavad and how he had clung to his dead father. 'Is there any hope?'

Alexia opened her mouth to say something but hesitated. I knew she held little hope herself and that in a way my question had been unfair. 'Sometimes we have to believe in something we can't see or feel, just so we have a reason to keep going. The problem with you and me is that we are supposed to be a source of hope to others.' Alexia turned and peered into the flickering fireplace. 'We can't give up . . . even when we want to.'

She turned away, and I knew she was trying not to cry . . . and failing. She hardly made a sound but, when I stood and walked to her, her face was wet with tears.

'Alexia?' My heart ached from the sorrow I could feel in her. 'Why do you keep trying to swallow your pain?'

Alexia looked down at her feet. 'Because I should be able to bear it. All this . . . It's nothing less than what I deserve.'

'Grief is hard, but coupled with guilt I'm sure it's almost impossible to bear. Please, don't do this to yourself.' I put an arm around her shoulders and felt the tension she was forcing on them. 'It is not your fault they died.' Alexia shook her head, her tears falling on the cold stone floor. 'It's not your fault,' I said, now holding her close.

Alexia couldn't reply. She leant her head on my shoulder and wept.

'I loved him so much, my Ethaniel,' she said once she'd recovered a little.

'Ethaniel?'

'My Ethaniel, my husband. I wish you could remember him. And Jeri—he would have been king one day. And because I fled to Hunt, thinking I could save him, he died. I led my son to his death. And I left you to be treated with cruelty . . . If I had just accepted my defeat . . . All those soldiers, my men, dead. Gone to battle at my orders, to defend a kingdom we lost . . . Zavad's father, Lezan—where will it stop? The weight of it is unbearable.' She trembled. 'And as for my grief, my grief alone . . . I don't even know where to start. I feel ill just thinking about it. I have lost everything important to me, except you. All I want is to see them again.'

I said nothing, knowing that no words could even begin to heal her yet. I just held her close and let her cry until she was exhausted. I was relieved she was sharing her burden, as painful as it was. Carrying it on her own had been having a visible effect on her health, and I was certain that was why she'd been so pale and weak.

She was almost asleep in my arms when I heard someone arriving on horseback outside the front door. I reached for Elhian's sword but, before I could pick it up, Darj rushed in. 'What is it?' I asked. It wasn't like Darj to be anything but composed and in control.

He ignored me when he saw Alexia and knelt by her side. 'Is she hurt?' he asked.

'Well, yes, but not in the way you imagine,' I said.

Darj pressed his lips together, understanding. Again, he seemed to recoil, as if he was responsible for the queen's pain. 'Alexia,' he said as she opened her eyes, 'I'm sorry, but we have to leave. We're in danger.' He took her hand. 'Can you ride?'

'I think so.'

'Good. I have three horses waiting.'

'Only three?' Alexia asked. 'What happened to Brenna? Is she all right?'

'She's fine, but we can't wait for her. They know we're here.' Darj helped her stand and led her outside to the horses while I ran to get Zavad.

The boy fought against me, refusing to come outside, and in the end Darj had to come back and carry him. 'What happened?' I asked him while Alexia wasn't nearby. 'Why do we have to leave now?'

'They know we're here. I heard them singing,' he said. '"Tonight she dies, tonight she fries, just like her son, oh won't it be fun!"'

The mockery in the song repulsed me.

I followed him outside and we all rode up the mountainside, far enough to be out of danger but close enough to still see the cottage.

We watched. A few minutes later men ran up the three streets leading to the house, securing all exit points.

They burst into the cottage. Angry yells filled the night when they realised it was empty.

We listened to them arguing, fighting. One man was killed in the fray. They tossed black liquid on the roof and on the floors inside, and soon the house was alight.

Alexia saw the flames and turned her face away. 'Thank you for keeping us safe,' she said to Darj.

'If we somehow survive this, you can thank me then. In the meantime, let's just get to Casmodia.'

13
CASMODIA

With winter beginning to settle in, the mornings were becoming dark and cold, like the sun was freezing and delaying in its ritual rise. It could hardly be seen as it climbed the sky in Casmodia—snow fell across the mountains and whitened the tips of ancient trees instead. It was eerie and soundless, as if white death was creeping over the high peaks. Below was the Gap that linked Casmodia with its broken enemy to the south. The wind whistled through it like a tunnel.

It wasn't until midday that the sun broke through the clouds. I stood at the edge of a sheer cliff and placed a rugged blue stone in a small hollow on a tree branch. I held it there until the sunlight caught it, causing it to shimmer. I did this twice more before the sun disappeared again. I laid false tracks to the right and tread carefully to the left to re-join my companions.

We'd been followed for the last two days and it was my idea to create a diversion with the stone. Darj had found it hidden in the rocks of the Casmodian Mountains. It was like the one in Elhian's sword, but it needed the sun to make it glow. It was my hope that whoever was following us would see it, think we were heading in that direction, and follow the false tracks.

'I did it,' I said, catching up with the queen and general as they rode along a narrow path.

'Good,' Alexia said.

She was deep in thought and had been for days. For almost a week we had been making our way through the mountains, ever closer to our men but still without a plan as to how to set them free. Zavad's small, white arms clung to Alexia's waist. He'd wrapped her green cloak around himself as best as he could and was still sleepy.

We were trying to find the quickest and safest route to Casmodia's capital, Semanez, a city Alexia said was built in and around the hills and named after Casmodia's first known tribal leader. She told me it had been over a year since she'd last visited. Ethaniel and Darj had been with her, as had I, but of course I couldn't remember. 'I was aware of the growing tensions between my kingdom and Casmodia,' she explained, 'and upon my visit I also found them determined to make war. I did my best to negotiate, but Cades wanted something from me I could not give. Then days, weeks, and months slipped by without a whisper of conquest, and I grew hopeful but never content.'

When evening fell, the four of us made camp in a small area sheltered by close growing pine trees. Alexia unsaddled the horses while I searched for firewood with Zavad. Darj took the queen's bow and arrows to hunt dinner. He returned with two rabbits just as I finished making a fire. I let him skin and cook them. 'It's Jag following us,' he said. 'I saw him with a group of men following your diversion.'

'Good,' I said, secretly amazed I could fool the Casmodian general.

It wasn't until much later, once the sun had set and Zavad was asleep, that Alexia finally voiced her thoughts. 'There had to be someone helping on the inside for the Casmodians to get my sword,' she said.

Darj glanced at me.

Brenna.

She looked at him as he poked the campfire with a stick, and I could tell she suspected he knew something. I couldn't speak for him, but I sometimes found her perceptiveness unnerving. 'Say you are he,' she went on, 'that if it weren't for you, the Targian kingdom would still be standing. Say that Adaliah and I are your prisoners—no, gifts, sent to honour the Lord of Semanez.'

Darj shook his head. 'I will not let you compromise your dignity.'

'We won't be staying that long, but they will take us into the lord's chambers and that's what we need if we are to find information.'

Darj caught my eye. 'What's your plan?' he asked, but before I could think of what to say, Alexia kicked his shin.

'It will work!'

'And where does Zavad fit into it all?' Darj asked.

The boy was sleeping. 'You'll see,' she said.

The next day we travelled towards Semanez, but not in the way I had envisioned. Instead of skirting the city to find a secret way in, Darj rode with us towards the front gate, adapting a bold persona that would be imperative to our plan. Alexia and I had our hands bound and faces covered.

A large, round man with a single key hanging on his belt paced the stone wall over the gate. He stopped and lent on the wall with a frown, watching as we drew closer. Once we were in hearing range, he called down to us.

'I am Lord Parrian,' he said. 'What business have you here?'

Darj dismounted his red stallion. 'I have a gift from Cades himself for those who stayed behind to protect what is his.' He revealed our faces—two tired and dirty girls. 'Straight from the queen's palace.'

Parrian smirked. 'They'll have to be cleaned up a bit.'

'I will ensure this, my lord. Just show me the way.' Darj stepped towards the gate, too confident in my eyes, but convincing.

'Wait,' Parrian said. 'Who's the boy? One of their sons?'

'Certainly not. This is my son. I hoped you would let me show him around the city. It is enough to inspire any young boy.'

Parrian slanted his head as he studied Zavad. 'I have a son, too. Perhaps he could show yours around our great city.'

'Thank you.' Darj waited for Parrian to open the gate, but the lord still hesitated. My heart began to quicken. *He knows we're lying. Surely he knows.*

'You don't look like a Casmodian,' he said at length.

'Not by birth,' Darj said, thinking quickly, 'but in heart. I have risked much for Cades, and he said to show you this, to let you see where my true allegiance lies.' He lifted my saddlebags on Bagred and drew out Elhian's sword.

'The sword of Cades himself! Either you have killed him, or he gives you much honour in letting you carry it.'

'Cades lives, even as I am standing before you,' Darj said.

'I don't doubt it. Open the gate!' he shouted at two soldiers.

The loose chains rattled as the doors opened out like heavy butterfly wings. Darj gave a nod of thanks and led us in while Parrian came down to meet him. He reached his hand out to Darj with a grim smile. 'This is appreciated. Things have been too dull in Semanez.' He examined us with small dark eyes. Alexia turned her face away, but I held his gaze. 'Most of my comrades are in Targe and beyond,' he said to Darj, still watching me, 'riding in the name of glory behind one of the greatest leaders Casmodia has ever seen. And I'm here, babysitting women, children, and young, inexperienced soldiers more concerned with their drink than their duty. You there!' he shouted at one. 'Get back to your post!'

A great castle loomed behind him. It did not look as inviting as Alexia's palace in Liane. It was made from dark-grey stones that needed cleaning. Tall turrets gave it a powerful feel, but also an oppressive one. Snow covered the rooftops. I imagined it was just as cold inside. 'I'm permitted to stay there in my own chambers during Cades' absence,' Parrian told Darj, 'but I would give even that up just to ride to battle. It's a cold morning, isn't it? I often wonder what possessed Semanez the Great to choose this place as his base. An avalanche has drowned it on more than one occasion. But it is hard to get to, is no grounds for a fierce battle, and gives any approaching enemy a disadvantage . . . ' He trailed off. 'My men will take you to my chambers. Clean these women up and I will meet with them tonight.'

When we entered the lord's chambers in Cades' castle alone, Darj breathed a sigh of relief. 'We made it.'

Just as he spoke, the door opened behind us and Parrian walked in with a boy a few years older than Zavad. 'This is my son,' he said. 'He wants to show your son around.'

'May I come?' Darj asked. 'These ladies can get themselves clean.'

'Come with me,' Parrian said. 'We can eat. Talk.' He looked at Alexia and me. 'You two: my maid will prepare a bath and give you fresh clothes. I'll be back later.'

Zavad circled Parrian as if seeing a Casmodian for the first time, a real enemy up close. 'What?' Parrian barked.

Zavad ran back to Alexia. She put a hand on his shoulder and urged him to leave with Darj. Zavad obeyed, and the four left.

The door closed, and the latch slipped into place.

Alexia glared after them. 'And where is the mother to that son of his?' she asked. 'He looks at us like that and he's probably married.'

'This part was your idea, remember?' I said.

Alexia opened her mouth but a response failed her.

'So . . . I take it we're not having a bath?' I asked.

Alexia examined her dirty fingernails. 'I hope someone appreciates the sacrifices we're making.' She pulled the key Zavad had just stolen off Parrian out from under her cloak and opened the door with it. She peered outside and, seeing that no one was there, walked up the passageway with me by her side.

We followed Darj first, wanting to listen in on their conversation for a few minutes before we continued with the next part of our plan. We hid behind our hoods again and ducked past the castle's servants more than once, but we had a bit of luck when Parrian took Darj into a private room. We concealed ourselves around the corner until the food had been delivered, and then stood on either side of the door.

Through the small gap between the hinges, I watched as Darj poked the half-cooked meat on his plate and tried not to watch or listen to Parrian tear through his share like he was trying to kill it a second time.

'Those women . . . Were they the queen's ladies-in-waiting or something?' Parrian asked.

Darj nodded. It seemed as good an explanation as any, I supposed.

'Do you have any recent news about Alexia Elryane?' Parrian asked.

Darj took a small bite of his mutton and chewed it slowly. 'What was the last you heard?'

'That Cades had ensured Jeri's death and that she hasn't been seen since. I heard they burnt him alive, and that her screams could be heard right across the land.' A nervous scowl passed over his face, but then he laughed. Alexia remained composed but her eyes had clouded over with raw anger.

'That's about all I know,' Darj said. He hid his anger well—only we heard the edge in his tone. 'There were rumours when I passed through Egra that she was hiding there, but nothing to confirm it.'

'All I hope is that the A'zyon Warrior doesn't find her.'

Darj acted surprised. 'Her cousin? She's dead, isn't she?'

Parrian laughed. 'You don't know about the fifty?'

'The fifty what?'

Parrian leant closer, like he was about to reveal a secret. 'Fifty Casmodians were sent to find and bring them to Cades. The soldiers were found dead on the way to Egra, most of them without wounds. Just defeated. Just like it was at Kest River.'

Darj was now genuinely surprised, as was I. 'Kest River?'

'Yes. She escaped after a month of custody and they hunted her there and killed her. Two men stayed with the body, but they were killed, without wounds. What's even more unexplainable is that she was later found alive!' He shuddered. 'That Adaliah is not just a warrior. Cades even gets edgy about her. If she finds Alexia, Cades could have real problems, and we don't want that do we?'

Darj shook his head.

'Mind you,' Parrian continued, 'Cades has taken over so much of Targe that there really is no going back, and a young girl who can't remember anything is powerless anyway!' He laughed into his drink.

I kicked at a door until it burst open.

Alexia stood back and watched as it fell to the ground. 'Well,' she said when the dust settled. 'I was going to try the door knob.'

'It would have been locked like the others,' I said as we lifted the door back onto its hinges. I didn't tell her I'd imagined it was Parrian. 'We haven't got time to pick through every door in Semanez.'

We walked into a cold, stone library.

The room had six equal sides. The only window was in the ceiling. The walls were covered in spider webs and lined with shelves that were sagging under the weight of books and ancient documents. I ran my finger over their dusty spines while Alexia perused through the scrolls and letters that lay on a large table in the middle of the room.

'What are you expecting us to find?' I asked.

'Surely a Lord of Casmodia would not be ill-informed of his liege's plans,' Alexia said. She picked up a letter and read it aloud. '"To my Lord Parrian, protector of Semanez, the foremost city in our almighty kingdom, accomplice in magnificent deeds" . . . ' She skipped down the page. 'I assume there's a point to this. Ah. "Fenellar has been conquered. Please make preparations for more Targian men . . . " He was sending my men here, but how could Semanez house so many thousands of them? They were already coming in droves before this.'

'Semanez has been emptied of its own men. There could be room.'

'He wouldn't give them the privilege of staying in Casmodian houses.' She picked up another letter and glanced over it. 'This is

Parrian giving instructions to the elders of other towns. Crisock, Ignallia, Ruebed and Tiathi. Each of them is training so many thousands of my men, turning them into Casmodian soldiers.'

I stood behind Alexia and read the letter for myself. Then, I heard someone coming. I motioned to Alexia to hide behind the table while I stood just beside the doorway. I saw a shadow pass across the floor and held my breath.

'Are you in there?' a familiar voice whispered.

Alexia stood and I smiled with relief. I opened the door carefully but knew young Zavad wouldn't compromise us.

'Come in,' Alexia said. 'Tell us what you've found out.'

He entered the room and I shut the door again. 'Not all of your men are here,' he said.

'Yes,' Alexia said. 'We found that out, too. There are some here though, aren't there?'

'Yes, many. Parrian's son said they are all in underground prisons.'

'Underground prisons?' I asked. 'Do you know where they are or how to get to them?'

'Parrian's son pointed to one of the grates that covers a passage underneath.'

Alexia put a hand on Zavad's shoulder and kissed his temple. 'Where would we be without you?'

The boy beamed.

Later that night, Alexia and I waited until Parrian stumbled back to his chambers with a drink in his hand. Darj stood behind him as the lord scanned the room for his 'gifts'. We were sitting on his bed. Thankfully, we had been able to have a quick bath and were in fine dresses that felt too good after the worn clothes we'd been wearing. Zavad, also clean, lay by the fire feigning sleep.

'You are beautiful,' Parrian said, though whether he meant Alexia, myself, or both, I don't think even he was capable of distinguishing. He gave us a broken smile, but Darj unsheathed his sword and brought the hilt down on the back of his head. The lord stumbled and fell face forward onto the floor, unconscious.

'Thank you, Darj,' Alexia said, putting on her cloak.

Darj dragged Parrian's limp body onto the bed. I put on my cloak as well and pulled the hood down, while Alexia dressed Zavad with a coat and scarf. Then, we left the castle and went out into the cold night.

14
THE FIRST REGATHERING

Zavad led his three guardians to the large grate he'd been shown with a speed that impressed even Darj. 'This is the one Parrian's son showed me,' he said.

Darj knelt next to it for a closer look. 'There's a stairway down there. Is this the only entrance?'

'How should I know?' Zavad asked. I realised he looked tired and had probably had enough of travelling with Casmodia's most wanted enemies. 'No one could see the city in one day. It's even bigger than Liane!'

'All right,' Darj said, realising he had antagonised the boy. 'I don't understand why this one is unguarded.' None of us offered a suggestion so, using his sword, Darj broke the chain and lock that secured the grate and lifted it up as quietly as he could. 'Go!' We hurried down the stairs and Darj came in after us, bringing the grate back down over his head.

We made our way through the dark, damp tunnels. They lit up as I walked ahead with a burning torch. 'I wonder how long they have been down here,' Alexia said, trying to keep up. Her face had paled again.

We began to see just how extensive the undergrounds of Semanez were. We passed numerous intersections, guessing our way to the Targians and hoping for the best.

'We could split up,' I said, not wanting to be stuck there all night. The small dark passageways were making me anxious.

'On no account will I risk us losing each other,' Darj said. 'Besides, can't you hear that?' We stopped moving and listened. There were shuffling sounds and a few tired groans.

'Are . . . are we being followed?' Zavad asked.

'No,' Alexia said. 'It's them. It's my men.'

'Please, stay here,' Darj said to Alexia and Zavad. 'We'll call you if we need to.'

For once Alexia didn't argue. I walked with Darj further up the path where we discovered a dark room dug into the side of the tunnel. It was barred with strong steel rods and the only way in and out, from what we could see, was through a small gate that was secured with another lock and chain. 'Just hide your face for now,' he said to me. I took a step back and pulled my hood down while he rattled the gate, testing its strength and stirring the men inside at the same time.

One of them came towards the bars. 'Who are you?' he asked in a deep, hoarse voice. His smell of sweat was overpowering even from where I stood.

'My name is Darj Ryder.'

'General Darj Ryder?' The man pressed his face up against the bars.

'Yes.' Darj pointed to his armband.

The man stared at it. 'It's Darj, men! The queen's general!' The others crowded around the bars to see for themselves. 'My name is Ival Fort,' the first man said. 'I was a soldier in Gristern before I was captured with several others and brought here. What brings you to Semanez? How did you get in here unnoticed?'

'I'm here to free you, so you can help us fight back. We are planning to go into battle as soon as we can release our prisoners.'

'Targe is lost, isn't it?' Ival asked.

'Targe as a kingdom is now under the rule of Cades, yes, but it lives on in us.'

'But what is there to fight for? We've not only lost Targe but our queen, too. Our people are dispersed, and our homes are gone.'

'So we will re-gather, we will rebuild. And,' Darj leant closer to the men, 'your queen is not lost.'

Ival's face dropped. 'What?' A hum of disbelief filled the cell. 'She lives?'

'Yes, she does,' Darj said, 'but do not ask me to tell you where she is yet. The Casmodians must not even hear a whisper of it.'

The men muttered their agreement.

'But even if we release all the men in Semanez, we won't have enough to fight Cades,' Ival said.

I knew Darj feared the same thing. A lot of our plan was riding on an unspoken agreement with the Casmodian prince. 'We hope to have others, but we must start with you.' He raised his voice when he continued. 'Now, listen to me. I'm going to release you so you can follow me out of here, then some of you will go with Ival to set the others in Semanez free.' He unsheathed his sword and slashed it against the lock and chain. It fell to the ground and the gate swung open. 'We will split up and leave this city tonight even if we have to burn down the walls!'

At this point I walked back to Alexia. She was gripping her stomach but turned away when she saw me. Zavad looked concerned.

'Alexia? What's wrong?' I put my hand on her shoulder, forcing her to turn back to me.

Alexia cupped my face with a clammy hand in what I think was an attempt to reassure me. 'I'm fine.'

'You are not.'

'I'm fine. Darj is releasing the men. We must be ready to move.'

'Alexia—'

'Please, just leave it.'

I could hear the general directing the men. 'Release the Targians in Semanez,' he said as they began to pass us, not realising who we were. 'Regather the lost.'

'There's three of them,' Ival whispered to those of us who stood behind him, waiting to come out of the grate. While the Casmodians had left it unguarded before, they had now come to ensure no one from the depths could escape.

Or so they thought.

'Be ready to run at them as soon as I break the lock.'

The Casmodian soldiers laughed. Ival raised himself onto his toes and said he could see them sitting around a small fire, drinking ale.

'Now!' he said. He pushed up against the grate and it gave way. Two men rushed out while he held it up. They ran at the Casmodians and pushed them to the ground. One stole a sword and impaled all three, one after the other. They returned and moved the grate to the side to help Ival and the others out. Darj held back and pulled Alexia, Zavad and me out last.

Alexia and I hurried away with Zavad to get our horses.

'Quickly,' Alexia said as she mounted and pulled Zavad up in front of her. 'Darj will be waiting for us.'

Semanez was already crawling with Targians, many of them driven wild by lack of food and light. They started setting houses on fire, and the sky lit up with flames. Alexia hesitated at the sight. We could hear screaming. 'Come on,' I said. 'Darj will not let women and children die.'

I rode Bagred and led Guntar as we made our way towards the western wall where we planned to hide amongst the men. Soldiers fought in the streets around us, and we passed many dead bodies, both Targian and Casmodian. Ahead of us, men brought horses and wagons to a large armoury, where the Targians' weapons had been stored after their capture. They filled the wagons with as much as the horses could pull, not just with weapons but with various other items we would need on the road, including a few tents and beds. Once they had taken as much as they could, they, too, began to head for the western wall. There, Alexia and I held back while the Targian soldiers ran at the guards at the gate and killed them all.

Darj nodded to us when we arrived, recognisable to him by our horses. He ordered the gate to be opened, pushed through the men and mounted Guntar. Flames engulfed the great castle, Cades' own residence. Some of the men had used oil to accelerate its downfall and now it burned on the hill like an angry volcano, the first act of Targian revenge. Whatever was happening in our homeland, at least we had achieved this, at least we had shown the world we would not give up yet. Darj eyed Alexia as she stared up at the castle, trying to assess her reaction. I wondered if it would ease any of her grief, but when I saw the look she gave Darj in turn, I knew it brought her no pleasure.

I thought of Parrian lying unconscious in his chambers. Had he woken in time to get out? We hadn't intended this end for him. What would happen to his son? I wondered if Alexia was thinking about the same thing.

That night, two and a half thousand Targians left Semanez, leaving it crippled as a sign that we were not yet defeated. Some men, as ordered by Darj, stayed to keep the city under Targian control.

The rest of us went on to battle.

15
ON THE ROAD TO TIATHI

After seven days of travelling, we camped in the wilderness on the road to a smaller Casmodian town, Tiathi, where we planned to free more of Cades' prisoners and integrate them into our army. Darj and Ival organised men to distribute the food they had found—mostly salted beef, dried apples, and oats—and then made sure every man had a sword. 'My scouts have reported that a battalion of Casmodian soldiers are heading towards Tiathi Basin,' Darj told us. 'Whether they know about Semanez yet or not, I don't know, but they certainly know we have men now and we must be ready to meet them in battle soon.'

Later that night, I stood outside the tent Alexia, Zavad, and I were sharing. We kept away from the army, our identity not yet revealed to them to keep us safe. I practised with Elhian's sword, wearing a long linen shift and concentrating hard in hope that my focus would alleviate some of the fear I was beginning to feel again.

I heard someone approaching behind me and knew by the heavy steps that it was Darj. He unsheathed his sword and brought it down as if to strike me, but I raised Elhian's sword to meet his. In two swift moves, I pushed him back and disarmed him. He moved to retrieve his sword, but I tripped him with my foot. He fell onto his back, and I pointed my sword at his chest.

The general raised his hands. 'All right! I surrender!'

I grinned, lowered my sword, and let him get to his feet.

'You were always impossible to catch unawares,' he said with a smile. 'Why aren't you ever afraid?'

I laughed hollowly. 'All I know is fear, Darj. Not because I'm afraid of dying. Not because I'm afraid of fighting or going into battle.' I looked up at the night sky, daunted by the millions of bright stars shining down on me. 'I go into battle, but I don't remember how I became a warrior, who taught me, or what it is that makes me want to fight. But I am afraid of losing everything I love, like Alexia has. More than that, I fear I will never remember who it is I love, who I trust, what I fought for, and who I really am.'

Darj put a hand on my shoulder. 'No one can tell you who you are. Just respond from your heart.'

'But Darj,' I said, suddenly feeling emotional and lost, 'I'm scared I'm fighting for something I don't or didn't believe in.'

He didn't say anything straight away, and I appreciated that. I wasn't looking for empty sentiments. 'Is there anything you believe in for sure?' he asked.

'Are you talking about Ru'ach?' I asked, thinking about what Lezan had said to Alexia in the cave that night about something called the Great Spirit.

'Well, that's not quite what I meant. You always believed in him though, even as a child.'

'Did I?' Something else I had forgotten. 'Now I don't even know what he is.'

'Ru'ach is the breath that gives life and purpose to the earth and all that live on it. Very old writings and traditions say he burst forth from

Kest River and gave it life. He protects all of the living and strengthens us whenever we call on him. He is nowhere . . . and everywhere. Mostly we feel him here.' He put a hand over his heart. 'He is the wind that encircles us . . . connects us to each other. Cazine called upon him to give his good power to the swords.' Darj grimaced. 'Unfortunately, that power was corrupted by evil.'

I thought about this. 'It would be nice to have someone watching out for us,' I said, 'but I don't know what I think or believe anymore.'

'I find I need something to believe in to guide my steps. In my role as a general . . . as a man, I have to have some way of knowing right from wrong.'

'Isn't war wrong, though? You describe Ru'ach as being all about life, but war is all about death.'

'That's true, and it's our job to make peace where we can, but when evil knocks on the door and threatens everything you stand for, everything you love, you have to unsheathe your sword. You have to fight back.'

'Yes . . . I agree, and I know we need all the help we can get, so I hope Ru'ach is on our side. And I do believe I was taught to fight for a reason. I believe that what has happened to Alexia should never happen to anyone. I believe Cades is wrong, and that Targe should right that wrong. But Darj, no one fights just for their kingdom. They may fight for Alexia, but these men also fight for a woman, for their families, for their homes and livelihood. But me? I don't belong anywhere. Without a memory, my old life never existed. What's my reason to fight? How can I trust you? Alexia? Elhian? Myself?'

'You love Alexia . . . As you said once, your heart has not forgotten what your mind has.'

'Yes . . . But . . . Don't get me wrong. You won't be able to stop me going into battle. If it is what I have been trained for, if this is what Ru'ach has given me life on this earth to do . . . I will fight for Targe and for Alexia, and I will do so proudly. But when it's all over, what will I have? What will I do? Who will I be?'

Again, Darj didn't rush with a response. 'Once, you were full of confidence,' he said. 'Now you're full of questions. I remember the day you first came from Kest to spend the summer in the palace, barely fourteen but better with a sword than most soldiers I know. I knew then you would grow to be great. When you arrived on the field of the Battle of the Yellow Forest, you saved the lives of so many men, but what everyone admires is that you're more than a heroine. You're human. Most people would've left that boy to die on the side of the road, even Lezan, but you saved him. You're brave because you don't agree with fear, even when you feel it. You don't have to fight for Targe or your cousin, but you're choosing to because you feel it's the right thing to do. That's what makes you the Adaliah I know, the Adaliah I have full faith in, the Adaliah I'm proud to go into battle with. The principles of your faith haven't left you. In essentials, you are not so very different from the person you were.'

I was touched by his words. Darj often seemed tormented, and I got the sense he blamed himself for Alexia's situation much more than he should. But Lezan had told me the truth when he'd said Darj was my friend.

I decided to ask him something else that had been on my mind for a while. 'What was Alexia like before . . . before all this?'

Darj sighed and lowered himself to the ground. He ran his hand over the tips of the long grass around him. Snapping one in half, he put it in his mouth as I sat down next to him. 'She was more herself, if you know what I mean.' I raised an eyebrow at him, confused, and he tried again after taking the grass out of his mouth. 'She wasn't as closed up as she is now. When things bothered her, she would share them. She was deeply connected to Ru'ach, too. She had to be, to cope with her role. Now, I have no idea what's going on in her head. I don't think she hates Ru'ach, but she has certainly disconnected herself from him.' He smiled at me. 'You know, she was quite playful with Jeri and Ethaniel, a very warm person. She and Ethaniel loved each other so much . . . Losing him, and then Jeri . . . it's like shattering a glass vase and trying to put the pieces together again. No matter how well it's done, there will always be cracks, signs of a past hurt. Alexia will never be the same again.'

I shifted my position, trying to get comfortable on the hard ground. 'Was I there when Ethaniel . . . ?'

'Yes. It was at Cades' hand. Alexia was . . . ' He shook his head. Apparently, no word could describe how Alexia was. 'You were infuriated. You were going to kill Cades on the spot.'

'Why didn't I?' *It would have stopped a lot of trouble,* I thought, irritated with my past self.

'Because you had to get them out.' He met my eyes. 'You say you have no reason to fight. Alexia has lost everything, and she still goes on. You can, too.'

'She's not well, you know.'

'I know.'

'Alexia?' I gently shook my cousin the next morning.

'Ethaniel?' she murmured.

'It's me, Adaliah.'

Alexia opened her eyes and sighed. 'I wish I could stay with my husband.'

'Were you dreaming?'

A small smile played on her lips. 'Yes. I was back in the palace and dressed in a royal gown.' For whatever reason, I imagined her in a sparkling blue dress, her hair up and under a beautiful crown. 'Ethaniel was coming back after a long absence. Jeri was so excited to see him . . . Ethaniel picked him up off the ground and swung him around, and then he came to me and kissed me with a passion I'd forgotten.' She ran a finger over her lips as if Ethaniel's touch still lingered there.

We shared a smile as Darj came in. 'The army is moving out,' he said. 'Tiathi isn't far from here, so we're leaving camp set up. Alexia, as soon as the men in Tiathi are freed, we will ride on to the Basin for battle.'

He'd explained to me earlier that the Tiathi Basin was a sunken expanse of land that turned into a shallow lake any time rain endured for a week or more. It was free of trees and other obstructions. There'd only been enough rain to make it damp in the recent days, so overall it provided a good place for a battle.

Alexia propped herself up. 'Where's Zavad?' she asked. The boy had slept in the tent with the two of us.

'He's on your horse waiting for you,' Darj said. He turned to me. 'Do you remember the other route I showed you?' I nodded. He'd pointed it out to me on a basic map. 'Good. I'll meet you both at the Basin.' He paused. 'Keep safe. Both of you.'

Darj would later tell us how he and the Targians ran at Tiathi. According to his account, they lost a few men to archers but broke through the weak, wooden gates and killed the few Casmodian soldiers who stood against them.

Civilians screamed and hid in their houses, but Darj, true to the man I had come to know, didn't ask anyone to leave. He and his soldiers simply ran to the garrison where the Targians were being held prisoner, tore down the door, and released another eight hundred men by noon.

No innocent lay dead. The women and children were safe. His men, despite having lost so much, had retained their integrity. Both Alexia and I knew how important that was to Darj, how important it was in the rebuilding of Targe. Darj didn't leave any of them behind this time—Tiathi wasn't as important as Semanez, so the men were more valuable on the battlefield.

Darj, Ival and the other captains made sure the new men were given weapons and any armour that was available. Each man was outfitted and sent to join the rest of the Targian soldiers who gathered in formation just outside the town walls. Some of them were young and had never fought. Some had been taught to fight by the Casmodians. Some had lost much in battle. Others were farmhands and labourers who knew nothing about war except for what it had taken from them. Yet, they were all ready to fight back.

Darj mounted Guntar, raised his sword and rode from one end of the men to the other so that even those at the back could hear him shouting 'Arjla divala', an old, patriotic call to battle—one I would come to hear myself soon enough.

'Whatever your background, whatever you have lost, why ever you are standing here today, you are all the queen's warriors! We will fight together for that which has been taken from us!'

16
THE RETURN OF THE A'ZYON WARRIOR

Alexia, Zavad, and I took a narrow but safe route and, as it was a more direct path, we arrived at the Basin well before the Targian army.

We came to the peak of a small hill at the east of the Basin and were at once taken aback by the sight that lay before us.

Thousands of men stood in the lowlands below—a Casmodian army with blue banners flying high and, across from them, another army, smaller but also impressive. They were mostly dark-skinned, and they held red banners. At the front of them was a single Casmodian astride a white horse, a young man even I recognised.

'It's the prince,' I said, astounded. 'With the Jazmardians!'

'Thank you, Ru'ach,' Alexia breathed as she closed her eyes. 'It must have been them that drew the Casmodian army here.' She looked out at the blue soldiers. 'Wait,' she said, confused. 'They have Jazmardian warriors with them as well.'

Not sure what to make of this, we watched as Elhian's cavalry rode into position. The prince's horse pawed the ground. He stood with an army but, as the only Casmodian on his side, he stood alone as well. I wondered at his bravery to stand against his own soldiers in such a way, to defy his father so brazenly. Reaching for the sword by his side, he waited until the leader of the Casmodian army began to approach and then rode out to meet him.

The two figures in the middle of the Basin were small in the distance, but much depended on their conversation. I could feel Alexia tensing beside me and knew she wanted to be down there, too, having her say, perhaps even having her revenge.

Both armies were quietly waiting.

'What do you think they're saying?' Zavad asked.

'That is Officer Hae,' Alexia said, missing his question and pointing to the man talking with Elhian. 'He has a scar across his brow where Cades punished him for being late to council. The missing finger on his left hand was for bringing back bad news about a large shipment, and yet he is still loyal to Cades. He tried to kill Darj in the Battle of the Yellow Forest, you know. He wanted to send his head to Cades in a basket.' Zavad gasped at this. Alexia patted his shoulder. 'Don't worry, Zavad. If anything, Darj will be the one to overcome him, I am sure.'

Elhian and Hae finished talking, and Elhian cantered back to his army. He rode to two Targians. I recognised them as the two who had been in Liane's prison, Xander and Raggin. Elhian *did* have a plan for them. The three of them held their swords high and the Jazmardians behind them lifted their weapons, too. Elhian glanced around the Basin like he was looking for something. He seemed hesitant to go into battle and, of course, did not know that Darj and his men were near.

Alexia looked up at the sun. 'Darj should be here by now.'

Just as she spoke the words, Elhian's men suddenly broke formation and began looking around with a sense of urgency.

'They can hear something,' Zavad said, turning his head to the breeze.

'It's a war-cry,' I said.

The two Targians standing with Elhian responded to the cry on the wind with a loud 'Arjla Divala!'

'What does that mean?' I asked.

'It means "with him we stand",' Alexia said as Darj and his men appeared over the north-eastern hill. 'It is ancient Targian, and it refers to Ru'ach.'

The Jazmardians came to life at the sight of their allies—singing and calling out in their own tongue and banging their weapons against shields. It was stirring watching our men riding to join theirs and unifying against a common enemy.

'Let's go, Adaliah,' Alexia said. 'Zavad, you must stay here.'

'But I want to come,' Zavad said. 'I want to fight.'

'And one day you shall,' Alexia said, 'but not today.'

Her tone left no room for argument. Zavad sat on a rock with tightly folded arms and a red face, and he didn't look at us when we said goodbye.

The closer Alexia and I came to our army, the more we could hear the yelling and cheering that was being exchanged between the allies, and the more empowered I felt. We were riding with our cloaks and hoods on, keeping our identity quiet until the right moment, just as we had discussed with Darj. It was only Alexia's arrows with their gold-tipped fletching that could have given us away, but no one seemed to notice them.

Alexia and I hid amongst the men as Darj pulled his horse up beside the prince. 'I can't tell you how relieved I was to come over that hill and see you and all these men here.'

Elhian gave a small, nervous grin. 'It took you long enough.'

One of the Targians from Liane prison—a tall man with shoulder-length black hair—rode next to Darj and gripped his forearm.

'I'm so glad to see an old friend!'

'And I you, Xander,' Darj said.

Ival made his way to Darj as well. 'Our men are worried, now they have seen the army,' he said. 'Even with Elhian's men, they don't think this battle can be won.'

Darj rode back to his men.

A young soldier yelled out to him before he could speak. 'We don't have enough,' the soldier said, 'and they are heavily-armoured and well trained!'

'Yes, they are,' Darj said. 'But remember, Ru'ach is with us, and we must fight against this evil. These men have come into our kingdom and taken our homes. They have killed our loved ones and will continue to do so unless we stand up to them and fight back!'

'We are mostly militia,' the same man called. 'We'll be killed!'

'We are stronger than them!' Darj yelled back, leaning forward in his saddle. 'We are the soldiers of Targe and the sons of Ru'ach. We know that love is stronger than hate. We know that life is stronger than death! Evil will not prevail if we hold fast and raise our blades as one!'

'Hae is leading them. He is one of their best warriors. He was there at the Yellow Forest!'

Darj fell silent, turned, and looked at the man that led the Casmodian army ever closer. 'Yes, they have Hae,' he said. 'But we have the A'zyon Warrior.'

A hum of disbelief filled the air. 'The A'zyon Warrior?' Elhian asked.

Ival's eyes lit up as the question echoed over the army.

'Yes,' Darj said. 'Both Queen Alexia and Lady Adaliah live!'

The people cheered. This caused me to feel a wave of emotion, which in turn motivated Bagred to become restless. I patted his neck and tried to keep him calm.

Despite the overall bustle of hope at our names, there were still some who doubted. 'Then where are they?' an older, more robust soldier asked.

Darj looked up at the hill we had ridden over, and I realised even he hadn't seen us arrive. Everyone followed his line of sight, including Xander and his friend Raggin, who kept patting each other's shoulders in excitement. Raggin was shorter and plumper than his friend and didn't have nearly as much hair.

Silence fell over the army as they waited for the 'A'zyon Warrior' and their queen to make their appearance, not knowing we were amongst them.

'Well? Where are they?' the same soldier asked again.

I reached down and pulled out Elhian's sword. The light shone brightly, but it didn't feel dangerous. I looked at Alexia and she nodded. We pushed back our hoods and I lifted the sword high, sending the light upwards. It was vivid and beautiful.

Elhian turned and saw us first. 'They're here!' he yelled, raising his sword into the sky as well.

It took a second for the rest of the men to realise what they were seeing and to recover from the shock, but, when they did, they responded with an 'Arjla divala!' that was so loud, I'm sure it must have unsettled even the Casmodians.

'The A'zyon Warrior has returned!'

'Queen Alexia lives!'

Bagred reared in excitement while the men cheered again.

I moved towards Elhian and handed his Faith Sword back to him. He smiled his thanks and gripped it. In turn, he gave me the blade he had been using.

Darj offered a hand to the queen as she dismounted and, as soon as her feet touched the ground, everyone—including Darj, Elhian, the Jazmardians, and me—knelt before her. The sound of so many kneeling at once created an immense but invigorating sound of unity, and I felt prouder than any time I could remember.

Tears filled Alexia's eyes. I knew she had doubted if her men would ever again be able to honour her as they were now. 'Arise, my soldiers,' she said. 'Go into battle with your warrior. The time has come for us to take back what was stolen!' Everyone stood and saluted her.

'Blessings upon the queen!' Ival shouted, and the men echoed the cry.

'It's time to go,' Alexia said to me.

I hesitated. Even after all this I didn't want to leave my cousin.

Alexia hugged me and held me close, and then drew back and kissed my cheek.

'It doesn't seem right that so many people have faith in someone so full of fear,' I said, looking down as my pride and hope faded. 'Someone like me.'

'You are the A'zyon Warrior,' Alexia said with a smile. 'Fearless. With you on our side, we cannot be defeated.'

'I will try not to let you down.'

Alexia shook her head and remounted her horse. 'You could never do that.'

She gave Darj a nod and he turned to the men. 'All archers follow Her Majesty!' he called. Men equipped with bows and arrows formed rank behind Alexia, and she led them up to a crag on the hill.

Then, Darj and I moved to either side of Elhian.

17
THE BATTLE OF TIATHI

My breath quickened as I watched the Casmodians begin their charge towards us. I turned my head to the sky.

Ru'ach, I hope you're on our side.

A cool breeze blew past my body and lifted my hair. My mind became silent and calm, and I felt something stirring in me. I didn't recognise it at first. I couldn't remember feeling it before. It filled me with warmth, slowed my breathing.

Courage.

He is with me. I can do this.

I looked forward. Bagred snorted in anticipation. Without thinking about it a second more, I charged at the head of the men with Elhian and Darj close by. The rest of the army shouted and followed. They were loud and fierce.

Ival eyed the space between the Casmodians and us. He raised a green flag adorned with twelve gold stars. The Targian flag. It fluttered in the wind and triggered a volley of arrows that arched into the sky and into our enemy. Men fell to the ground. Another volley of arrows followed, and another. More men fell from their horses. As we drew close, Ival lowered the flag, and the volleys stopped.

I made the first strike. As soon as my sword clashed with another, the transformation was complete. All fear left. I was the A'zyon Warrior.

The air filled with screams of agony, shouts of loss. One man next to me lost his hand. Sweat flew as men took their swords back and flung them forward into their enemy. Some attacked the horses, forcing their enemy to the ground.

I saw the one they called Xander fall when his horse was speared. Its front legs collapsed first as it dropped to the ground. Xander got to his feet and pulled a Casmodian down from his horse.

A sword tip ran along my side. I turned to my attacker and pierced him with my blade, then grabbed his sword before he fell so I had one in each hand.

I could see the blue light somewhere to my left and knew from the horde of men that was surrounding Elhian that he was their target. He slashed a soldier to the ground and impaled another. I'd been right. He was well trained.

Arrows sped through the air at individual targets. I glanced up at the crag and spared a thought for Alexia. A lot of Targians had fallen already—a blur of red seemed to be everywhere I looked. I knew one of the archers near Alexia carried a white flag, ready to be flown should she call for a retreat. I couldn't see it yet.

'We're losing,' Darj said, appearing beside me with a red-faced scowl.

He was right. We were outnumbered and our men were neither well-nourished nor strong. The field was already littered with bodies.

'We've come too far to walk away now,' Elhian said.

I battled a toothless warrior and saw Hae walking towards me with a rope over his shoulder. The scar on his brow was clear—it gave him a disfigured and pitiable look.

I hoped he wasn't coming for me. I was tiring, and everyone seemed to be targeting me now, or so I felt. I'd dismounted when a soldier had forced one of my swords out of my hand, but now I was re-armed. Still, I had blood trickling down my arm, sweat pouring off my face and a burning sensation in all my muscles. One man was running towards me with his sword high in the air. I threw one of my blades at him. It landed in his chest and he fell backwards, skidding in the dirt.

I tried to catch my breath. Blood was running down Darj's neck from a head wound that looked painful. He wiped his arm across his sweaty face and saw Hae as I had, walking in our direction.

Darj ran at him. He tackled Hae to the ground from the side and the two rolled in the dirt. They got back on their feet and clashed swords. Darj ducked an overhead swipe and lunged at Hae, who sidestepped him. Darj struck at him again.

It was while they were fighting that I saw the inevitable flash of white on the hill. 'Ival!' I shouted. 'Darj!'

The two men saw the flag swinging from side to side.

Darj kicked Hae down. 'Retreat!' he yelled. 'Retreat!'

The men about us turned and ran, yelling the word until everyone could hear it.

Before I could follow, two more Casmodians attacked me. I struck at one and then the other. One fell but the other only stumbled. I kicked his stomach, and he grabbed it in pain. The other soldier got back to his feet and struck my middle where I had been nipped with the sword. I fell to one knee in agony but managed to impale him.

A sword burst through the chest of the other solider—Elhian's sword.

'Let's go!' he yelled.

I struggled back to my feet, remounted Bagred, and rode away from the Casmodians.

Help us, Ru'ach!

I saw Raggin searching the bodies on the field ahead. 'Where is Xander?' he asked Darj.

Before Darj could respond, someone lying amongst the bodies called out, 'I'm here!' Raggin ran and helped him up, both then joining our retreat.

The archers were riding down the crag, coming down to meet us. I assumed Alexia was riding behind them, but my attention was drawn away by a deep, horn-like sound that suddenly echoed in the distance.

I paused. The enemy was still chasing our men across the Basin, but we all slowed at the sound. I looked up ahead, where we had first entered the Basin, where we were running to now.

The horn sounded again. Darj raised his hand to halt the army. The enemy was close behind, yet Darj's mouth had curved into a small smile.

Elhian and I rode up beside him. 'What is it?' I asked.

Darj pointed up ahead. There were spear tips moving in the sky. Then, a line of men began to appear over the small ridge, followed by a whole battalion of warriors.

Two of them were on horseback, and one of them wore a crown.

The remaining Jazmardians who fought for us began to shout in their own tongue. It was only then that I recognised the first rider as Naclen, the refugee from Fenellar. 'Who is the crowned one?' I asked.

Elhian stared at him. 'I do believe it is Hazaka Cazren, King of the Jazmardians.'

18
THE SECOND ATTACK

There was no time for greetings when King Hazaka reached us with his men. His soldiers hurried to join our ranks, and Darj turned our army around to face the enemy once more. I breathed quickly, rallying the strength I needed to fight again. The Targians formed rank behind Darj while the Jazmardians who had fought for Elhian now hurried to Hazaka.

'Attack!' Darj yelled, raising his sword. The air filled with shouts and the sound of horns.

As the only Casmodian on our side, Elhian must have felt alone, but he held his sword up high and was the first to ride out.

'Get her!' Hae shouted later, pointing at me with his sword.

Darj seemed to appear out of nowhere and struck at him. 'How quickly the flow of battle changes,' Darj said. We were all on foot again.

'It's not over yet!'

Darj's first strike had been blocked, but he caught Hae off-guard with a strong blow. Hae dropped his sword and Darj pushed him to his knees, pressing his sword into the Casmodian's chest. 'You are more right than you know,' he said. 'This is only the beginning.'

Darj ran his sword into Hae's side.

Hae fell onto his back, his empty eyes staring up at the sky.

With the extra men we soon had the advantage. Those left of the enemy started to withdraw, but I still had three soldiers determined to kill me before admitting defeat. They kept just out of range of my sword and danced about me. I had been tired before and was exhausted now. My reactions were slowing, but when one moved behind me and I jabbed my sword under my arm almost blindly, I hit him. I withdrew the sword and heard him fall to the ground.

I engaged with the second soldier, but the third moved out of my line of sight, and I didn't realise what he was doing until Darj yelled my name and I heard the panic in his voice.

I killed the man in front of me and turned on my heel. The man behind me was about to strike.

I knew then that I would die. I had neither the strength nor the speed to respond to his attack.

But he stopped. He fell down in front of me, dropped his sword and rolled. Blood spilled out from under him.

I turned him over and saw the now-snapped arrow that had killed him and saved my life. The fletching was green and gold-tipped.

Looking up, I saw my cousin riding towards us with an empty bow in one hand. Zavad was sitting in the saddle in front of her.

'Alexia!' I called in surprise.

Darj's face filled with pride. He raised his sword to her and shouted, 'Arjla divala!'

The cry echoed across the Basin as the men began to realise the battle was won.

'Victory!' Darj yelled fiercely. 'Victory!'

The men roared.

But I didn't celebrate. Something told me Alexia was in serious danger. I heard Lezan's voice in my head: *You must keep your cousin safe.*

I peered at the hill Alexia had just descended. At the base, on the edge of the battle, and not as far away as I would have liked, I saw a tall man dressed in blue, a single bald Casmodian soldier with a bow and arrow. Even from where I stood, I knew it was Jag Warhin.

'Alexia!' I shouted again. 'Get down! Alexia!'

But Jag released his shot.

His aim was almost as accurate as the queen's. The arrow hit Alexia's left shoulder from behind and her body seized up.

Her face turned white. I shouted her name again. Her clear blue eyes searched for me, but she fell as if in a slow faint. All sound ceased as I watched her legs slide off her horse. She hit the ground at a sickening speed. Her body went limp, and she didn't get up.

Some of the men ran after Jag, but he'd already disappeared. I hurried to Alexia, as did Raggin and Xander. Darj caught her horse, helped Zavad down and ran with him back to the group of us that now surrounded the queen.

I was holding her hand and trying to bring her around.

'Don't,' Elhian said, arriving as well. 'We need to remove the arrow while she's unconscious.'

'It didn't go all the way through,' Zavad said. He leant into Darj, looking at Alexia with distress.

'That's not a good thing,' Elhian said with a grimace. I glanced at him in horror, and then he spoke the words I feared. 'We'll have to push it through.' He looked to Darj, who nodded and turned Zavad around so he couldn't see. Elhian lifted Alexia's upper body and pulled back her clothing just enough to bare her shoulder. He felt for the arrow and, with a strong, swift thrust, he pushed the arrowhead through to the front. It burst through her flesh and blood poured down her cloak.

I let out a cry of pain on her behalf but watched as Elhian snapped the arrowhead off and removed the shaft from behind. He smelt the arrowhead for poison and, satisfied there was none, threw the bloodied wood to the side and asked Raggin for some wine.

'What makes you think I have wine?'

'I've seen you drink it; it's in your saddlebag. Get it now!'

Raggin did as he was asked and handed the prince a cloth as well. Elhian poured the wine over the wound and wiped the excess away.

I watched his thick brown fingers dab the gash and remembered how he had tended me in a similar way. I found it fascinating that the same hands that wielded a sword so well in battle still had in them such a careful touch.

'Does anyone have anything we can use as a bandage?' the prince asked. Alexia's blood was still running down her front. Raggin went to his horse again and returned with a long, skinny piece of material. Elhian wrapped it under her arm and over her shoulder as many times as the cloth allowed.

Darj and Raggin made a stretcher using spears and the clothes of dead men. By then, Elhian had done all he could.

'Why were you with her, Zavad?' I asked.

'Jag found me in my hiding spot,' the young boy said, his lips trembling. 'He and another solider grabbed me and took me to Alexia. She saw us and shouted at Jag to let me go. He joked about how her husband and child were both dead, which made her really angry because he killed her son. She aimed an arrow at him. It was the fiercest thing I've ever seen. They argued—'

'What about?' I asked.

'He told her it was her fault that her son had been in Hunt in the first place, her fault that he died. She shot her arrow at the other soldier and killed him. "Let him go or you're next," she said, but I knew she was worried about hitting me, so I elbowed him between the legs really hard. He let go of me and I got away. He tried to grab me back, but I was quick. Then, he hurried away. Alexia and the archers wanted to ride down to help with the battle, and I begged her to take me with her. I wasn't going back to my hiding spot after that.' He sobbed. 'I thought Jag had run away and that we were safe. But he hadn't.'

I squeezed the boy's shoulder gently.

Alexia turned her head and groaned. 'My child . . .'

'What?' Elhian asked.

I held her hand again as she opened her eyes. The groan soon verged on a dull scream as the pain began to register.

Darj pulled a vial of powder out of his own saddlebag. He leant over her and spoke calmly. 'You're going to be all right. Open your mouth—this will help with the pain. I took it from an apothecary in Hunt.' She did as he asked and he tapped a bit of the powder onto her tongue, which she swallowed. I realised how much she trusted Darj but was glad she did. It soon settled her breathing and the pain in her eyes faded a little.

Raggin and Xander carefully lifted her onto the stretcher and, with the help of two other soldiers, began to carry her away. Zavad walked by her side, his small hand gripping hers. I let them go so I could find Bagred and help the others.

Before I could do either, the sound of a horse's hooves came up behind Darj and me.

King Hazaka Cazren was riding through the soldiers, smiling in a way that made me wonder if he thought he'd just won a game. There was something about him that, unlike the Targians, seemed untouched by grief and hopelessness. In place of that was a youthful gaiety, evident to me in the way he was cheerfully waving to his people as he passed.

Hazaka saw Darj and eyed him. Darj was standing in the midst of many men and was not dressed singularly, but it was he Hazaka rode towards.

'Well, Targian,' he said as he stopped his horse in front of us. Naclen joined us, too. 'It seems we arrived just at the right time.' He dismounted and grabbed Darj's forearm in a friendly greeting, then bowed his head to me.

'A little earlier would have been nice,' Darj muttered.

'Yes, well, we came as fast as we could. Young Naclen here gathered most of these men but would not leave until he found me. What he did not know was that I was already trying to find him or Prince Elhian, and so we missed each other! Nevertheless, we are here now. And we have defeated the Casmodians. And some of my own people. I must work to win back their loyalty. Oh, we are a cursed kingdom!'

Darj nodded vaguely, presumably as confused as I was. 'Well, I'm pleased you're here.'

'As am I,' Elhian said, entering the conversation. 'And I'm glad you haven't joined Cades.'

'Joined Cades? The man who not only stole my sword but split my kingdom in two and is using my own men against me? Ha! I think not.'

Elhian smiled. Naclen stared at the prince with a youthful pride that told me Elhian was not welcome company as far as he was concerned.

'You must come to our camp on the other side of Tiathi and stay with us,' Darj said. 'We have little food, but I'm sure the men are capable of catching some and providing for you and your men.'

King Hazaka gave his 'most grateful thanks,' adding, 'my men will make preparations as soon as we take care of our wounded, and bury those who did not survive this worthy cause.'

I went to find Bagred, and when I did, I leant against him, fatigue and pain both settling in.

'Adaliah?' Elhian put a hand on my shoulder.

I blinked. 'We . . . We must help the wounded.'

'Yes . . . ' His voice faded.

I turned in time to see the colour draining from his face. 'Elhian?'

He turned away from me and vomited.

'Are you all right?' I asked, not sure what to do. 'Were you injured?' I imagined he'd been kicked in the stomach.

'No . . . ' He remained doubled over with his hands on his knees, vomited again, and then straightened and returned to me. 'I'm sorry,' he said, lowering his gaze and rubbing the back of his neck. 'You would think after all my training in healing and warfare that the sight of blood would not cause such a childish reaction.'

I stared at him, surprised. 'But you didn't flinch when you pushed the arrow through Alexia's shoulder.'

'No, I always seem to cope at the time. In battle, healing wounds. It's only later that my body reacts and realises how sickened it is.' He gave a tired smile. 'As you can imagine this is not a trait Cades was proud to find in a son.' He checked to see what injuries I had sustained, noting the cut across my middle in particular. 'You're exhausted.'

'Yes.'

'Today you fought like three men put together. Everything they say about you is true. I have never seen a greater warrior than you.'

'Because I killed? Or because I survived?'

'Because you are strong and quick and intuitive. Many warriors are just one of those things.'

'I won't ask which one you are.'

Elhian smiled. It was warming, not like Hazaka's. It made me believe in myself. Perhaps I could trust him.

'Adaliah, you should go. You need to be with your queen when she wakes. There are more than enough men to help here. I will see you back at camp.'

I thanked him and mounted my horse, but before I could dig my heels into Bagred's sides, a Targian soldier stopped me.

'Excuse me, my lady,' he said, bowing. 'Could you please confirm the rumours? Some of us have been in prison since the Battle of the Yellow Forest. Is it true that both the queen's husband and our prince have died?'

I studied the man's concerned face and wondered how many others were only just discovering this. I answered with a nod. 'Ethaniel was killed by Cades himself, and their son by his right-hand man.'

I expected him to be sad, but the grey look of grief and shock on his face surprised me.

'We cannot bring them back,' he said, almost to himself, 'but we must remember them.'

19
ELHIAN'S STORY

Alexia tried to prop herself up in bed that night when I walked in to check on her. Elhian had already cleaned her wound again, stitched and redressed it. He'd placed a green paste of herbs underneath the bandage to stop the cut from getting infected. He seemed to be managing the sight of her broken and bloodied flesh this time and hadn't vomited since leaving the battlefield, but I did notice how pale he looked afterwards.

'I know it was close,' Alexia said now, 'that there were many wounded and dead, but I hope my father can be proud. Targe has defeated the Casmodians on their own land. The next challenge will be regaining land in our own kingdom.'

I handed her a plate of food but said nothing.

Alexia took the plate with her good arm. 'You're angry,' she said.

'Yes, I think I am.' I sat down on my bed and pulled off my leather boots. I bent my toes back and forth, trying to get feeling and warmth back into them. 'You saved my life today, and I am grateful, but I wish you wouldn't put yourself in such danger. Your people are worried about you . . . You are all I have, and I care for you.'

'It wasn't a choice,' she said. 'I was not about to let my cousin, my only living relative, be killed, especially not when I had the power to do something about it.'

'Alexia, if that arrow had hit you just slightly to the right, you would have been killed.'

She shrugged her shoulders and then grimaced in pain.

I leant back on my hands. 'Lezan asked me to look after you—'

'You have looked after me.'

'Yes but . . . He also said you might become the most wanted woman in history. What was he talking about?'

'I don't know,' she said, but then she pressed her lips together and looked away. Moving her thin pillow to a better spot, she lay down with her back to me and gave a small groan as her body readjusted to the position.

I was about to leave the tent—I wasn't yet ready to sleep myself—but Elhian pulled the flap back and Darj was standing behind him with Zavad. 'I thought I'd come and check on the patient,' Elhian said with a nod towards Alexia, 'and Darj has asked me to tell you all that happened while I was away.'

Alexia turned around and pulled her blanket up to her neck in a show of modesty. 'You will forgive me if I don't get up,' she said.

'I would chide you if you tried,' Elhian said good-naturedly. He sat next to me. Zavad rested on his small bed and Darj took the only other place at the foot of Alexia's.

'So, what happened after I left the palace?' I asked.

Leaning back, Elhian told us how he tried to talk to his father after my escape in one last attempt to stop him. 'I think he suspected me of helping you to leave, but he thinks I'm weak and incapable of instructing a servant, let alone a woman or an army. He told me to forget you. "A woman is the death of every man if they aren't stopped. Didn't your mother prove that?" Little did he know that comment confirmed in my heart what I needed to do. He told me they had conquered Hunt and, of course, almost finished the royal line.' He gave Alexia a look laced with guilt and shame. 'Then he said something about "the Zalems" being appeased, whatever that means, and that he had done too much to be slighted by nothing more than a girl.' He gave me a fond smile. 'I think you've proved to him now that you're not to be underestimated.

'But I knew Cades wasn't telling me everything about his plans and that made it difficult to plot against him. I knew we would need to make a stand soon, but I also knew we couldn't do it on our own. I wondered if the Jazmardians could help and thought they might once they heard we had the A'zyon Warrior on our side.'

'You had more faith in me than I did,' I said.

He didn't respond to this, but Alexia gave me a curious look. 'Do you remember the two Targian prisoners in Liane, Raggin and Xander?' Elhian asked. 'Jag had told me they'd both tried to kill Cades. I went to get them and explained that they stood against my father and that I did, too. They agreed to help me with my plan but only for your sake, Your Majesty.'

Alexia smiled faintly. 'I remember them. They stood up to Cades when he came into the palace, before Ethaniel . . .'

Elhian looked away. 'Yes.'

He told us how he arranged to meet them at the stables later that night. 'Raggin wasn't convinced the Jazmardians would fight for me. I knew it was a long shot, but I was hoping they would fight for themselves. After all, once Cades is finished with Targe, he will invade Jazmarda. I can't just watch him take over the rest of Targe and then the Rhea Lands. I can't stand by while he and his army kill children, rape women, and make slaves of the men.' He picked at his thumbnail. 'I don't know what I am exactly and if I'm honest, I constantly fear my father's evil lies in me. But I know who I am not, and I am not my father.'

I don't know about Alexia and Darj, but it was then that I believed in him.

'The three of us travelled into Kest and crossed the river. By then I'd realised my father had sent a soldier to track me. I caught him and found out he'd been ordered not to harm me. That's the odd thing about Cades—he wants me dead, but not until he has another heir to the throne. Even now he will not risk leaving his kingdom to an unknown commoner.'

Darj and Alexia glanced at each other.

'Were Raggin and Xander good companions?' I asked.

'Silence was Raggin's greatest enemy. Xander was more patient with him than me. "When was the last time we saw mountains as lovely as these, Xander?" he would ask. "Yesterday," Xander would reply. "And the day before that." The two bantered the entire trip, but I think that helped me get through the uncertainty, somehow.

'We pushed through thick scrub, trying to find a path into Jazmarda, and came to a small hut. There were notes nailed all over one wall inside, but the script was in ancient Targian, which none of us could read. I think it had something to do with the Keeper of Kest, your father.'

He met my eyes, but I encouraged him to keep going with a wave of my hand. I knew I wouldn't remember anything.

'We searched the hut for secret passages and when I kicked the wall, a part of it bounced open. Behind it was a large stone door that had some sort of complicated encryption on it. It had a place for a key and lots of scratches and dints, like someone had tried to break into it.'

'A tunnel entry,' Alexia said.

'Yes, that's what I thought.'

Neither volunteered an explanation, and Elhian went on before I could ask. 'We arrived at the edge of Jazmarda the next morning and came across a sort of road guard. I explained who I was and why I was there, but he said that Jazmarda had joined with Cades, and would not give me entry. I couldn't believe they had been drawn into his campaign when they must know that if he conquers Targe, they will be next. I said it was impossible, but he told me Jazmardian soldiers had already left to take their place in Cades' army.

'The man told us that Targe was defeated, and that Cades had sent fifty men to kill you. I asked him how he knew, and he pulled Naclen out from behind a tree. He had been captured on his way to Liane.

'The poor boy was bound much more than necessary and, seeing him there, helpless, I did something I don't do very often. I lost my temper. I kicked the man and we fought. Raggin and Xander untied Naclen.

'I got him in a position of surrender and was going to let him live, but he pulled out a knife to stab me, so I impaled him first.

'It was only because of Raggin that I kept going after that. Only then did he reveal that he knew King Hazaka personally. He said he'd worked in Amaz's court for a while as a messenger to Jazmarda, where he met Hazaka and got to know him. He found it hard to believe Hazaka would side with Cades. This gave me hope, so we pressed on. Naclen came with us, although he made it clear it wasn't for my sake—he refused to even speak to me because I'm a Casmodian. I can't blame him, considering what my father has done to his kinsmen.

'We rode into Etarbelec, travelling in shadows and pressing on beyond the point of safety.'

'What was it like?' Zavad asked. 'The city?'

Elhian smiled as he thought back to the different and strange place. I wondered if I had been there before, but even if I had, when Elhian indulged Zavad's question, none of it sounded familiar. 'It's hot, and doesn't have the serenity of Liane, at least, the serenity Liane had under Queen Alexia. The houses are sandy and red like the dust. It's a very busy city—people were rushing through the streets and talking loudly. The people there are dark-skinned with golden tattoos. The women all braid their hair and tie it up with brightly coloured ribbons, and their children play barefoot in the street.'

'Mother would never let me do that,' Zavad said, wide-eyed.

'Raggin and Xander went to the Red Temple, where Hazaka is known to spend time away from his wife, while Naclen and I went to the High Court.' Elhian looked up. 'That reminds me. Lezan—what happened to him?'

'He . . . died,' I said, not knowing how else to present the news.

Elhian shook his head. 'I thought so. I met his brother Kadram at the High Court and he seemed to know that Lezan was in trouble. I wish I could have thanked him for all he did for us. Kadram knew who I was even though I was trying to pose as a traveller from the west. He told me that Hazaka had indeed been overthrown, disarmed of his sword and stolen of his army, just like . . . ' Elhian glanced over at Alexia. She raised an eyebrow, daring him to go on. He didn't. 'But he said that Jazmarda was a large kingdom, and that while some had joined with Cades, many others did not support him.

'Naclen and I caught up with Xander and Raggin after that. They hadn't found Hazaka, but they'd talked to a priest who said that if we gathered the men, they would follow us, and that they would send a message to Hazaka to meet us on the Grey Plains.

'The four of us split up and did just that. I was the first to reach the plains with a battalion of militia. A scout told me that more Jazmardians had joined with Cades and were forming an army. I knew we were running out of time. Xander and Raggin brought their men the following day, but Naclen didn't arrive. I thought he had abandoned us until today, and yet it was he who found the king and brought the men who gave us victory.'

'All that matters is that we did have victory,' Darj said, 'and that we have shown Cades we will not be so easily defeated.'

20
RISING WITH THE DAWN

I woke the next morning to the sound of a horn. It was before dawn, and I still felt tired, having talked to the others until past midnight, but I threw back my covers and wrapped a fur skin around myself.

I passed through the flap of the tent. The whole army was ready. They were holding torches and walking in lines towards something. They began to sing a song in unison. It was low and sad, but strong and hopeful at the same time. The song spoke of a journey, of life and death, of life being victorious over death.

Just as Alexia came out of the tent behind me, also looking to see what was happening, I saw Darj, Hazaka, and Elhian standing together. The night air was brisk, and I rubbed my arms as I walked over to them. 'What's going on?' I asked Darj.

'It's a tribute.' He pointed out two large stone structures up ahead. They were made of white stones piled on top of each other, stones that came from the nearby riverbed. They formed two solid, tall rectangle walls only one stone deep but five stones wide and about ten stones tall.

'What is this?' I asked Darj.

'It's a memorial service.'

Two men walked to each of the structures and lit the two small bowls of oil that sat on top of them. A sense of familiarity descended on me. 'Have I seen something like this before?'

Darj turned to me. 'Yes. The men did this for you, when your father died. There was only one memorial tower then though, of course. Do you remember?'

It was the question everyone kept asking me. 'No, but it does feel like something I've seen before.'

'Tell me, what are they doing?' Hazaka asked Darj.

'Well, it's not only a goodbye to Ethaniel and Jeri but, as the dawn signifies, it's done as a reminder that after death, there's life. After dark comes light. It's a commitment to live on, without those we love and because of them, at the same time. It's giving them a special place in the hearts of Targe for all eternity.' He eyed Alexia, the wounded woman walking towards the men. 'And it honours the family members of those who died . . . It's saying we understand the loss. You're not alone. Ru'ach is with you, with them.'

'That's beautiful,' I said.

Alexia paused in her step, standing at the back of the men. They had left a path in between them that led to the two memorials, but Alexia hesitated. I knew that for her, taking another step was a big commitment, an acceptance that they were dead. It meant facing the Great Spirit again. Tears were already on her cheeks. The men sang to her husband and her son. And to her.

The night breeze blew around us. It felt warmer now. *Ru'ach is the wind that encircles us,* Darj had said. It encircled Alexia now as she looked to the sky. She seemed to mutter a prayer and then took a step.

The men knelt for her as she walked past them. Their singing grew louder, and her steps more confident. I watched as she walked taller with pride, her long dark hair flowing out behind her. She cradled the arm of her wounded shoulder against her chest like she was protecting her heart. Then, when she reached the space for her in between the two memorials, she knelt, and the men's singing faded.

Darj and Elhian knelt as well, so I did the same. Silence fell over the camp, and soon the breeze flapping through the tents was the only sound.

We stayed there until a golden line cracked the dark horizon in front us. We watched as the yellow sphere appeared curve by curve. It filtered the sky and clouds with shades of red, purple, pink, and orange. Once the entire circle of the sun was visible, Alexia rose, and so did we.

I felt the warmth of the rays on my skin, the strength of the men around us. I got the sense that our family was near. The horn sounded again, and the men started singing louder and stronger than I had ever heard.

Alexia stood and turned towards her men. They bowed and Ival yelled, 'Blessings upon the queen!'

The army resounded it loudly. It brought a smile to the queen's face and mine, too.

Alexia walked back, the men bowing to their queen again as she passed. 'My cousin has strength again,' I said to Darj, wiping away a tear.

Darj stood with his hand resting on his sword. He watched Alexia's dignified walk. She was no longer looking at the ground but reaching her hand out to the people who loved her. 'That is not just your cousin,' he said. 'It is Her Most Glorious Majesty, Queen Alexia of Targe.'

21

THE ROYAL COUNCIL

I tried to get some more sleep after the ceremony finished, but the men were up and talking, and I had too much on my mind to relax anyway.

I left my tent for a second time and stood outside the door. I saw Raggin ahead of me, stitching the wounds of his friend and roughly pulling the thick thread. Xander was both dirty and quiet. 'Why are ya looking so sad?' Raggin asked, talking loudly enough for me to hear from the tent. 'We just had a historical victory! We're back with our queen and A'zyon Warrior! Did you see that girl fight? By Ru'ach, she's amazing. You should be rejoicing.' Xander forced a small smile. 'What is it?' Raggin asked. 'Tired? Hungry? Cold? It's not love, is it?'

Xander scoffed. 'No. I haven't even been anywhere to meet women.'

'Ah, so it's lack of love then?' Raggin asked, chuckling at the sight of his friend's disgusted expression.

'Shut up Raggin.' Xander closed his eyes.

I saw King Hazaka walking to the two men, wearing a long red cape and his crown. 'Raggin,' he said, the cape twirling around to his front. 'I never knew you were so good with a needle and thread. Perhaps you could fix the atrocious tear in my undergarments once you are done here.'

'I have my limits, sire.'

Hazaka laughed a little too long. 'Yes, well, I suppose you are wondering why I came over here. I am gathering . . . Well, at least I am trying to gather . . . ' He looked about him. 'I have found it an unfulfilling task so far!'

'Gathering what?' Xander asked irritably. I couldn't blame him. Hazaka was getting under my skin as well.

'The leaders of our great kingdoms. I think it is time we had a Royal Council to discuss our next move, since I believe I have missed out on too many decisions.' He laughed and flicked a piece of grass off his shoulder. 'Tell me, have you seen either of them?'

Raggin pinned Xander down by his shoulder when he tried to sit up. 'No, not since this morning. I would help you look, but I don't trust this man to stay still while I'm gone.'

Xander tried to resist Raggin's hand. 'How's your wife, sire?' he asked. 'Queen Telitha?'

Hazaka's expression soured, but he soon laughed again. 'Ah, she is well. The same as ever, but pregnant with my heir, so I am feeling patient of her for now. I just hope she does not have a daughter, or I shall begin to feel outnumbered!'

'Congratulations sire,' Raggin said, smiling and showing a missing tooth. His line of sight travelled past the king. 'There they are—the prince and the queen.'

I looked where he was pointing and hurried to meet them before Hazaka arrived first.

I walked up behind them and discovered they, too, were in conversation. 'I'm not sure, Elhian,' I heard Alexia say. She was nursing her arm and seemed to be in pain. 'But I will not forget how you fought with us.'

'Yes, but we must take the next step. I know you well enough to know you always say you're not sure, only to come up with a flawless plan right when we need it.'

'Ha, I have no such talent. Besides, why have I been allocated the job of coming up with a plan?'

'I'm not sure . . . Perhaps because people are more likely to listen to you.'

I took this opportunity to make myself known. 'And this coming from someone who convinced thousands of men to join a fight they could ignore?' I asked.

The two turned. 'Indeed,' Alexia said. 'Besides,' she added quietly, 'if I ever was, the time of my being of use to you or anyone else will soon draw to an end, I fear.'

Elhian and I were about to protest—I couldn't understand why she would think such a thing—but it was then that King Hazaka reached us.

'The very gentry I wished to see,' he said importantly. 'May I request a council of the leaders of our three great and majestic kingdoms?'

Alexia pursed her lips to stop a less than polite answer escaping. I'm sure her sore shoulder was not aiding her forbearance. 'Hazaka, your every sentence is a conquest,' she said and, even though I don't think she meant it as a compliment, he smiled and thanked her. 'A council, you say?'

'Indeed, to discuss our next move as allies.'

Alexia raised an eyebrow. 'I see you men think alike. Very well, but if we are to have such a meeting, I would like to request the presence of Darj, Adaliah, and a comfortable chair.'

Hazaka leant back and folded his arms. 'Darj is a good soldier,' he said, 'but he is not royalty, and she is nothing more than a girl!'

Anger flickered in Alexia's eyes. 'It's because of Darj Ryder that we survived and that the Targians were able to join you on the field yesterday.' She leant forward as she spoke. 'He has much experience and knowledge in warfare and is also a trusted friend of mine and of my late husband. As for Adaliah,' she said, gesturing towards me, 'she is not only my cousin, but also quite possibly the reason we won yesterday!' I glanced away, convinced she was stretching the truth now. 'On top of that, if anything happens to me, she is next in line for the crown.' This was not something that had occurred to me and I looked at her in shock. I was glad I hadn't known that when she was on her deathbed in Tarcraig. 'Her involvement in our affairs is imperative for the survival of Targe and, having seen her fight yesterday, most likely for Casmodia and Jazmarda as well.'

I watched Zavad build a small tower out of white stones as I gazed through the flap in the tent. I wanted to go and help him, but Hazaka was droning on again about Jazmarda's place in the three-way alliance.

It was the fourth day after the battle. Alexia was reclined on a bed, her shoulder still aching, but the look of pain on her face was not because of that. I wanted to slip out, but I knew I had to support my cousin. Zavad was having much more fun, though. He knocked down the stones and started again. The second tower he built was much stronger and more stable. I was proud of him.

'If I were him, I'd add a west wing,' Darj whispered to me.

I analysed the potential architecture. 'No, I think a drawbridge first.'

'Adaliah?' Alexia asked. Her tone indicated that her patience had almost been exercised. 'What do you think we should do next?'

'Free the rest of our men, as we've both said before,' I said, watching as Zavad scattered the stones again. Apparently, the tower still needed improvements. I admired his determination. 'We have more than enough resources to complete the task.'

'And then what?' Hazaka asked. He raised his hands in frustration as he waited for me to speak, but I said nothing. I didn't have the answer.

'And then go to Jasteria,' Elhian said. He was walking the perimeter of the tent for a third time.

'Jasteria?' Alexia asked, sitting up. 'That city was one of the first to fall. It is one of Cades' tightest strongholds in my kingdom.'

'Exactly. We need to hit him where it will do the most damage. Remember, the greatest thing you can hurt is his pride. Jasteria was one of his grandest conquests, after Liane, and maybe Egra. Each of us could lead a battalion and—' Alexia stood and turned aside. Elhian paused, but she indicated with a wave for him to continue. 'And surround the town.' His enthusiasm faded as Alexia moved to the opening of the tent and leant on the doorway. 'Are you unwell?'

'I'm fine,' she said with a dismissive wave. I narrowed my eyes at her, wondering what she was hiding. 'Tell me, how many battalions would you need?'

'As you know, Jasteria has six equal sides. The best attack would be a six-fold attack.'

'And who would you have lead these men?'

Elhian hesitated again, confused, as I was, by her questioning. 'Well, Darj, Hazaka, Adaliah,' he counted three with his fingers, 'either Ival, Xander or Raggin . . . Myself, and you of course.'

Alexia began to pace. 'When would you plan such an attack?'

Elhian turned his palms up and shrugged his shoulders. 'But—and I'd like your opinion Darj—it would take at least four weeks to be ready for it I think.'

'I don't know . . . ' Alexia muttered before Darj could reply.

For the first time during the meeting, I began to pay full attention. I watched as Alexia rubbed her wounded shoulder and avoided eye contact. The queen opened her mouth as if to say something more, but then shook her head and walked towards the door of the tent.

Darj stepped after her and put a hand on her shoulder, preventing her from leaving.

'Ah!' she said, flinching. She turned to him with clenched teeth, rubbing her shoulder again. 'Darj!'

'What's going on?' Darj asked.

'Look, I am no warrior—'

'You are our best archer, and you saved Adaliah's life,' Darj said.

'I know you're only a woman,' Hazaka said, 'but—'

'Only a woman?' Alexia repeated dangerously. I put a hand on my forehead, deciding Hazaka was not a very perceptive man.

Hazaka ignored her and went on. 'You should know how important it is for you to be with your men, to lead them to battle.'

Alexia now did not restrain from glaring at him. 'Do you think I'm not aware of this?' she asked, raising her voice.

'I think you are avoiding the next move. Elhian made the suggestion—'

'I am content with the plan. There is a small likelihood of success without grave loss, but I believe we are in the company to make it work. I simply . . . ' She took a deep breath and blew it out again.

Darj peered at her with an expression somewhere between irritation and bewilderment. 'I do want you to be safe, but—'

'If you see any flaw in the plan, know anything we do not, it is vital that you tell us of it,' Elhian said.

Alexia closed her eyes and rubbed her shoulder again. 'I just believe it's going to be a bit more difficult than we think.'

'When has a battle ever been easy?' Hazaka asked.

'Alexia,' Elhian said. 'We are your friends. Your confidence will not be betrayed. Now, tell us: what's going on?'

Alexia sat on the edge of her bed and tried to stretch out her arm. She watched as Zavad played with his stones, finding joy in the simple pleasure. I think she missed her son all over again, but she didn't speak the words.

'I just . . . ' she began in a whisper. We all leant forward to ensure we heard whatever she was going to say. 'I want to fight, and I will. No one will stop me from that. But I don't think I should agree to go to battle without at least telling you that I am already more than three months pregnant.'

22
AMATHEA'S KNOLL

Amathea's Knoll, a soft hill re-named after Alexia's parents, was a peaceful place to sit. Now towards the end of autumn, the leaves had fallen, exposing the trees' gnarled and knotted trunks naked to the icy wind. Underneath the frosty ground and wet foliage were hundreds of bulbs that would cover the hill in yellow, blue and scarlet flowers once the winter broke, or so I was told.

On top of the hill there stood the ruins of an old abbey that had been destroyed in a battle fought between King Amaz and the Bone Hordes—barbarians from the desert east. Trees grew inside the abbey walls now, and its floor was made of green grass. It was still tall and grand. It still felt like a sacred site.

Ru'ach . . . please be near us.

A quiet breeze filtered around me, and I felt that he was.

Alexia told me how Ethaniel had brought her to the abbey when they were courting, years before. As the princess and only heir, the entire kingdom had been waiting to see whom she would choose as her consort. She said she was subject to many suitors and entertained some to please her father and the court, but her heart had only ever belonged to one man. On that day of spring, he knelt amongst the flowers in the abbey ruins and asked for her hand in marriage, and she accepted. She had been seventeen. My age.

Now, carrying his child and sitting atop the bleak summit, I think she longed for him more than ever. We were just southwest of the Tiathi Basin in Targe: less than a day away from camp, but over the border and in our homeland. I had been desperate to talk to her properly following her announcement but, after deciding to go ahead with separate attacks on the other Casmodian villages, we had hardly had a chance to be alone. There had been two weeks of fighting, and it all blurred together. We'd lost soldiers and gained no land, but Cades no longer held Targian prisoners. We had freed all of our men and were planning for our attack on Jasteria.

'How long had you known?' I began when Alexia offered no conversation. While the news of the pregnancy explained a lot and I'd had time to get used to the idea by then, I was still incredulous and trying to understand how a pregnant queen would influence our approach to the war.

'Since just before Jeri died.'

'It is . . . it is Ethaniel's, isn't it?' I whispered.

'Of course it is!'

'I'm sorry, it's just that . . . I don't remember when or how or where he died . . . '

'It was the night before the Battle of the Yellow Forest.'

'When he died?'

'No, I mean . . . He fought in the battle and was killed when he came home to the palace to escort us away. What he didn't know was that a few men, Cades included, had followed him. It was the night before that our child was conceived. What upsets me most is the irony. For over a year we had tried to give Jeri a little brother or sister and never succeeded, and now, when they are both gone, on the one night when a child was the furthest thing from our minds, we did succeed. This should be such a joyous thing, and yet I am wrestling with resentment.' She looked up at the front of the abbey where the sun streamed through the grand window frame. 'I don't understand Ru'ach's reckoning, or why he is asking me to do this now, alone, or why this child must grow up without a father.'

'I don't think Ru'ach did this to you,' I said. 'Darj said he is good. This is evil's doing.'

'He still let it happen, though,' she said softly. 'He is supposed to be our protector. He could have stopped Cades. He could have stopped Jag.'

'They are the true enemy. If you're going to hate anyone, it should be them.'

She turned to me, her expression an uncomfortable one. 'That is the Targian's choice—love or hate. But Cades is the one who's full of hate. I don't want to be like him. I don't want to hate Ru'ach, or anyone. I will always choose love. I'm just . . . sad.'

'Were you happy when you found out you were pregnant?'

'I . . . I was bewildered. At first, I was too lost in grief . . . I'm so tired, Adaliah,' she whispered. 'But . . . this child has given me a reason to press on, a reason to fight, to live, even though sometimes I resent having to do so. I take comfort in knowing that Ethaniel and Jeri will live on. I just wish this child could have known them. They both would have been so excited.'

I said nothing for a while. A part of me was hurt that she not only hadn't confided in me about the pregnancy and sought protection but had actually gone to great lengths to hide it instead. Part of me was angry with myself for not seeing it or even considering it. Part of me was relieved that Alexia's secret had not been life threatening . . .

but then . . . 'The most wanted-woman in history,' I said, remembering Lezan's words. 'Lezan knew, didn't he? He was worried for you, because . . . Because if Cades finds out that you're carrying the heir to the Targian throne . . . '

Alexia exhaled slowly. 'Actually, it's a little more complicated than that . . . ' I wondered at her, but she brushed it off. 'The point is I have put you all at risk, just as Darj said.'

'Darj was only angry because he worries about you.'

I remembered the silence that had followed her announcement. We had all stared at her like she'd just said she was going to give birth to a horse. Elhian and I were speechless, but Darj voiced daggers at her. 'Now I understand why Lezan was so hard on you that time! You have been risking much more than your own life. You have been putting the whole royal line in harm's way!'

I don't think Alexia was used to his criticism. I knew she only meant to protect those she loved. Darj knew that deep down, too, I was sure. He was just thinking about how she'd placed herself between us and the archers on the road to Egra, how she'd been shot in the Tiathi Basin and come off her horse . . . All the times when the child could have been lost.

'Part of me feels peaceful, knowing I will be a mother again soon,' Alexia said now, 'but I also know I won't be able to rest in that peace until the child is born and secured away from Cades.' She leant into me. 'I hope the two of us can achieve at least that.'

Back at camp that afternoon, Alexia went to find Zavad, and I followed Darj and Elhian on a deer hunt, not wanting to be left alone with Hazaka, who was going on and on about glory and honour to his men.

'Perfect,' Darj said when Elhian shot a deer. An hour had passed by then and that was the first word the general had said.

Elhian brushed through the grass to the dead animal and pulled out the arrow. The two of them picked the carcase up and flung it over Guntar's back. Riding Bagred, I held onto Guntar's reins while they tied it down.

'Darj, how long have you been the queen's general?' Elhian asked, mounting his white horse, Leuk.

'Oh, ah, since her coronation, three or so years ago. Do you remember Will? He was the general before me, but he fell sick and died. The council was not happy when the queen promoted me—I was younger than all of them—but there was no one else for the job, I think.'

'You do well protecting Alexia.' Elhian glanced at me as he said it.

'Alexia.' Darj grunted her name under his breath and fiddled with his stirrup.

'I'm sure the queen is proud to have you lead her army, as I would be.'

If Darj was moved by this, he didn't show it. 'Thank you, but whether she is or not is beside the point. Her husband is dead. Her son is dead. Her kingdom is lost. I have failed her as her general, and as a man. She will only ever see me through those eyes now.'

'Darj, that's not fair,' I said. I'd known he blamed himself for things, but no idea how much.

'Yes,' Elhian said, furrowing his brow. 'She lives, and her child with her. Targe will go on.'

Darj mounted his horse with the deer behind him. 'Perhaps.' He took the reins from me.

'Do you have family?' Elhian asked him as we began to ride back to camp.

Darj was silent until the prince repeated the question. 'I had two sisters,' he said. 'One married a merchantman from the White Isles, and I've only seen her once since. I write to her when I get the chance. She has three sons and two daughters now. The other lived to see her only child die, and she . . . well, she took her own life not long after.'

Darj's red horse paused of its own accord, allowing us to stop by him. 'I'm sorry,' I said, even though I must have known that once.

'I don't mean to be hard on Alexia,' Darj said, 'but I will not stand by and let her fall into the same fate as my sister.'

We wandered on, quiet in the surroundings of our own thoughts. I wondered what other things Darj had endured and how he remained so strong and convicted. I thought about the courage Elhian had to stand against his tyrannical father and his own kingdom's army, a feat I knew would take great strength of mind. Alexia had lost everything but still retained the respect of her people and, even though she was reduced to a tent in the wilderness, she never complained.

I should not be the one they give titles like the A'zyon Warrior to. I am anything but fearless.

We came to a small brook and I noticed broken twigs and unsettled dirt at Bagred's hooves. We hadn't passed this way before so I knew the tracks weren't ours, but before I could wonder any further a stag, tall and grand, appeared on my left. I was glad Darj and Elhian didn't see him—I didn't want him to become our dinner. He had been drinking from the brook but raised his head and looked at me, then moved away. I watched him go and then noticed something else—a pair of legs hanging down from a branch. Further inspection revealed that the legs were attached to a small boy. He saw me looking at him and tried to hide behind some leaves.

'I'll catch up with you,' I said to the men before turning Bagred up the brook. 'Zavad,' I called. 'Come down.'

Two angry eyes peered over the branch. 'How did you find me?'

'What are you doing?'

'I want to go to Kest,' he said, climbing down.

'Why?'

'Because I want to see my mother!' Tears dripped down his dirty brown face, leaving white, snail-like trails down his cheeks. I dismounted and tried to hug him, but he pulled away. 'I want my family.'

'I know. You will see them again soon.'

'I will never see my father again though, will I! And now 'Lexia will have her own baby and forget all about me. She's the reason my papa is dead, isn't she!'

I hid my shock at his anger and accusation, feeling both protective of Alexia and pitying of the boy. 'No. You cannot blame Alexia, Zavad. She loves you and so do I.' I put a hand on his shoulder. 'And you know, her child's father was killed, too, just like yours. It will never know its big brother either, but I hope it will know you.'

'Zavad!' Alexia called, walking over to the boy when we returned and tucking him under her arm. 'Where have you been? You're freezing! Come and warm yourself by the fire. Where did you go?'

'I want to see my mother.' Zavad pulled free of her and walked away.

Alexia watched him settle next to Xander and Raggin by the camp-fire. She gave me a questioning look and indicated for me to follow her inside our tent.

'I've been thinking,' she said, sitting next to me on my bed. 'There would be many women in Kest longing to see their men. So many will never see them again.' She gestured towards the soldiers camping outside. 'They are weary and hungry. Perhaps we should go to Kest, before Jasteria. What do you think? Perhaps you will be able to find something to help your memory there, and that could be the difference between victory and defeat for us.'

'Do you think that's possible?' A part of me had given up on ever having my memory returned.

'Adaliah, do you remember anything about Kest, before you woke?' I shook my head. 'Nothing at all?'

'Alexia . . . ' Perhaps I was overtired, but for whatever reason I suddenly felt annoyed and emotional. 'Every day people try to probe my memory, and it's always the same. I remember nothing! All I have is bad dreams, of darkness and chaos and pain. But none of it makes any sense!'

'Adaliah . . . I'm sorry—'

'Are you?' I asked. 'Or do you just need me to fight for you?'

Alexia flinched at my sharpness but remained calm. 'I have never asked you to fight for me,' she said, pricking at my conscience. 'If you wish it, you can leave now.'

'And go where? I turn around and all I find is darkness.' I could tell she didn't know what to say. I didn't even know what I wanted her to say. She turned to leave me alone, but my eyes filled with tears, and I didn't want her to go anywhere. 'Alexia, what do I do? What if I never remember?'

'Oh Adaliah . . . ' She sat with me on the bed again and put an arm around my shoulders. She held me close, and her tenderness made me cry even more. 'This is not the Adaliah I once knew,' she said fondly. 'This is not the Adaliah who could always find a smile in every situation and who was so clear about what she believed.'

'I'm so scared,' I whispered.

'Yes, we are most afraid of what we cannot see, or cannot control. But even if I don't understand him, we have Ru'ach who connects us all with love, and we have each other. Fear flees when there is love, and I love you, my dear cousin.'

She convinced me to lie down and stayed by my side until she thought I was asleep. With her nearby, the fear really did begin to fade once more.

Later, I heard her step outside. She was soon having a discussion with Elhian and Hazaka that I could hear through the thin tent walls.

'I want to take my men to Kest,' she said. 'They need to know if those exiled are all right, and so do I.'

'Well, send a scout!' Hazaka said.

'If they do not have enough supplies they will die.' The irritation in her voice was unmistakable. 'Everything we accomplish at Jasteria and thereafter will be wasted.'

'You are being far too dramatic! I do not—'

Alexia's tone changed and I could tell her tolerance for Hazaka had just dried up. 'I don't care what you do or do not think, Hazaka. My people will be going to Kest with or without you.'

'Alexia,' Elhian said.

'How dare you insult me in this manner?' Hazaka asked. 'We are supposed to be working together!'

'If we were working together you would have fought with us when I sent word before the Battle of the Yellow Forest!'

'Alexia?'

'You know full well I was unable to respond to your letter.'

'Yes, just like the other six leaders I beckoned to help. Not one came to our rescue. We were left at Cades' mercy, so do not talk to me about working together.' I could hear real anger in her voice.

'We fought together for victory at Tiathi!'

'And we will fight together again at Jasteria. My plan is simply to take ten days to go to Kest with my men and to then return to this very spot.'

'Ten days is too long!'

'Alexia!'

'What?' she snapped at the prince at last. I smiled to myself, knowing Elhian's patience would be tested as well.

'Would you both sit down please?' There was silence for a moment, and I assumed they were doing as he asked. 'I know where you are both coming from, but I think you are both missing the point here.'

'Which is what?' Hazaka asked, sounding bored.

'The fourth sword. It has to be in Kest. I'm sure Cades has men looking for it there. We should get it before he does.'

'But where would we start?' Alexia asked.

'At the hut I found,' Elhian said. 'There's also the chance something there will spark Adaliah's memory.'

Alexia chuckled to herself in a way that made me suspect that had been her true plan all along.

'But whether she remembers or not,' Elhian added, 'the fate of our kingdoms could well rest on her shoulders, and we need to keep her safe.'

'Well,' Hazaka said, 'I think that is one thing we can agree on.'

23
THE WHITE STONES

I brushed Bagred down the following morning, alone and away from camp. I spent more time than I normally would untangling his mane and tail before cleaning out the dirt in each of his hooves. I ran my hand over the bare patch of skin that had grown over his wound. He nuzzled me and, leaning my head into his neck, I found his smell comforting.

I walked with him back to the camp and came across Darj kneeling beside Zavad. The boy was sitting in the middle of an impressive array of white stones and pebbles.

'What are you up to Zavad?' Darj asked as I stopped by them. 'You must have cleared an entire river bed!'

'I'm building a road, back to my mother,' he said, trying to get the smooth stones to sit next to each other.

'Zavad, we are going to Kest in the morning, to find your mother,' Darj said.

Zavad looked up from his labour, his eyebrows now high in his dirty forehead. 'Really?' he asked.

'Yes—the queen has decreed it.'

'Can I take the stones with me?'

'We would need several carts to carry all these,' Darj said.

'Please?'

'No, Zavad. Now, Queen Alexia wants you to get clean before you see your mother again.'

'Clean?' He repeated it like it was a foreign word. 'But what if Mama doesn't recognise me?'

Darj and I laughed. 'She will,' I said, 'and we will tell her what a brave boy you have been.'

Darj ruffled his hair. Zavad grinned and ran to find Alexia, his tattered clothes breezing behind him.

Darj and I looked over the boy's collection of stones. Some of them were worn, some were white, and others more of a dull grey. Some were round and others had sharp edges. Darj took a handful and let them slip between his fingers. He seemed deep in thought.

'Are you all right?' I asked.

He nodded but didn't look at me. A triangular-shaped stone stayed in his hand. He ran his rough fingertip over its smooth surface and slipped it into his pocket.

'Are you going to Kest?' I asked Elhian later.

'Yes. Adaliah, I don't know if Alexia told you, but I want to go back to that hut. If we're looking for the sword, I think that would be a good place to start and being there might help you remember.'

'What are you suggesting?'

'That you and I go and find it. Perhaps you could even take me to the spot where you woke up, and then we could work backwards.'

'Why is everyone so keen for me to remember?' I asked more tersely than intended. It wasn't that I was angry with him—I was just tired of letting people down every time my memory failed. I knew it frustrated them, but they seemed to forget I was the one living in the mist.

Elhian's steady brown eyes made me feel ashamed again. 'For your own sake. Is that not enough?'

He was only nineteen, still a boy in many ways, but Elhian had a way of making people respect him. 'When do we leave?'

'In the morning. We will travel to Kest with Alexia first, and then we can go south to where I found the hut and near where you were . . . hurt.'

I agreed but could no longer meet his eyes. I wasn't sure why, but I wanted him to think well of me. The words had never been spoken, but I felt a bond with Elhian. Perhaps it was because we were the younger two of our companions. Perhaps it was because he was the first one to make me feel safe after I woke in the river or that I felt he understood me as I was. Perhaps I just respected what he was trying to achieve and wanted to help him do it.

The truth was I could hardly understand what was happening in my mind, let alone in my heart.

I had some of Zavad's stones in my pocket. Pulling them out, I picked one that was a rough circle. Then, I picked another that formed a single point and held it out to Elhian. 'From Zavad's road, because we're all trying to get home.'

He opened his palm to me and, after I dropped the stone there, he took my hand in his and kissed it with a tenderness I wasn't expecting. 'I know you are as lost and fearful as I am,' he said. 'But you are not alone.'

Alexia and I woke when a flock of a hundred or so white birds flew across the camp at daybreak, screeching, squawking, and starting the morning as the flurry it turned out to be.

'Ival Fort,' Alexia said later as a group of men gathered inside our tent, awaiting instruction, 'tell my men to prepare to leave.'

Ival left to obey.

The queen was sitting behind an improvised table, leaning back into a chair and looking regal despite her tainted dress and less than clean skin. 'Xander, if you wouldn't mind assisting him . . . Raggin, please ascertain from Hazaka if his people intend to join us or to stay here and wait for our return.' Xander and Raggin gave a bow and left as well. 'Where is Naclen?' the queen asked for a second time.

Elhian hurried off and returned with the youth in question. 'Ah, Naclen,' Alexia said, 'please take a horse and ride ahead of us to Kest. I want you to send word that we are coming and ask the people to arrange themselves into groups according to the village in which they were born. I think this is the quickest and easiest way to reunite a kingdom.'

Naclen hesitated.

'What are you waiting for, soldier?' Darj asked. 'You have your orders.' Darj nodded towards the door and Naclen left without bowing.

Now with only Darj, Elhian and myself left in her presence, Alexia turned to the prince. 'Elhian, I need you to take my stitches out before I tear them out with my teeth.'

Elhian hid a smile as he moved towards the medicinal equipment we had acquired in Tiathi for that very purpose. He bent down on one knee beside her while I pulled her long dark hair out of the way, removed her cloak and helped her get her arm out of her sleeve.

Elhian frowned at the purple and black haze that was on both sides of her shoulder. 'It still has a lot of healing to do, but the wound itself has closed over. The dead skin is probably what's making you itchy.' Using very fine tools, he pulled out the twelve small stitches on her front, where he had forced the arrow through, and then the five on her back.

'Darj,' Alexia said now, 'please find Zavad and get him ready for his trip home.'

'Kest is hardly home, Alexia,' Darj said.

She gave a sad smile. 'But a mother always is.'

Later, Darj gave Zavad a leg up onto a horse while I mounted Bagred. Around us were many more mounted soldiers, waiting to ride back to their families. Hazaka and his men were not among them, having sent a message back with Raggin that they would wait for our return.

'Adaliah,' the boy said, panicking. 'Where are my stones?'

One of the soldiers nearby overheard him and rode over, pulling one of the stones out of his pocket. 'We all took one son, to help you carry them home.' Some of the other men nearby held up the unique stones they had chosen as well. 'We heard what you were doing and wanted to keep them to remind us of what we had, what we are fighting for, and of you, the boy who brought us home.'

Zavad's wide eyes gave the smile his mouth could not. 'Thank you,' he said.

24
TOWARDS KEST

Alexia let her cloak fall to her feet. I was already in the hot spring, diving under the water like a fish. Remembering how good it felt to be clean, I rubbed my face with my hands in an effort to turn my skin from a dirty brown to a fresh white. I flipped onto my back and, losing myself in the grey sky, called out for Alexia to hurry up.

Alexia removed her dress so she, too, was left in only a thin shift. She ran her hand over her stomach, which was now announcing her secret. Without her many layers of clothing, Alexia was notice-ably pregnant, about sixteen weeks along. She was weary but I still thought she was beautiful. She stepped into the pool and dived in past me.

Darj had reminded Alexia we would be passing by these springs on our way to Kest, and after that she had been determined to visit them. The army camped on the road nearby but, as we swam in the warm water, it could have been just us in the world.

'How did you hide it so well?' I asked once we were both satisfied we were free of dirt. 'Have you felt sick each morning?'

'The sickness didn't limit itself to the morning. Still, it seems to have faded now, for which I am thankful. I was running out of excuses for leaving the group abruptly all the time.'

'When will it be born?'

'Early in the spring.'

'Aren't you terrified?' If she was, she was hiding her fear a lot better than I could have. But then Alexia had a lot of practice hiding her true emotions. It was part of her role.

She scoffed. 'Terrified of what? Cades killing it, or both of us? Losing this war and my kingdom forever? Giving birth to a child that will have no father? Being a queen and a mother in the midst of this darkness? Why would I be terrified?' I touched her arm, realising how stupid my question had been. 'I'm sorry,' she said. 'I don't mean to get so angry. The only good thing about losing your family is you know you have survived the worst life can offer and that nothing else could ever match it.' Alexia put her hand over mine. 'Except it happening again. I fear for this child, Adaliah. And for you. You will be careful looking for the sword when you go, won't you?'

Elhian and I planned to go to the exiles with the others first, as Darj had suggested it would be good for them to see I was still alive. Only then would Elhian and I turn south to see this hut of his and look for the fourth sword. 'I want to stay with you.'

'And I with you, but we will meet again soon, before Jasteria.'

'Promise me the Casmodians won't find out about your child,' I said, meeting her eyes. 'Even if we lose every battle and town and soldier, your child must live.'

Alexia smiled. 'We will do our best.'

'Are you finished yet?' a bored male voice called from behind a rocky interface. Elhian was keeping watch with Darj.

'No!' I called back playfully. I swam behind my cousin and massaged her shoulders, taking care not to aggravate her wound. I could feel the tension in them and tried to ease it.

Alexia sighed and seemed to relax. 'Should I ask Elhian about his true intentions before you two go?' she asked.

I stopped mid-motion. 'What? No . . . '

'Well, he is a good man, and strong, no matter what Cades says.'

'I don't think now is the time for that.' I continued the massage but felt my cheeks flush. 'What makes you suggest that anyway?'

'Experience.'

I wanted to ask her how she and Ethaniel had met, but worried that thinking about it would upset her. For the first time, as I felt the tight knots in my cousin's back and neck, I appreciated not having a memory.

'How do you know we can trust him?' I asked. 'If he's on our side, why didn't he save Ethaniel, Jeri—my father?'

'I'm certain he knew nothing of Cades' plans. One day you'll remember, and you'll laugh to think you ever doubted him.'

'Adaliah! Alexia! Please!' This time it was Darj getting impatient.

'Oh, go and kill something for dinner!' Alexia yelled back.

'We wanted to catch fish there!'

'Fish don't live in hot springs,' we heard Elhian say.

'Yes, but they may not know that,' Darj said.

Only when our skin started to go wrinkly did we give in. We dried and dressed in the beautiful gowns we had used with Parrian in Semanez. Mine was purple and gold, Alexia's was blue, green and gold, and both were velvety and warm. We called the men, and Darj and Elhian came out from behind the tree.

They approached the two of us and hesitated with surprise. Alexia looked beautiful, feminine and fresh, but Elhian smiled at me. 'Lady Adaliah,' he said, bowing from the neck.

As Alexia put on her cloak and hid her growing stomach, I sensed his even gaze upon me and suddenly felt shy.

Later that night, Naclen returned from his quest and came and sat by our campfire to give his report.

'Did you find them?' the queen asked, sitting between Darj and Elhian.

'Yes,' Naclen said. 'Casmodian soldiers are posted around the camp, which spreads further than I could see. Thousands upon thousands of people are there, Your Majesty, with bare shelters and little food.'

'How did you get to them if there were so many soldiers?' Darj asked.

'As I was watching them, I heard a Casmodian sneaking up behind me. I killed him and realised I could use his uniform. I dragged his body away and swapped our clothes, including his helmet to hide my black hair. Then, I rode straight into the camp. I found a few Targians gathered together outside a tent. I told them to come inside with me and explained who I was, but I had trouble convincing them I was from outside the camp even after I took off my helmet. But once they realised I was telling the truth, they were very excited. I told them that Targe is regathering, that we'd had victory at Tiathi. They could hardly believe it, or that the two of you are still alive.' He nodded at Alexia and me. 'When I told them the army was coming to reunite with them, one of the ladies began to cry. I gave them your message about organising themselves into the towns in which they were born, and they said they would spread the news, and would do so subtly so the Casmodians would not even notice.' He shrugged as he took the bowl of stew Darj was offering him. 'And I came back to tell you we will have to fight to see them.'

Two days later, Alexia and I crawled up a small hill with Zavad, peeking out over the top to see the situation of the exiles for ourselves.

'They look so cold,' I said, my heart going out to the small children I could see hugging themselves in the icy breeze.

'But not hopeless,' Alexia said, eyeing some of the adults. 'They know we are coming.'

Darj appeared on another small hill further around the encampment. He was carrying a tall, green banner, which he thrust into the ground. Some of the exiles noticed him and began to call to each other in excitement. This, however, alerted the Casmodian guards as well. One of them sounded a horn. I didn't know what their signals meant or if they knew who Darj was, but the sound that rang out seemed to speak the word 'intruder' and 'attack' all at once.

A group of about thirty or forty began to run towards Darj, but apart from his horse rearing he didn't move. In fact, he yelled 'Arjla divala' at them, the words baring his teeth and making him fierce.

'I think he's enjoying this,' Alexia said.

The group of Casmodians drew closer. More of their comrades came out from amongst the people to join them. There were soon a hundred or more of them, racing towards a lone man . . . or so they thought.

Another minute passed, and then our best soldiers as chosen by Darj appeared on the hill behind him.

Even Alexia smiled to see the look on the Casmodians' faces when they realised. They stopped running, yelled at each other, called out commands. By then, Darj, Elhian and the rest of the chosen soldiers were charging at them.

Alexia turned Zavad's face away from the bloodshed that followed.

'Look how swift and eager they are,' I said.

'It's because their family and loved ones are in sight,' Alexia said.

The exiles were mostly getting out of the way of the fight—it was taking place right amongst their tents—but I spotted more than one who impaled a guard when they could.

'Are the Casmodians bad people?' Zavad asked.

I turned to Alexia, hoping she would answer. She nodded vaguely.

'Why?' Zavad asked.

'Because they kill good people for no reason other than to empower themselves.'

'But your people are killing them now.'

'Yes, to release all these men, women and children, your family included.'

'Isn't Elhian the Prince of the Casmodians?'

'Yes.'

'Then why don't you hate him?'

'Because he is a good person,' Alexia said. 'A person's goodness isn't defined by their race and kingdom, but what they choose to fight for. Elhian chose to fight against his father when many would have cowered.'

It was another hour before the cries of 'Arjla divala' were heard like a wave across the people. The last surviving Casmodians ran for the hills, and we cheered to see them go.

'It's done, Alexia,' Darj said when he reached us, smiling at her in a way he hadn't done in weeks.

We led the army down to their families. With stern faces, the men resisted temptation to ride ahead and find their loved ones, but this yearning eased as the people separated ahead and bowed before us, before Alexia. Many of the exiles had tears in their eyes. Some moved closer to the queen and kissed the bottom of her cloak as she rode past. For the first time, I saw how the people loved and needed her, but I was also moved when they cheered my name, rejoicing to see me alive as Darj had said they would. It was an odd feeling, being loved for a life I couldn't remember. Many spoke blessings over us all; many were too moved to say anything.

Most were searching for their families. The first reunion happened when one soldier found his young wife and daughter gathered with the other villagers from Jeriton. He dismounted and threw his arms around them. Soon soldiers were breaking away at every second, and the air felt light with a laughter and a joy Alexia and I found hard to share. We knew there'd be no family waiting for us.

We rode on until we came to a smaller group. There, Alexia asked a young woman which part of Targe she was from.

'Fenellar,' the girl said without lifting her head.

Alexia tightened her reins and stopped, and I did the same. 'Fenellar?' she asked. We looked at the few hundred people standing with the girl. 'Where are the rest of you? Thousands of people live in Fenellar!'

'They have died, my queen, or they fight in your army now.'

Alexia seemed to recognise the girl's voice. She dismounted and walked to her. 'Look at me,' she said. The girl hesitated before slowly lifting her head. 'Brenna!'

The maid's face was drawn, dirty and wet with tears.

'What happened to you?' Alexia asked. 'Where have you been?'

I tensed, wishing we had told her the truth before this. Darj had wanted to protect her, but now I felt she wouldn't appreciate having to find out this way.

Brenna knelt before Alexia and clasped her hands together. 'Please, have mercy my queen.'

Confused, Alexia looked at me and then at Darj, who had been discussing something with Naclen. Rage rose into his face when he saw Brenna. He dismounted and pushed the maid away from Alexia before unsheathing his sword.

'Darj!' Alexia said.

Brenna was trying to scramble away on the grass. Still on Bagred, I reached for my sword, too, although I don't know why.

Naclen ran over. 'Brenna? Darj, that's my sister!' Naclen took her hand.

His sister?

He had mentioned that his sister went to live in Liane some years ago. *It was Brenna?*

'Move away or I will kill you both,' Darj said with a cold tone I hadn't heard before. It was violent. It was protective. He stood between them and the queen.

'Darj,' Alexia said, 'I demand you to explain what is going on.'

'What has she done?' Naclen asked.

'Ask her yourself,' Darj said.

Naclen turned to Brenna. She was sobbing hysterically, like some people do when they're afraid for their life.

'Tell them what you did!' Darj yelled, pointing the sword at her throat. Naclen tried to push him away, but Darj kicked him down. 'Tell your queen what you did!'

Brenna spoke through her tears. 'I . . . I was the one who took your sword. I loved a Casmodian . . . I did it for him. He is now dead at Adaliah's hand.' She glared at me.

I bristled at her accusation. 'The price all those who fight against Targe will pay,' I said.

'Go on,' Darj told Brenna.

She returned her gaze to the ground, sobbing again. 'I took the sword from your chambers. All . . . all of this is on my head.'

I turned to the queen. Her concerned gaze became cold and emotionless as she registered the weight of her maid's confession.

'And tell her what happened at Egra!' Darj said. I was glad he was not my enemy.

Brenna tried to catch her breath. 'I told them where you were. I told them so they could kill you.'

Naclen moved away from her as if her words had repelled him. 'Treason,' he said. 'High treason.'

Brenna bowed again in front of Alexia, her forehead touching the ground and her tears dampening the grass. Alexia peered down at the dark head of the girl who had once served her daily, and turned away.

I saw how Alexia held Zavad's hand tightly as we walked to the few people who remained a legacy to Hunt. Zavad was dragging her forward and I stayed by her side, wanting to support her but not quite sure how.

Ahead, a woman came out of a small tent with a newborn in her arms. Her hair was matted, her clothes torn and muddy, but her vibrant blue eyes told us that Zavad's mother lived.

Alexia stopped walking, and Zavad turned to hurry her. He realised she was looking ahead and, following her line of sight, turned to the woman whose children now clung to her clothes. He yelled to her and dropped Alexia's hand.

The woman saw him, and a sob rose out of her chest. It was a sob filled with joy and pain and grief. She handed her babe to another and knelt down to him. He ran into her arms and the two cried together. Brothers and sisters soon surrounded them. There were eight altogether, including Zavad and the baby sister he had never met.

There were many tears, but I noticed how Alexia blinked hers away.

Zavad eventually emerged from his family and called for us. His kin turned to see Alexia and I standing near them. His mother curtsied before moving towards the queen, her new daughter in her arms again and her restored son by her side. 'We called my daughter Jenny, after your mother,' she said, showing Alexia her child. 'If I had known the service you provided my Zavad, I would have called her Alexia, in honour of you.'

Alexia smiled. 'I am honoured even so, but it was Lady Adaliah who saved him from death, and he who did me the service. Zavad has helped us in many ways, so I will ensure your family will always live in comfort once Cades is subdued. I can give you a home in Liane, if you like. I know what you have lost.'

It was a generous offer, and I could only imagine what it would mean for this widowed woman and her family.

But the mother simply nodded and said, 'I know I have suffered no more than you, Your Majesty.'

Elhian and I discussed our plan to leave the next day before going to bed, but I lay awake and restless well into the night. It felt colder than usual, and I was concerned about leaving Alexia. I was also fearful that the journey Elhian and I were about to take would prove fruitless. *Then what will we do? How long do we have before Targe is broken forever?*

I don't remember falling asleep that night, just waking later to find Darj in our tent. He was crouching in front of Alexia, who was sitting on the edge of her bed trying to catch her breath.

'What's wrong?' I asked, sitting up.

Her hands were shaking and white. Darj covered them with his. 'Just breathe,' he said to her. She was gasping.

I moved over to them and put an arm around her. 'What happened?' I asked, feeling her shudder under my touch. She leant into me.

'It's her nerves,' Darj said when Alexia didn't answer. 'I heard her call out. Be calm, Alexia, for your child's sake.'

A tear escaped from under her long dark eyelashes. She put a hand on her chest, trying to steady her heart. I rubbed her back until her breathing became more regular again.

'I'm . . . I'm all right,' she said.

Darj indicated for her to lie down, and I moved out of the way so she could. He placed warm furs over her and propped her head up with a pillow before returning to his tent. I held her trembling hand until she found sleep. I hoped Ethaniel and Jeri would visit her in her dreams again and questioned whether anything we did could make a difference when so much damage had already been done.

25
PARTING WAYS

I could tell my cousin was having a pleasant dream by the time morn-ing broke, and, after seeing the way she'd been that night, I didn't want to be the one to wake her now. Instead, I began putting on as many layers of clothing as I could bear to protect myself against the growing cold. Bagred was outside, saddled and waiting. I put on my green cloak over my clothes and collected the plain sword I'd been using since returning the other to Elhian. I shivered as I walked across the frosted grass. I slipped some supplies into the saddlebags on Bagred—dried fruit, nuts and thin bread—and stroked his neck.

Darj stood with Guntar nearby, brushing him down with strong and purposeful strokes.

'You will safeguard her, won't you?' I asked. 'And make sure she eats properly? She's too thin for a mother-to-be.'

'Since when were you the expert on this?' he asked.

'Since I was a woman,' I said matter-of-factly. 'Are you still angry with her?'

'Angry?' Surprised, he stopped brushing. 'She's impossible some-times, and she takes too many risks for my liking. It's not good for a queen to think she's invincible—'

'Oh Darj, she hardly believes that.'

He ignored me. 'I worry about her, and I'm angry about the war, but I don't think I could ever be truly angry with her.'

'Then you must start talking to her again. She's starting to take it to heart. She does appreciate you and she'll need you now, even if she doesn't admit it openly.'

Darj laughed. 'I've never met a royal woman, yourself included, who ever needed help.'

I wasn't sure how to respond to that. 'But you will look after her?'

He put a hand on my shoulder. 'You know I will, or die trying. You can travel in peace.'

Elhian was coming towards us. His dense brown hair was falling over his face in a wild way, but he didn't brush it aside. He led Leuk behind him. 'Are you ready to go?' he asked.

'Yes, but Alexia's still asleep.'

He considered the sun. 'We need to go as soon as we can.'

I re-entered the tent and sat by my cousin while the others waited for me outside. After brushing the hair back from her face in an attempt to rouse her, I gently touched her stomach out of curiosity.

She woke with a frightened start.

'Adaliah,' she said. 'Sorry. I forgot where I was.' She propped herself up.

'Sorry, I didn't mean to startle you,' I said. 'What were you dreaming about?'

She smiled and lay back down. 'Ethaniel, before we were married. We were kissing in the palace hallway when my father came upon us. He told him to either marry me or remove his hands from my waist, then muttered something about me being like my mother. We were duly embarrassed, but as soon as he left Ethaniel kissed me again.'

I smiled at her, wondering if it was a dream or a memory. Perhaps it was both.

'You're leaving,' she said, now focused.

'Yes.'

'I know Elhian is in a hurry, but I want to address the people while you are still here.'

Darj, Elhian and I sat on our horses as the queen mounted hers. The people began to gather in front of us, brought together by Xander and Raggin.

'Alexia! Alexia!' a small voice called. We both turned to see Zavad scrambling up the small hill we were on with an older sister and little brother not too far behind.

'Zavad? What are you doing?' the girl asked.

'I'm coming with you,' he said to us, puffed. 'And you Adaliah.'

'Zavad, you must stay with your family,' I said. 'Remember how much you wanted to see your mother?'

'But I will miss being with you both. And you may need me.'

Alexia leant down to touch his face. 'I know we will, but I also know your mother needs you even more than we do.'

'Come, Zavad,' his sister said, holding their little brother's hand. 'Michel is hungry, and Mother is waiting for us.'

Giving in, he kissed Alexia's hand and mine. I thought again of the little body I'd found on the side of the road. At least I had the joy of knowing he was now with his family. At least I had done something right, something that had brought life instead of death. He ran down the hill with his sister and brother.

Alexia pressed her heels into her horse and moved forward. The people turned to her and fell silent. They looked up at us with such expectation. Not for the first time, I worried that I would disappoint them. News had spread that I was without my memory, and I often received looks of pity. I found this disheartening at first, but Elhian said it was only because they cared about me. Whether it was true or not, I drew some comfort from the thought.

'My Targians,' Alexia began, 'tomorrow, we must leave. I know you have suffered, but I must ask those of you who cannot fight to stay here yet a little longer until all that must be done, is done. I see you and know that Targe was never conquered. I am proud to see that Targe is not just embedded in old stones and farmlands but in each of your hearts, which are more precious to me than any castle or city. It is for you that we go to retrieve our homeland. You deserve to be free from evil, and to live in peace and safety. It is my duty to protect you with the help of the Great Spirit, who will breathe life into all that has withered under Cades' darkness.

'While we go to face battle, while I cannot promise that every man here will return home, I can assure you that even after the darkest of battles, there is victory, that even after a life of death, death will bow to life once again!' She paused and looked at Darj, who indicated with a smile for her to go on. Her secret was getting harder to hide by the day, so they had decided to use it to bring hope now. 'It is with great joy that I tell you that I am expecting a child.' She pulled back her cloak and flattened her dress over her stomach to prove her point. A hum of whispers spread over the people, both the exiles and the army.

Raggin was the first to speak. 'Blessings upon the queen!'

The people echoed the sentiment and shouted many other excited blessings that I felt sure would reach the ears of Cades even if he were deep in Targe. Even without my memory, I felt proud to be Targian, and the hope I saw in the people's faces stayed with me for a long time.

Alexia laughed quietly before raising a hand to silence them. 'While my husband and son are no longer here to enjoy this child, I am proud to offer it not only as my child, but as the child of Targe. It will live to see Targe in its glory once again because of the sacrifices made now. We will leave tomorrow for Jasteria. Once our work is done, we will return to take you home.'

I held my cousin tightly when it was time to go, wanting to take as much of her with me as I could.

'Come back to me in one piece,' she whispered.

I hugged her again. 'I will see you soon.'

'Adaliah,' Darj called as we began to ride out. I looked back over my shoulder. 'Protect Elhian for us.'

Elhian scoffed with mock indignation and I grinned, listening to the men laughing behind us as we rode into the morning fog.

26
BAGRED

'Recognise anything yet?'

I shook my head. The landscape was familiar, but I knew that was only because the loud river we were riding beside was the same one I'd woken in. I shuddered to remember the fear I'd first felt when I realised I was being hunted. At least some things had changed since then.

'They say the river is powerful, living water,' Elhian said as Leuk stepped over the rocks that were hidden in the grass, 'that Ru'ach himself first entered the world here.'

'I could believe that.' I looked up ahead, paused, and then quickened Bagred's pace with my heel. I turned him into a shallower part of the river. 'This is where I woke up.' I pointed down at the spot. Elhian rode to catch up with me. 'This is where everything starts for me. I cut my hand on that rock and pulled myself to where we are now.' Bagred began to back out of the water. 'Whoa, Bagred,' I said.

'Bagred?' Elhian asked, turning sharply. 'You called the horse Bagred?'

'Yes . . . ?'

'Why? Do you remember that name? Why did you call him that?'

I frowned. 'Well . . . there was a tree near here with a sword that had that name engraved in it.'

Elhian turned his head towards the sky in a gesture that I think was more a mixture of annoyance and relief. 'Adaliah . . . I never knew you had called the horse Bagred. I've only ever heard you say, "my horse".'

'But why is it so significant?'

'You better take me to this tree,' he said, turning Leuk away from the river. 'Bagred was the name of your father.'

I felt a rush of emotions, none of which I could name. I couldn't even think what that meant. Alexia had only ever spoken of him as the prince, her uncle, 'your father', and I chided myself for never questioning what his name was. I turned my horse around and took Elhian to the tree where the sword remained even now. The bloodstains were gone, presumably washed away by rain.

Elhian went to work prying it out of the trunk. 'This isn't the Life Sword,' he said.

'I wouldn't think my father would leave it here in the open.'

'But perhaps it's the key we've been looking for.' With one more heave, the sword fell to the ground.

I picked it up. Its metal-laced handle felt familiar somehow. An image filled me, a vision of fighting a great battle, of leading cavalry . . . But it faded and was gone.

Elhian watched it pass through my eyes. 'Maybe it's the sword you used,' he said, 'at the Battle of the Yellow Forest, perhaps. You must have taken it after he died.'

'Perhaps.' I ran my finger over the engraving of his name in the blade. He'd only died about four months earlier. Just four months earlier, I hadn't been an orphan. 'Did you ever meet him?'

'Only once. He was tall, even more so than his brother, the king. He was a fine warrior, one of the best, and he taught you everything he knew. He loved his brother, but you were his greatest pride.'

'Then why can't I remember him?'

Elhian grimaced. 'Because my father is a tyrant.'

I looked at the name again. 'I want to remember him, Elhian. I want to remember what it was like before.'

The sun was falling faster every day, but we made it to the hut before it disappeared all together that night. We tethered Bagred and Leuk to a tree outside and Elhian led me in, the new sword in hand.

The hut had one window, a small fireplace, a table, a bed covered in leaves, and a wooden floor that looked like it was turning into dust. While Elhian made a fire, I took off my cloak and perused through the documents that were pinned to the wall just as Elhian had described, but they meant nothing to me either. 'I bet Alexia could read them,' I said. 'We should take them to her.'

'Yes, of course. I should have thought of that.' Elhian moved the bed back and showed me the locked stone door. 'This is it,' he said. 'This is what we need a key for. Perhaps the sword . . . ?'

I tried to stick the sword point into the keyhole, but it was far too big. 'I guess it was never going to be that easy,' I said.

'No . . . ' We studied the door like it was a puzzle. 'Maybe we should rest until morning,' Elhian said. 'It might make more sense then.'

He offered me the small bed to sleep on and I didn't object, but it wasn't until I lay down that I realised how tired I was. My muscles felt heavy and worn.

Elhian lay on the floor by the fire, supporting his neck with his rolled-up cloak.

'When did you know you would have to fight against your father?' I asked, staring at the wooden ceiling.

'When he beat my mother for telling me to be kind.'

I turned to look at him, but his eyes were closed. He was taut, but his thick soldier's build seemed to be naturally that way. He breathed out, and I watched as he relaxed. Being with him felt . . . comfortable, somehow.

'What was she like?'

Elhian smiled to himself as he thought of her, but it wasn't a happy smile. 'She had great visions for Casmodia, but she did not have the opportunity to carry them out. She told me stories of Ru'ach and his loving help, but as Cades' wife . . . I would watch him hurt her and beg him to stop, and he would turn to me and tell me to be a man. I began to think that if being a man was to be like him, it was a curse.'

'What changed your mind?'

'I came to Targe with my father when I was fifteen. I met Alexia, still a princess—Jeri was just about to be born—and I met her father. *He* was a great man, Adaliah. I wish you could remember him. He showed me what true kingship meant, as well as true manhood. The things he told me: how Ru'ach anointed our positions to help others, how we were placed on earth to make a difference . . . That made sense to me. With Cades, I always felt his philosophies were wrong somehow, even when I was too young to understand why. It was on that trip that I decided to model myself by King Amaz instead. Unfortunately, my father noticed this, and it was then that things began to fracture between us. I challenged him publicly on more than one occasion, and he did not thank me for it. He never intended to have a son with a brain or a conscience. He broke my jaw once when I quoted King Amaz. It was hard not to hate him after that.'

I was quiet as I thought about all he had told me, as I tried to imagine what the King of Targe must have been like. 'Did I meet you at that time?'

'Yes,' he said.

'Were we friends?'

Elhian opened his eyes and turned his face to me. 'I hope we still are.'

I must have fallen asleep not long after that, but the darkness that filled my mind was not the night. I was soon groping into the nothingness again, being hunted again.

Kill her!

I was trying to get away, but there was an invisible, powerful force pushing me towards my attackers. I was screaming.

End her life!

Elhian shook me by the shoulders. 'Adaliah?' I instinctively fought away from him. 'Adaliah!'

My heart was racing, but I saw the prince and it calmed down again.

He helped me sit up. 'Are you all right?'

I took a deep breath. 'Yes.'

'These dreams . . . Can you tell me what they're about?'

I shook my head. 'They are broken images. I think it's my memory trying to piece itself together, only to shatter again.'

'Would you like me to sit with you until you fall asleep again?' he asked.

'Yes, please.' The fear of the dream was still lingering. I forced a smile, but it was full of irony. 'My sleep is filled with nightmares because I can't remember. Alexia's mind is a nightmare because she can't forget, and somehow between the two of us we are supposed to restore order!'

Morning seemed to break late over the Valley of Kest. When I woke, I realised Elhian was gone from the hut, but he returned with two fish before I could wonder where he was.

'To keep our strength up,' he said.

'Is there anything you can't do?' I asked as he began to fillet them by the fire.

He laughed. 'I make it my business to learn as many skills as I can. Unfortunately, not one of them can help me do what I really want to.'

'What's that?'

'Give you your memory back.'

I checked on the horses and brushed them down until the fish were ready to eat, and then we ate in the hut to keep out of the cold.

'What do we do if we can't get in the door?' I asked as Elhian chewed into the white flesh.

'We ride back to Alexia. We are already running out of time.'

I was glad that, like me, he was not keen to linger. We both wanted to re-join the queen near Jasteria before any possible battle.

I studied the sword from the tree as I ate. The elaborate handgrip was all white, except for one small piece that was definitely silver. It was shaped like an arrow and embedded into the handle. I put my food aside, lifted the sword, and gently pressed the arrow. It popped out and fell into my hand, half the height of my palm and thin like a key. The small arrowhead was as sharp as a real one.

Elhian raised his eyebrows. 'How did you do that?'

'I don't know,' I said, equally surprised. 'Should we try it?'

Elhian nodded. He continued to eat as I slipped the silver arrow into the keyhole. Nothing happened at first, but I moved it half a turn and tried again. This time, the door sprang open with a release of dust, revealing the tunnel behind.

Elhian and I finished our breakfast first, but then began to explore what turned out to be an extensive passageway. It seemed a long time before we came to an intersection. There, the air was cold and still, and the smallness of the space began to make me uncomfortable. At first it was just a feeling of wanting to keep moving, but then my breath started to quicken. I could feel myself beginning to panic. It wasn't the sort of feeling that preceded a fight, where overriding my fear was a possibility—rather, the fear was taking over me. My chest tightened and my breaths shortened. I was fighting back the urge to sit down and hug my knees. I felt dizzy. Elhian was carrying a torch he'd lit in the hut's fire, but the darkness seemed difficult to keep at bay. It was closing in on me.

Elhian put a hand on my shoulder. 'Close your eyes. Imagine you're in a field.'

I pictured myself by the brook near Mount Dennell, where the plains were wide and open.

'Take deep breaths.'

I took one, but it was then that my head started to ache. My mind began playing games with me again, flipping visions around and stealing them. In one of them I heard a little girl's laughter . . . I saw a beautiful lavender room . . . I saw a small black cube, and my withered body locked inside it. I closed my eyes, trying to make the images stay so I could understand them, but they flittered in and out until my mind was like a deserted battlefield filled with rotting corpses.

'Focus on the field,' Elhian said.

I forced the other pictures out of my mind and did as he said. I imagined wildflowers, and a warm wind. I painted a sunrise behind them. A few minutes later, I was able to open my eyes again.

Elhian patted my arm. 'Sometimes the battle of the mind is the hardest one we fight.'

'How did you know to do that?'

'I've fought my own battles. Everyone has.'

I nodded as we looked at the two paths once more. They seemed identical to me, but I felt like I should know which one to follow. I bit my lip. 'Let's take the right one,' I said, trying to sound confident.

Elhian led the way through the hilly tunnel. I focused on following his boots and continued to beat the fear down in my mind every time it tried to raise its head.

Arjla divala. With him I stand.

I can do this.

Eventually, the dirt floor changed to wooden slats beneath our feet. Our steps echoed through the tunnel and Elhian's torch soon became insignificant as we walked towards natural light and a featherlike breeze.

What we found was a small castle built into the side of the mountain. Part of it was carved into the stone. Part of it hung on the side of the mountain but was concealed with vines and purple flowers. Through the gaps of the leaves there were beautiful views down to the Valley of Kest and into the Targian plains. Kest River had carved a deep ravine that came close to the castle; I could hear the water below. The stone structure, propped up by intricately engraved white columns, had three levels that jutted out at unusual but beautiful mezzanine areas on top of each other. The faint smell of coriander and jasmine hung in the air. The whole place was open but sheltered, spacious and almost like living outdoors except for the marble floors and stone furniture and curved staircases.

'The Keep,' I said to myself. I felt queasy and put a hand on my stomach as I walked into the main living area.

'You're not expecting, too, are you?' Elhian asked with a mischievous smile.

'Not as far as I can remember,' I said. 'No, it's just this place. I know it, but I don't.' I followed my feet up the first set of stairs, where there was a white bed laid out behind mauve silk drapes. My head felt physically pained as I sat on the bed. I massaged my temples, trying to make the memories reveal themselves. It was like there were boulders disturbing the flow of my mind, and they wouldn't move.

A thin silver crown was beside the bed. I touched it with my fingertips. 'Was this mine?' I asked Elhian as he came into the room.

He picked up the diadem. 'Yes, the circlet of Lady Adaliah Elryane, the comeliest woman in court.' He placed it on my head. It was light but firm.

I met his eyes, but Elhian looked away and walked out to the nearby balcony. I took the circlet off and followed him. 'What's wrong?'

'Nothing. I just . . . ' He cleared his throat. 'I just hope the damage Cades has caused can be righted.'

'But what will you do once he is subdued?' There was still a lot I didn't understand about Elhian—to me he was shrouded in mystery, like my mind. I had come to believe in him, but I was still amazed at his defiance of his father and his unusual loyalty to the Targian monarchy.

'*If* he is subdued, you mean.' He took a deep breath. 'I will start by ensuring Alexia is returned to her throne and then go and make something of whatever's left of my home. I will have to earn the respect of my people, especially those who have supported Cades' cause. Without an army, without men, I will be relying heavily upon your cousin's goodwill.'

'Is that why you fight for her now? To ensure her alliance once you return to Casmodia?'

'There are many reasons why I fight for Targe. That is one of them, as is King Amaz, but those reasons are not what truly motivate me.'

Not willing to ask him what did, I placed my hand over his. Whatever his reasons, I was glad he was on our side.

I walked through the rooms again later and was struck by a portrait of a strong looking man dressed in Targian royal regalia. I felt my heart swell with emotion, even though I couldn't justify it.

Elhian noticed how I covered my mouth with my hand. 'What is it?'

'I know I'm staring at a portrait of my father,' I said, 'and yet I don't recognise him. Do you know how unbearable that is?'

I moved towards the painting for a closer look. I didn't know what liberties the artist took, but in the portrait my father had a firm but warm appearance. I could imagine him playing games with me as a child but instructing me to fight as well. I thought of him not as a man of smiles or laughter, but rather a serious prince who was pre-pared to die for his duty, like Darj perhaps. Whether my imagination was correct or not, I couldn't be sure, but it gave me some comfort to think of him as someone I once knew and loved, as someone who once loved me.

Beside him was a picture of a lovely young woman. A plaque indicated that she was called Princess Cassondra Elryane.

'Your mother,' Elhian said gently. 'Apart from her name, you had no memory of her before either.'

I remembered that Alexia had said she'd died with my younger brother in childbirth.

Now I was fighting back tears. It all seemed so unjust. I was at a time in my life when I needed and longed for my parents more than ever, but they had both been taken from me.

On another wall was a picture of myself in which I looked much grander than I felt now. Looking at it, I realised I had been harbouring a fear that the person I was said to be was not the person I was. But the name 'Lady Adaliah C. Elryane' was engraved on a plaque at the bottom. It was me. I was Prince Bagred and Princess Cassondra's only living child, the Queen of Targe's only living relative. I'd been painted wearing a beautiful lilac gown that was draped elegantly across the floor, and the same circlet as I'd just found was on my head. I reached out to touch the portrait as if it were a ghost.

The painting next to it was the royal family, as was. An older, very impressive man sat on a chair in the middle—King Amaz, according to Elhian, not long before he died. On his right was his daughter and heir, Alexia, and on his left, a handsome Ethaniel. Alexia held Jeri as a babe in her arms. 'He had his mother's eyes,' I said with tinge of sadness. I stared at him and his father, feeling their loss in a much more personal way.

As I touched Jeri's face, an arrow flew through the room and landed in his body.

Both Elhian and I turned. Someone had followed us in.

27
THE CHASE

Six Casmodians were behind us. They ran at us, but Elhian made the first strike.

I impaled one of the men, but another kicked my sword out of my hand. I knocked him down with a kick that tore my skirt. I bent down to retrieve my blade and fought on.

A strange but familiar light caught my eye. I saw a soldier running down the stairs and back towards the tunnel. He was holding a sword . . . a different sword. That was where the light was coming from.

'Elhian!' I shouted.

He pulled back to see what I was looking at. 'I can handle these men,' he said when he saw it. 'Get the sword. It's the Life Sword!'

I elbowed a soldier out of my way and ran down the stairs. I hurried into the tunnel, the light just ahead of me. I pursued the soldier all the way back to the hut. Through the window, I saw him riding away.

Don't let him escape!

I ran outside, untethered Bagred and set him going before I had even properly mounted.

I began the descent into the Valley of Kest and spotted the soldier again further down the hill. A branch scratched my cheek, but I didn't feel the pain of it. My eyes never left his back. We reached the bottom of the mountain and raced towards the river.

I glanced over my shoulder. I hadn't meant to go this far without Elhian. What if the prince was injured? What if I got lost?

Keep going.

Our horses waded through the high water and as Bagred was the stronger horse, I was soon closer than ever.

I rode after the soldier into the Targian plains, my fear returning and tightening my stomach. Hours passed but somehow, he was always just ahead. Frustrated and tired, I was forced to stop for Bagred's sake. The poor horse was exhausted. With the onset of darkness near, I pulled him up and made camp alone, hoping Elhian would understand why I had kept riding and wondering if that's what he'd expected me to do. As I rested, I wondered about renaming my horse, but I'd grown used to it and it gave me some comfort to use my father's name regularly, like he was with me.

I kept a keen lookout on the horizon, towards which the soldier had continued to ride. I knew he would have to stop soon as well or risk killing his horse. I comforted myself with the thought of beginning the chase again in the morning. I remembered what Alexia said about the sword, how if it fell into Cades' hands it would give him great power, power that would bring more death. It would quicken his victory, and Targe as it existed now would be lost. I couldn't turn back, no matter how alone I felt in the open plains.

Early the next morning, before the mist had risen off the ground or the birds had woken in the trees, I fetched my leathers from Bagred. I secured a cuirass over my dress and pulled it tight. I put on two pauldrons to protect my shoulders. There was no sign of Elhian, but I couldn't let the soldier's trail fade, not when so much was hanging in the balance.

I doused the campfire and, taking a piece of paper from my saddle-bags, left a charcoal note under a rock in case Elhian came by:

Let me go on. You must return to the one with child.

For four days I chased the man across Targe until Bagred and I were weary from both hunger and fatigue. On the second day, it started snowing in the lower parts of Targe, and I couldn't rid myself of the ice chill. We crossed another wide stream known as King River—the longest in the kingdom—and by then I was thoroughly cold.

While I rode, my thoughts shifted from my task to Alexia, who would now soon be near Jasteria with King Hazaka, as per their agreement. As Elhian hadn't reached me, I hoped he had found my note and obeyed it. I felt lonely on the road by myself, but it was of more comfort to me knowing he would reach her even if I couldn't. He could explain what happened, and he could support them if battle arrived before I did. Cades already had two swords—Alexia's and Hazaka's. If there was something I could do to prevent him from getting mine, I had to do it.

I ignored my aching body and pushed poor Bagred on.

Soon there was a thick layer of icy dust on the ground. Bagred sloshed through it on the fifth morning. It was becoming harder for me to track the soldier and to find food for both my horse and myself. I hadn't expected it to be like this or to take so long.

I'd been riding in a daze for the better part of the morning when I suddenly realised I was travelling on a track between fenced fields. I paused and looked up ahead. Not too far in front of me was a large city with tall green walls, now sprinkled white. I realised with a start that it was the city I had once seen in a dream, the one Alexia and Naclen had called Fenellar. It was the first time my mind had successfully communicated something to me. My surprise transferred to Bagred, who reared with a snort.

I calmed him with a pat and looked around for shelter, or somewhere I could wait until darkness fell. There was a thin cluster of trees nearby. I rode there and dismounted. The soft crunch of the snow under my feet didn't stop me from hearing the quail, which I hunted and cooked after finding as much dry kindling as possible. Then, I brushed Bagred down while waiting for the sun to set.

Once night came, I tethered my horse to a tree and put the fire out. I pulled my hood down over my face, concealed my sword under my garment, and headed to the walls of Fenellar on foot.

From a distance, I could hear the laughs of women and the jibing of men. The closer I drew, the more I saw that Fenellar, once one of Alexia's greatest sources of pride and wealth, had become a brothel.

Wall guards drank and sang out-of-tune melodies while women dressed in ferocious colours danced around them. They had long dark hair and bare hips that moved about in the winter air, mesmerising the men. Still far enough away to be unnoticed, I headed down the south side of the wall to look for a less populated entry. I came to a smaller gate guarded by two men and, after studying them for a while, I was about to keep moving when one of them disappeared behind the wall. I walked towards the remaining guard to seize my chance, though I had no idea what I was going to do.

He was young and not very alert, which was soon explained by the empty cup in his hand and the wooden keg he was leaning his foot against. When he saw me coming, he raised his cup and shamelessly looked me over. I was repulsed at first, but it gave me an idea of how to proceed. Before he could say a word, I reached him and stopped his mouth with a light kiss. A group of men further down the wall jeered.

'Open the gate,' I said in a low voice, 'let's go in.'

The man nodded dumbly and led me inside. Then, a look of doubt passed over his face. 'What's your name?'

'Don't worry about that,' I said, trying to think fast.

The guard grabbed my wrist and twisted it enough to hurt. It was all I could do to maintain my pretence, but I needed information from him. 'Clair,' I said, trying not to wince at the pain. 'My name is Clair.'

He let me go. '"Clair." That's a pretty name. Come with me—I'll show you what real men are all about.' He spoke with a definite slur.

'Did they retrieve the sword?' I asked as I was led through the empty, cobbled streets. Somewhere nearby, Cades had shot a woman with an arrow, and Naclen's friend Quion had died.

He glanced over his shoulder at me. 'What do you know of the sword?'

I feared I had already given myself away. 'Nothing, I just thought someone said all four had been retrieved.'

'Well, you heard wrong. Elhian still has Casmodia's.'

'Of course . . . ' I tried to sound like this was news to me. 'But the one from Kest—'

'Is now in the citadel after weeks of searching. You ask a lot of questions for a beggar girl.'

I paused and put a hand on his shoulder, turning him to me with my best attempt at a seductive smile. 'Can you show me?'

He raised an eyebrow at me and began taking me in another direction.

We walked down two more streets before arriving at a building that looked similar to Alexia's palace in Liane, only much smaller. It had the same white-grey stones with tall turrets that the guard said held rebellious Targian prisoners, the few who, with the women at the wall, had not been sent to Kest.

Better that they had been.

The guard took out his key and opened the first wooden door. I followed him into a cold foyer, where two staircases disappeared behind stonewalls on either side of me. There was another door to open, but instead of using the key, the guard knocked.

Another Casmodian soldier opened it a fraction and peered through the crack, but relaxed when he saw his friend. 'What are you doing at the citadel?'

'Guess who this is?' the guard who had brought me asked. 'The A'zyon Warrior, who thought I would be another Parrian.'

28
INSIDE THE CITADEL

I knocked the guard down with the hilt of my sword, elbowed his friend and used the hilt on the back of his head, too. They both fell to the ground at my feet, unconscious.

You're so stupid, I told myself. I'd taken it for granted that the soldier would have been as gullible as Parrian, and I hadn't even picked up that he'd realised who I was.

What kind of warrior am I?

I slipped into the main hall of the citadel. There, stone columns bordered both sides of the room, and on each one there were high horizontal bars bearing Casmodian flags.

I don't know where he came from, but a soldier struck at me with his sword. I ducked his strike and then, seeing archers aiming at me at the other end of the room, grabbed him to use as a shield. Three arrows hit his body and he fell from my grip to the floor.

I brought my sword down against the next approaching solider, deflected his strikes and, once I had the chance, impaled him. The next one managed to trip me and landed a cut across my back before I was able to roll out of the way and get back to my feet. I thrust my sword into his side. Out of the corner of my eye, I saw an altar at the rear of the hall and the handle of the sword that lay on it. My sword. I pressed towards it.

One soldier approached me from behind and brought a shield hard against my back. It antagonised the cut, and I stumbled forward, a searing pain writhing through me. As I lay there weakened, the men surrounded me.

I have to get out of here. I have to get the sword!

I realised I was beneath one of the flag-bearing bars. I jumped up, grabbed it, lifted my legs to my chest, and swung myself over the men. I landed on the floor again and stumbled on my first step, but then made a run for the sword.

It was a moment before the men pursued me; a moment was all I needed. I reached the altar just as the main door opened and more soldiers ran in, equipped with fiery arrows.

I reached for the sword, the Keeper of Kest's sword, the Life Sword.

It was long and elegant and engraved with beautiful swirls. The cross-guard and handle had gold embossing along the swirls, all of which brushed their tips against the smooth, dormant amethyst stone. Below the stone was a tiny butterfly engraved into the metal, and the embossed word *Life*. On the other side, *Death*.

A soldier shot a fiery arrow at me. A part of me heard the sound of its release. Others ran towards me, their heavy steps falling hard against the stone floor as they came closer . . . and closer.

I wrapped my bloodied fingers around the sword's handle. The arrow cut through the air towards me.

'I choose life!'

Suddenly, I had to grip it with both hands. The stone's light filled the room with a force that knocked down the soldiers and deflected the flying arrow to the ground. It burst out of every crack in the wall, out of every window, and made the citadel appear to be erupting with light. The force of it threw open the door of the main hall and I felt the rush of cold wintry wind on my face and in my hair.

Then, everything stopped. The breeze slowed and I was blinded. I saw in my mind's eye a tall, fit man handing me a sword and instructing me to use it. He disappeared and was replaced with a small child feeding a horse an apple and smiling at me with happy eyes. He, too, disappeared and Alexia stood there, on her own at first, and then with an army behind her. She was holding a bow and arrow and was prepared to shoot. But she faded, too, and the images, which had been so clear and defined, left my mind, and I opened my eyes.

There was no one left to fight. I ran past the felled men, back up the main hall and outside the citadel with the sword in hand. Using it, I fought my way past the men at the gate and ran through the snow to find Bagred.

29
AMBUSH

Five days later, I tripped on a log and fell forward into the snow. I struggled back to my feet and retook Bagred's reins. My eyes stung with tears of stress and exhaustion. I was travelling as fast as I could through landscape I didn't recognise. My confidence faded as I stumbled on. I was worried about my cousin. Two things had stayed in my core when everything else had faded: my love for my family and my ability to fight. 'Love and death can't both be part of me, can they?' I asked Bagred, but he was silent.

Maybe they can. Like the swords.

Somehow, I knew Jasteria would be more difficult to conquer than they thought. There would be much death—I was sure of it. Unless there was another way. I had to be there, had to fight for Alexia, for her unborn child: my family. They were all I had left.

And you Ru'ach, I thought, looking up at the cloudy sky. *I hope you are watching out for me.*

On the sixth day, I leant against Bagred as I tried to get my foot out of my boot, which was buried in ice-glazed mud. Exasperated, I gripped the pommel with one hand and slapped Bagred with my other. He sprung forward, taking me with him and freeing both my foot and boot. I let go of him and fell on my wounded back.

Coming across the army's tracks earlier had given me direction, but it was only my anxiety to get to Alexia and Darj that was keeping me going despite my longing for warmth and a good night's sleep. Would they be in the midst of a battle by now? Were Darj and Elhian fighting against defeat at that very moment? Had Alexia been harmed, or worse, captured or killed? My body shook at the thought as well as from the numbing cold. I forced myself up and mounted Bagred for the first time that day. He grunted, but I could feel some strength in him. I hurried him on.

By evening I was riding through tall, slim trees, something Elhian had told me about. I knew by them I was somewhere near Jasteria. The footprints in the path I was following were still clear.

I stopped when I heard movement. Bagred's ears twitched forward. I glimpsed a man stepping behind a tree, his silhouette contrasting with the snow-white floor. My eyes adjusted to the growing darkness and I saw another, and then another. Then, it was like the wood was full of them, crawling about like hundreds of silent insects. A thick fog was forming between the trees like a white blanket. It enfolded the men. They were moving stealthily, away from me.

I was behind an ambush.

The only thing to ambush nearby was the Targian army, the queen.

My mind raced. How many men were there? Had they surrounded the army? Did this mean Alexia had not gone to fight at Jasteria? Or had they fought and lost and what was left was about to be taken, too?

Biting my lip, I pulled out the Life Sword, hid the amethyst's light under my cloak, and moved forward. My father's sword from the tree— what I now called the tree-blade—remained sheathed.

A moment later, screams and shouting filled the night air.

I saw Elhian first—he was battling a tall, hard-hitting man. I recoiled when I realised it was Cades. The fear of our first meeting returned to me at the sight of him—I felt like a small child again. He was fighting Elhian with two swords, which by the colours of their stones I was able to identify as Alexia's and Hazaka's. Love and hope. Or perhaps by now he had corrupted them to hate and despair. Either way, the power of them was beating Elhian into the ground even though he wielded his own blue sword. I saw the rage in Cades' face and knew he hated his son as much as a man could hate anyone.

I rode to them. Bagred thumped across the ground, strong and determined. A powerful horse, he gained speed and certainty while my cloak flew about in the wind behind me. When we reached Cades, Bagred rose himself onto his hind legs and neighed. Cades attempted to strike him, but before he could I pulled out the fourth sword and the world filled with a new light. Bagred's hooves landed at Cades' feet and I brought the blade down against the king's, causing him to stumble backwards.

'Adaliah!' Elhian said, amazed.

I handed him the sword.

He nodded.

I joined the battle myself, slaying enemy soldiers with the tree-blade while looking for Alexia on foot. I found her on the other side of the battle, armour-less and barefoot in the snow. She struck two men across the face with her bow before loading an arrow and shooting a third.

I attempted to join her but was attacked by a man on my right. He pushed me back and struck at me twice. I only just managed to block his assault as I fell backwards. He struck at me on the ground and I had to roll out of the way. I kicked his legs out from under him and got up.

I glanced towards Elhian. Cades knocked him down with a violent blow. In the second I had to look at him, I saw blood on his face and knew he was unconscious.

I feared Cades would take the kill, but he walked towards Alexia instead. I remembered what Elhian had said—*he wants me dead, but not until he has another heir to the throne.*

The soldier at my feet was getting up but I pushed him down again and used his sword to pin his clothes to the ground. I hurried to reach Alexia before Cades did.

I was too late, but she had seen him approaching and was pointing an arrow at his heart. He didn't flinch. He continued to approach her. I followed him, glancing back at the unconscious prince and praying he would survive until we could get to him.

Alexia looked over her shoulder as if searching for a way of escape. I knew she was afraid of the same thing I was: that he would realise she was with child.

'Ally,' Cades said to her.

'Don't call me that.' Her voice was low and dangerous.

'Why not? Does it remind you of your dead husband?' He smiled and motioned to the bow she held. 'Put that plaything down.'

She drew the arrow back as far as possible. I heard the bow creak under the strain. Her hands were steady, but her expression was tinged with pain, and I remembered her weakened shoulder. The lights in

Cades' swords were increasing and while I didn't want to believe it, I knew she was no match for him.

Cades walked closer. The snow crunched under his boots. I held my sword up, ready to attack him from behind. 'Ally, you know what I want. Just give it to me now. It could all be over before morning. Think of the lives it would save.'

His voice was an old drawl that might have been beguiling once. Now, it was sickening. Alexia moved backwards, her arrow still poised.

Cades sheathed one of his swords. I thought he was conceding. But then he suddenly stepped towards her. I lunged after him and missed. Alexia shot her arrow, but he deflected it to the ground with the remaining sword and used his spare hand to grab her throat.

'Let her go!' I yelled. It was only then that they realised I was there, and then that he saw her stomach.

'What? You're pregnant!' He tightened his grip around her throat until she was forced to her knees.

I ran at his back, now determined to kill him then and there, but just as I was about to strike, he turned and hit me across my face with his hand. I fell to the ground in shock.

Alexia's face was reddening, but she didn't attempt to fight back. She couldn't. Her bow fell into the soft snow.

Cades forced her to look up at him, but her eyes betrayed nothing. The look of disbelief on his face turned to distorted delight. He released her but, before she could take a breath, he hit her across the face as he had me. 'You are a disgrace to your family line.'

'Stay away from her,' a familiar voice said. I looked up with surprise. Elhian was staggering towards us, blood still dripping down his face.

'Leave the queen alone.' He pushed Cades away from Alexia and the two began to cross blades again.

I rushed to Alexia's side. She coughed violently for a minute or so before standing and giving me a quick embrace. Her lip was bleeding. 'I thought I'd see you a lot earlier than this,' she said, picking up her bow. Her voice was hoarse.

'I came as fast as I could.'

I was just beginning to wonder where Darj was when I saw him fighting another man I had hoped never to see again—Jag. The Casmodian general was fighting like a wild dog. I saw him throw a handful of icy dirt into Darj's eyes. He kicked Darj in the stomach, and Darj doubled over. Darj stabbed Jag's arm with a dagger. Jag cried out, struck at Darj, and missed. Then, he ran away.

'Coward!' Darj yelled, but Jag kept running.

I fought and slayed a soldier while Alexia shot arrows fearfully close to my shoulder. Nearby, Elhian and Cades continued to fight. The four lights flashed around the trees, on the ground and in the eyes of the battling men.

Cades was smiling at his son like he found the situation amusing. Elhian charged towards him. He took three long steps before leaving the ground. He came down on Cades. The king fell backwards and dropped his swords. I hurried towards them.

Elhian pointed the Casmodian sword at Cades' throat. 'Call off your men.' Cades snarled at him. 'Do it!' Elhian yelled, pressing the sword in further.

The king gritted his teeth. 'Retreat!' he called. 'Retreat!'

His men hesitated, but when they saw that their leader was in a precarious position they began to pull back.

'This battle is no longer yours,' Elhian said. 'Neither is Targe. Neither am I.'

'Then kill me,' Cades said, spit flying from his mouth.

'No,' Elhian said. 'I'm not like you. You may try to kill me to further your own conquest, but I will not do the same.'

'Yes,' Cades said. 'That's because you're weak. Weak, like your mother was.'

Elhian pressed the sword down further on him. Everything in my being was willing him to win, but Jag returned. He was running towards the prince and before I could speak a word, he kicked the side of Elhian's head with a heavy boot, throwing Elhian off Cades. Elhian's sword fell, and he blacked out again. Jag grabbed the king's arm, wrenched him up and disappeared amongst the men, not only with the Targian and Jazmardian swords, but with the Casmodian one as well.

I later bent over a dead soldier and ripped some material off his clothing. I paused, my body registering how tired and hungry it was, as well as how stressed and battle-weary. It felt like every day was a fight for my life, and I didn't know if I could live like that for much longer.

I cleaned my father's sword with the cloth, found Bagred and slipped it back into its sheath.

Elhian stumbled as he walked to me. His face expressed the anger of a cornered stag. He held out the Life Sword for me to take. 'If you had fought him,' he said, but he pressed his lips together as if to keep his anger behind his teeth.

'He might have killed me.' I reached up and brushed the hair away from his head wound. 'He might have taken all four swords. His army wouldn't have fallen back. I might have failed. Who knows what we owe to you tonight?' I washed his wound with a clean cloth, anxious not to make him sick. My hand was shaking.

Elhian was still gritting his teeth, but the anger in his eyes began to subside. 'I would do anything to keep pain and death from you,' he said, 'but I've failed you before.'

'I don't need you to keep me from pain and death. No one can do that. From what I've seen, once it's set loose with a determination to take someone, there's no stopping it. We're just blessed it has yet to determine on us.'

Elhian laughed outright. 'What, you don't think that with Cades and his whole army after us that death isn't tapping us on the shoulder?'

I shrugged. 'That doesn't mean we have to turn to see who it is.'

Elhian smiled warmly and squeezed my hand. 'I got your note,' he said. 'You don't know how much I agonised over whether to obey it or not.'

'You did the right thing. I'm glad you were here before the ambush.'

His smile began to fade. 'Adaliah, you're shaking—'

'Yes . . . ' My legs were struggling to support me. 'I don't feel . . . '

'Adaliah?'

I reached out to him, but my legs gave way, and I slipped to the ground.

I woke just a few minutes later and, by then, Elhian had draped his cloak over me.

'What happened?' Alexia asked as she knelt by my side. 'Where are you hurt?'

'Nowhere new. I'm just . . . not myself.' I gazed up at Elhian. 'I'm more worried about his head.'

'It's thicker than it looks,' he said as he gave me some water. 'I just have a headache.' He stopped like he was waiting for something to happen. Then, he moved away and vomited.

'Are you all right?' Alexia asked when he returned.

'I'm fine.' He gave me an exasperated look. 'Just weak.'

I reached for his hand again. 'No. You are one of the strongest people I know.'

'I agree,' Alexia said.

He looked like he wanted to believe it but couldn't. He let go of my hand and gave me some more water while asking a soldier to bring food.

Alexia put a hand over her abdomen. 'There's a butterfly in my stomach,' she said with a smile, her voice still husky. She ran her hand over it with interest. 'My child knows what a chaotic evening it has been.'

'I think your child needs a little less excitement from now on,' I said. Her neck was still red, and I knew Cades' finger-marks would be visible as bruises in the morning.

Darj appeared behind her with folded arms. 'I'd agree if I thought she'd listen.' He, too, had blood all over his face and his eyes looked tender and sore from the dirt Jag had thrown in them.

'Excuse me?' Alexia turned. '*You* need a physician.'

'I'm fine.'

'Darj—'

'I'm fine!'

'Darj, you look like a slain deer left out in a sandstorm.'

'Oh, right, and you see those all the time I suppose?'

'Sometimes I think they compete for the honour of being the most stubborn,' Elhian whispered to me. I grinned.

'Would you just sit down?' Alexia asked in the end, exasperated. 'I will look at it myself.'

He tried to hide it, but I still saw Darj's grin as he relented and did as he was told.

30
THE CAZINIAN PAPERS

Raggin rattled two bags full of small coins. Sitting by a campfire in the early morning, I watched as he tried to lure his fellow soldiers over. 'Lay your bet now!' he called out to them. 'Make your guess!'

Xander stood next to him, sceptical but smiling.

'What's this?' a passing soldier asked. I listened in, curious myself.

'Oh, just raising a little money,' Raggin said with a scheming wink and a charming smile. 'Come on, lay your bet. Will the queen give birth to a prince or princess?'

Elhian came and sat by me. 'You have to admire his initiative,' he said.

The man pressed his lips together in thought. 'The odds are fifty-fifty. And how steep will your commission be? You'll be rich. I'm not sure I want to contribute to that!'

'But what if you win?'

'The winnings will have to be divided between thousands.'

Xander laughed but Raggin persisted. 'Yes, but if you bet just one tule and you are right in your guess, you will get at least two back, maybe more. You have nothing to lose.'

'Besides,' Xander added, 'I just know Raggin will divide any commission amongst the poor. Isn't that right, Raggin?'

I saw the glare Raggin gave him and couldn't help but smile. 'Just make a bet,' he said to the soldier.

'All right, I bet one tule that the queen will have a son.' The soldier let the coin drop into the bag. It chinked against the others. Raggin jolted the bag up and down and the coins all clattered together cheerfully.

'Do you accept xaws?' a Jazmardian asked, holding up a different sort of coin.

'Two xaws for one tule,' Raggin said firmly. The soldier complied.

Xander took down the soldiers' names before they left, and then Raggin turned to him. 'If you keep making comments like that you won't get your share of my commission,' he said.

Xander laughed. 'Neither will you if the queen finds out about this. The law hasn't changed—soldiers are still forbidden to gamble while on duty.'

At this point, Raggin realised Elhian and I were watching on, and he suddenly looked like a small child who had been caught stealing a treat. 'Lady Adaliah . . . ' He came over and gave a quick bow. 'You . . . you wouldn't bother the queen over something as trivial as this would you?' Xander followed him with a smug look, like he'd known this would happen. 'It's just a little fun,' Raggin said, 'to give our minds something to think about other than war.'

Not having any memory of the law Xander spoke of, I found the situation more amusing than anything. Before I could think of a reply Darj came over, too. In feigned seriousness, I told him what was happening as if they deserved punishment, but his response was to give a mischievous grin. 'I bet she has a girl.' He glanced over his shoulder and slipped a tule into the appropriate bag. 'But if the queen asks, I had nothing to do with this!' He winked at me, and I couldn't help but laugh.

Alexia later asked to speak to me with Darj and Elhian and, sitting down in her tent, I noticed how terrible we all looked. The bruises had formed around Alexia's throat as I'd expected, and now that Darj's face was clean of blood I could see the raw cut across his temple. Elhian had a bandage wrapped around his head and a lump that I could see even under that. I was the only one without visible wounds, but I still felt weak and shaky and had to recline while they spoke to me. My chest was tight again.

'Hazaka Cazren went to battle at Jasteria without us,' Alexia told me. 'You already know he resented us for taking time to visit the people in Kest. For reasons founded in ignorance and a want for glory—perhaps he wanted to prove he didn't need us, I don't know—he attacked with most of his men. Cades was there and subdued him with his misuse of the swords. On our way back from Kest, I sent Naclen ahead of us to scout the land. He reported that Hazaka's men were held in a stalemate, trapped in the snow outside the walls of Jasteria and surrounded by Cades' men. They are there even now.'

'I can't believe he would be so unwise!' I said.

'I don't think anything would surprise me as far as Hazaka goes now,' Alexia said. 'And yet, I do feel obligated to rescue his men, not for his sake but for theirs. We must still attack Jasteria, even if his actions have made this more complicated than it was to start with.'

'It will be dangerous, Alexia,' Elhian said. 'He has three swords . . . You were the one who told me what the Cazinian Papers said about them.'

Alexia quoted the words from heart. '"One will bring protection, two will bring upright power. If any are misused, death marks the last hour." Cades is misusing them. He has the swords of love, hope and faith, but with those he is producing the opposite.'

Elhian thought about this. 'Faith was given to Casmodia, so its perverted power—fear—will be the strongest force under Cades' reign I think.'

Perhaps that's why I feel so afraid all the time, I wondered.

'The thing is . . . ' Elhian stopped and rubbed his chin, mumbled something to himself, and left the tent.

Alexia gestured with upward palms, but Elhian quickly returned with a pile of curled papers in his hands. I recognised them as the ones we had taken from the hut in Kest. He spread them all out before her.

She looked down at them with a raised eyebrow, and then at Elhian, waiting for an explanation.

'The Cazinian Papers,' he said. 'I think. We found them in Kest.'

'You kept a copy of the Cazinian Papers in your saddlebag?' Alexia asked dryly.

'A copy?' Elhian asked with disappointment.

Alexia read through the parchment. She studied them one piece at a time.

'Well?' Elhian asked.

'This is my uncle's writing,' she said, 'and it's written in an ancient form of Targian . . . ' Alexia read over a chipped, brown section. 'You see, Queen Cazine wrote her prophecies down in Jazmardian, not Targian. It was she, along with the Casmodian and Targian kings of the time, who forged the swords.'

'Can these papers help us now?' I asked.

The queen picked up another piece and translated it into the common tongue. '"The purple butterfly will die and bring life where there is none".'

'Purple is the colour of Kest,' Elhian thought out loud, looking at me with concern.

'"The dragon, who will deceive the world, will find the woman with the twelve stars in the dark. There, his anger will be quenched".' Alexia read a few more lines in silence and pushed the papers away. 'It's nonsense,' she said. 'Take them away, Elhian. They are no use to us now.'

Elhian gathered the papers as Alexia left for some air. 'She believes it, doesn't she?' he asked Darj.

'Well, as you know there are twelve stars on the Targian flag, but there are also twelve stars on the points of her crown.' His upper lip curled. 'You know who she thinks the dragon is, and what he wants from her.'

Elhian shook his head, his cheeks flushing. 'But it will not happen.'

'What won't?' I asked. 'What is it Cades wants from Alexia? Lezan hinted at something as well, and I think it's time I knew.'

Darj sighed. 'He wants a child from her, a child that will replace Elhian as the Casmodian heir.'

'What?' The thought of him even touching her was vile. 'Why her?'

'Because he is perverted,' Darj said heatedly.

'Because she is a powerful and attractive woman,' Elhian said. 'He wants to have power over her, and his carnal desire fuels his ambition. Now he knows she is already with child . . . Who knows what he will do?'

'I feel like fish,' Alexia said that night.

'You hate fish,' Darj said.

'Fried,' she said, though I don't think she was talking to anyone in particular or in hope.

Even so, Darj offered to get one for her, and I volunteered to go with him. He seemed uneasy, and I wanted to keep him company.

'I'm sorry I didn't get back sooner,' I said as he waded into the river to retrieve a net some of the men had already set up.

'We're all glad you came back, Adaliah, particularly with your sword.' He pulled the net up and several fish flipped around. He picked one out, killed it with a small knife and began to walk back to camp. It seemed that whatever haunted the general, he wasn't ready to share it with me.

As we drew close to camp, we could hear Elhian and Alexia talking. We kept walking at first, but then Darj heard his name and stopped in front of me.

'He is a tense man,' Elhian said, 'but a good one.'

'I wouldn't have made it without him,' Alexia said. 'Though sometimes I struggle to be near him.'

'Darj,' I said, not wanting him to hear something hurtful, 'I don't think we should—' But he raised his hand to silence me.

'Why?' Elhian asked.

Alexia watched the hot, flickering flames of the campfire. They engulfed the air and suffocated it with black smoke. I could see the anger that shrouded her eyes. 'Because he held me back, Elhian. He held me back, and now Jeri is dead.'

My heart sank.

Elhian watched as she brushed away a tear. 'What happened?' he asked gently.

Alexia forced a small laugh to disguise a sob, but Elhian wasn't fooled. He remained steady and waited for her to speak.

Darj's face had a stony expression. He wasn't going anywhere.

'When my palace in Liane was taken and my husband killed,' Alexia said, 'Adaliah made a way of escape. She fought many soldiers off me. Darj was with us, and I had my son's hand in mine and was hanging onto it for dear life. Just as we were ready to ride out, another group of soldiers spotted us. Adaliah fought them off on her own and yelled at us to go, to leave her. We obeyed, as there was nothing else to do. She wouldn't come. You know what she can be like. When I glanced back before we went out of the gate, she had been knocked down and surrounded, and I was sure I'd lost her. Both she and Ethaniel had died protecting me. My heart was broken.

'We made it to Chettona and stayed there a while, and then we rode on to Hunt because Darj discovered Chettona was to be attacked next. I was ill and useless. Lezan found us and gave us a place to stay while Darj began organising a defence for Hunt, but Jag was too organised. He had been on our heels the whole time. Hunt was ravaged. All those people . . . all that death . . . And then . . . ' Alexia's voice broke but she forced the tears back. 'Jeri ran to help another, a little girl who was crying. I remember his hand slipping from mine. Jag caught him on his way. I ran to him. Jag threw me to the ground, grabbed Jeri's little wrist so hard I'm sure he broke it, and threw him into a burning house before I even knew what was happening. I ran to him. I struggled for him. He escaped at first. He ran out of the house—his shirt was on fire and there was smoke everywhere. The men surrounded him and tied him to a post. The fire grew and overshadowed him. There was no hope, but he was my son. Then Darj . . . Darj came and held me back. I fought against him with all my strength, but he would not let me go to Jeri. He made me turn away. And all the time I wonder, would Jeri be alive if I had made it? He didn't even see his fourth birthday. Why didn't Darj go to him, or at least let me? How can I ever really live without my Ethaniel and my Jeri?'

We watched as Elhian comforted her with an arm around her shoulders.

Darj finally looked at me. I saw the rejection in his eyes. 'Darj . . . ' I began, trying to think how I could justify Alexia's words and ease his wound.

'I've always known she resented me for that day,' he said, 'but why can't she see that the situation was hopeless? She would have been killed. How could I let that happen when Jeri was already lost?' I saw a tear in his eye. 'Does she think I don't feel the loss of Ethaniel and Jeri as well? That I wouldn't have given my very life to save them for her?'

I put my hand on his arm, but he pulled away and disappeared into the night.

The following day, the queen led a group of us down to the flat land on which Jasteria had been built against a shallow river. Darj rode in silence near Xander and Raggin. From the west, we circled to the north-eastern side to see Hazaka and his men for ourselves.

'Well,' Xander said when we saw the Jazmardians.

'Well,' echoed Raggin, cringing at the sight that lay before us. 'We should charge.'

'Great idea,' Xander said. 'I've always wanted to have a quick and painful death.'

'Why wait any longer?' Raggin said. 'I could finish you off now if you like.'

'I could kill ten men before you even got that blunt metal thing of yours out of its sheath.'

'Ha, sometimes it's not quickness that matters but perseverance.'

'Raggin, we have been friends since we were boys. If that's not perseverance on my part, I don't know what it is.'

'Stupidity?' Alexia asked distantly before returning to her thoughts. Elhian and I hid a grin while Xander and Raggin glared at each other. Alexia moved over to us. 'What do you think we should do?'

'They ambushed us,' I said. 'Perhaps we could ambush them, if only to save the Jazmardians.'

Alexia nodded. 'Elhian?'

He hesitated. 'I agree that that could work but, with all due respect, Your Majesty, I am not your military advisor.'

Alexia turned towards Darj. He was surveying the city with critical, clever eyes. He sensed her looking at him but met her gaze only briefly.

We began to ride back to camp. Raggin rode in between Elhian and me. 'You know,' he said in hushed tones, 'if the queen ever told you what she thought she was expecting, and you told me, I could make you both very happy.'

Elhian pursed his lips to hide a smile. 'Do you know what the queen is expecting, Adaliah?'

'A long day tomorrow rescuing a certain friend of someone we all know.'

Raggin rolled his eyes. 'I meant what is she expecting to give birth to?'

Elhian patted his friend on the shoulder. 'She's fairly confident it will be a child, Raggin.'

31
JASTERIA

Hazaka was hidden somewhere in one of the ditches he and his men had dug in the snow. Hundreds of soldiers lay in them, waiting out the winter stalemate. From what we understood, when Cades and his men left the city to ambush the Targians, Hazaka ordered a retreat away from Jasteria, but the Casmodians heard of the plan, and Cades sent some of his men back to guard Hazaka from the other side. They had been surrounded.

Dawn was breaking and, in the cold, I knew they were lucky to have survived this long. Some of them had tied the clothes of dead men over the top of the ditches, trying to hold the snow at bay. The material was flapping in the wind and snow. A storm was brewing.

'Now's our chance,' Darj said as the storm grew violent with increasing gales. Our men were shivering as we stood looking at Jasteria. 'The Casmodians have fallen back to the city because they believe the Jazmardians can't move in the storm. We must get them out now.'

'Our own men could be lost in the storm,' Alexia said.

'We'll be quick,' Darj said.

The men began to spread out across the field, searching for Jazmardians and helping them out one by one while archers took out Casmodian guards whenever they were visible through the snow.

I was with Raggin when we found Hazaka lying still. I thought he was dead at first and wondered what it would mean if he was, but then Raggin shook him, and he opened his eyes.

'Jazmarda,' the king whispered. The thought of the warm deserts of his homeland must have seemed like a dream amongst the white velvety powder that covered him. 'Where am I?' He drifted off again, but Raggin grabbed his hand and pulled him up.

Ten of our men died that day, but that was nothing compared to the hundreds of Jazmardians whose bodies were buried in the snow, a frozen testament to Hazaka's incompetence. As far as I could see, they had achieved nothing in attacking Jasteria alone. Darj and Alexia, having already endured so much death, refused to even visit him once he was saved.

A week later, while he and his rescued men continued to recuperate at our camp, we Targians surrounded Jasteria from all sides as per Elhian's original plan, ready for an attack. From a distance, Alexia and her archers aimed at the Casmodians on the wall. They concealed themselves behind trees, tufts of grass and ruined farmhouses, making each shot count. The Casmodians shot back so that arrows flew both ways, whistling through the air.

Using shields as protection, we made it to each of the gates with improvised wheeled contraptions that carried heavy, spear-ended logs, a project Darj had devised and overseen. The soldiers pushed them repeatedly with great momentum, piercing the doors.

I led my group of Targians into Jasteria, hoping the others were doing the same. An approaching rain cloud hung in the sky. The town was quiet and the Casmodian archers ceased shooting without any apparent order. I looked at the cottages and houses that lined the streets, knowing that Cades' men had to be somewhere nearby. The purple stone in my sword was shining like the sun on Kest River, but it was the appearance of a blue light that caught my attention.

Cades was ahead of me, alone. He had a sword in each hand: the blue and red. I couldn't see the green one.

He studied me like one would a painting. 'You caused me enough trouble before we killed you, and now you've come back from the dead to bring us even more trouble.' He stepped towards me. 'But, I am still prepared to make you a deal. Leave now. Forget this battle, and I will let you and your men live. Stay, and you and this army will die.'

The Targians who had entered at the other gates arrived behind him, including Darj and Elhian. Even then the king didn't seem concerned. 'I will torment your cousin until she begs for death,' he said, and then added with a lewd smile, 'after she bears me an heir or two of course. The point is I will kill everyone you love.' The king's eyes moved to his son's and I knew the words were meant for him as well.

I shook my head, not angry so much as annoyed. 'Do you really think that will stop these men?' I asked, gesturing at our soldiers. 'You can try and kill me. You can try and kill Alexia as you did her husband. You can take my memory, Elhian's crown, and even Alexia's dignity, but Targe will go on.'

The stones in the king's swords faded a little. 'I already know I will be successful.'

'The swords don't predict the future,' Elhian said as I walked closer to the king.

'Some things are indisputable!'

'Like the fact that Adaliah was dead at Kest River?' Elhian asked. 'How is it then that she is also here now, facing you—the very one who tried to wipe her into oblivion?'

Cades' expression darkened. 'I'm only a step away from taking the fourth sword and, with it, my victory. I need all four to complete my plan, and I am not going to let a child stop me!'

I began to move the Life Sword in a figure-of-eight. 'I don't believe the swords are the source of power,' I said. 'I believe in the power of the Great Spirit, Ru'ach, who gives us strength, and that the swords can only draw on that power, not the other way around. You may have three swords, but I don't believe they have any power to draw on from you. You have no faith. You have no hope. You have no love. That is *your* curse—your power is an illusion, and you will spend the rest of your life fighting to keep it.'

Cades' look was filled with hatred but for once, I didn't feel afraid. He brought two of the swords down against me.

I blocked him.

The light in my sword's stone outshone his. I pushed Cades away from me and the red sword slipped from his hand. It fell behind him, and he stumbled with surprise. A Targian solider picked up the sword.

'You are the one who is weak,' I said.

Cades' focus moved to his son. 'At least I don't let girls fight my battles.'

'No,' Elhian said. 'You murder them.' He stepped towards his father. 'Surrender now, and we will spare your men.'

Cades yelled an unfamiliar word and his men burst out of the surrounding houses. Some came through the windows, others down from balconies above. Our men met their opponents and, before long, the white patches of snow on the ground showed flecks of red. It began to rain, and water trickled in between the pebbles, forming tiny red rivers that ran between our feet.

I fought Cades and pushed him back again, then kicked at his hand. He grunted as the blue sword fell to the ground. The same Targian soldier who had collected the red sword now grabbed the blue one, too. I pushed Cades to his knees.

'You can't do this!'

I held my sword up at his throat. 'Move and I'll kill you.' I spoke braver than I felt but didn't want to prove to him I was the fearful child he thought I was.

Elhian ran to me with a rope. We tied it around the king until we were sure he couldn't escape. I was relieved to see him bound, but then I realised the Targian who had secured the two swords was lying dead on the ground.

The swords were gone.

Jag was riding away with them through the battling men.

Alexia and her archers continued to assault the city with arrows from the outside. I was left to keep guard of Cades while Darj, Elhian and our men fought and defeated the rest of the Casmodians. The battle had been much quicker than I could have hoped for but, judging by the amount of dead men that lay in the streets, not quick enough. I was once again surrounded by death, and my heart was numbed by it.

Before long, Alexia came hurrying into the city. Her archers held up shields to guard her as she walked towards us with a wet and smudged cloak around her shoulders.

She stopped near me and we stood facing each other, breathless. I continued to struggle with Cades, who was moving about like a trapped tiger. He yelled vulgar remarks at each of us until Elhian gagged him with a cloth.

'Well?' Alexia asked.

'Jasteria is ours,' Darj said.

He raised his sword, and the men erupted in a cheer of victory.

32
WAITING OUT THE WINTER

'Ival, please gather at least five wagons of supplies to send to the exiles,' Alexia said. 'There should be food stored here and some livestock. Jasteria always had a good harvest that lasted the winter, but I don't know how much the Casmodians have plundered. Send blankets and visit the apothecaries to see if there are any basic medicines my people will benefit from. Take whatever else you deem necessary and what we can do without and be ready to leave in two days if you can.' We walked towards the keep. It was to be our residence while we stayed in Jasteria. 'Darj, the men in your army who once lived in Jasteria, the ones who were never soldiers . . . '

'Yes, Your Majesty?' Darj asked.

'I want them to put Jasteria back to work. The blacksmiths, farriers, tanners, armourers, fletchers . . . I want them all working again. I want every horse tended to, every sword sharpened, and new, stronger bows and arrows made for my archers.' Alexia stopped, so those of us around her did, too. 'The next few weeks will be the worst of winter but with Cades now in prison, we have a bit of time. My first concern is getting supplies to all those in Kest before they are cut off. In fact, I'm sure we have physicians fighting with us. Find them if you can. I would like some of them to accompany Ival to Kest, to tend any of my people who may need them. My second concern is to refresh every man here and get him to his fighting best. No man is to fight again without decent armour and a full stomach. We will make the most of the bleak winter and wait out the next few weeks here.'

Naclen led Alexia and me to the chambers Darj had ordered him to prepare for us. He opened the first tall wooden door, waited until we walked in, and left.

Inside there was an inviting fire, a soft bed, and a table that had a large pot of warm broth waiting for us. There was a common but clean blue dress lying over the back of a chair with a long fur cloak, and someone had drawn a hot bath for Alexia. After spending the last few months in cold tents, it felt like we had stepped into the realms of luxury. We ate the broth together and then I helped Alexia take off her torn, soiled clothing so she could bathe. I left to view my own room. It was almost identical with a hot bath waiting for me as well.

I cleaned myself thoroughly before returning to Alexia's room. She was drying her hair in front of the fire.

'You look tired,' I said. 'You should rest.'

She didn't argue. She lowered herself on the bed and, shifting under the warm blankets, let out a long breath. She placed her hand over her stomach with a smile. 'Every time I start to worry, this child gives me a little kick,' she said. 'Bossing me around already, just like its father.' She closed her eyes. I imagined the playful banter that would have followed had Ethaniel been there to hear her. As she fell asleep, I felt he was nearby, watching over his wife even now.

The following morning, I replaced my leather with something more feminine. The purple and red dress laced up my back and I felt it looked pretty in the sun as I walked through the busy streets. Around me, the town was full of activity—soldiers were burying the dead, turning in their weapons to the blacksmiths, rebuilding the gates, and organising sentry duty on the walls. Ival and his group of men had already started collecting any spare food to take to the families in Kest. Some men were writing letters to their loved ones for Ival to deliver. Others were taking time away from the army. Some, including Raggin and Xander, had gone to fetch Hazaka and his men, whom we had left outside the walls until Jasteria was freed.

I was searching for Elhian when the shining stone in my sword distracted me. I thought of the directional light in the Casmodian one and tapped the purple stone to see if it, too, would show me the way. I had tried this on my travels from Fenellar to the Targian camp, but nothing had come of it. I was attempting to work out why when Elhian appeared behind me.

'You can't ask for what it can't give,' he said.

I turned to him. 'It doesn't give directions?'

'No, only the Casmodian sword has that ability, and its true power can only be accessed with faith. Access it with fear and it will point you in the wrong direction.'

'What do the others have?'

'Jazmarda's red stone can produce fire, which represents hope, because hope is like a light in the darkness. It's something that burns within us, just as despair is a feeling of darkness or being "burnt out". Access the stone without hope, and no flame will light. Within Targe's green stone is the elixir—honey-flavoured milk that can nourish anything, just like love. Access it with hate, though, and it becomes a poison, because that's what hate is.'

'And the Life Sword?'

Elhian took the sword and tapped at the stone. It fell out and opened, like two halves of an egg falling away from each other. Inside was a small contraption. Elhian picked it up. It unfolded in his palm, turning into a small, iron butterfly with glass purple wings. 'This sword,' he began with boy-like fascination, 'has the butterfly. It represents life. It is fragile and must be armoured to fight against death, just like us. It is used to send messages from one of the Ordained to another. If anyone not ordained touches it, they fall down, just as if they touch any of the other three stones.' I stared at the contraption with interest. 'Your father used it to carry messages to King Amaz and later, Queen Alexia. That is how you and the queen knew something was wrong when the messages didn't come for some time.'

'My father was killed when we went to find out,' I said.

'You remember?' Elhian asked.

I shook my head. 'No—Alexia told me about it before.'

Elhian gave me the sword again. 'Sometimes I think you are like the Armoured Butterfly.'

'Why?'

Elhian hesitated. 'Because you are beautiful and clever, but quick and dangerous, too.'

I laughed shyly. The fact that he looked embarrassed, too, only served to warm me to him even more.

After midday passed without any sign of the queen, I knocked on her door and opened it. She turned over in bed and beckoned me in with a wave of her hand.

I sat on the edge of her bed and touched her forehead. 'Are you feeling unwell?'

'No, I'm fine, just tired and aching.'

'That fire is keeping the room very cosy.'

'It's Darj. He's been looking after me. I'm told he cleaned this room out for me. He just brought me some more food as well.'

'He's a good man,' I said.

'Yes . . . ' She lay on her back. 'We had a fight after you left with Elhian, about Brenna. He felt I was too merciful in leaving her alive in Kest. She's under supervision, but I didn't order her death. He said I was making a mistake, and I was angry with him for keeping her betrayal from me. I'm ashamed of some of the things we said to each other.'

'Why have you let her live?' I asked.

Alexia sighed. 'Legally her crimes equal death—there is no escaping that. There's no excuse for what she did. The thought of her betrayal repulses me even now, but I want her to face trial and judgment like any other criminal, not killed coldly. I don't want to be like Cades.'

'I'm sure Darj understands that.'

'I hope so. He thought a lot of Ethaniel, you know. It was like losing a brother to him.' She rose and opened the window, wrapping a shawl around her shoulders against the breeze. 'How do you suppose Zavad is doing, and his brothers and sisters?'

'We can only hope they are all right. I miss having him around, but I'm glad he's away from this at the same time.'

'Yes. I'd like to invite the exiles back into Targe, but Cades' army is now under Jag, who has three swords and who I could say is even more unpredictable . . . There's no risk of them being killed in Kest, at least not by men.' She shut the window against the new snowflakes.

'The people are clever, Alexia. They had already constructed shelters and tents when we were there. They will look out for each other, and I know they will appreciate the supplies you are sending.'

'I hope so. I was thinking of sending Zavad a special something from us.'

'He'd like that.'

Alexia returned to the bed and sat down next to me. 'I have a good mind to just stay here until this child is born, now Cades is imprisoned.'

'I wish you would!' Alexia raised an eyebrow at me. 'I mean it would be the best thing for you and your child,' I said, 'that's all. You worry me. A queen should not be risking her life so much in battle, let alone a pregnant one.'

'But it's all right for you and Darj to do so, to say nothing of our fathers. This is my land and kingdom as much as anyone else's, if not more. I will fight for it in any way I can, for my child's sake if nothing else, and there's plenty else.'

'Do you have any suspicions as to whether you will have a boy or a girl?' I asked.

'I do, but I won't tell anyone in case it gets back to Raggin.' She smiled at my surprise. 'I see all, you know. Besides, you will all find out whether it's a prince or princess soon enough.' Alexia's eyes flashed with a little excitement.

'You're looking forward to being a mother again, aren't you?'

'Yes. Somehow it gives me more hope than anything.'

A comfortable silence fell between us. Alexia lay back down, and I settled in beside her.

'I'm glad you're resting,' I said. 'Being with child has been making you tired for some time, hasn't it? Let alone everything else.'

I looked over at Alexia when she didn't answer. She was already falling back to sleep with a faint smile on her lips, and I soon followed.

It wasn't until Ival left with the supplies and a fifty men escort that Hazaka found his spirit again. Alexia, Darj, and I were taking a weapon inventory in the main street when we heard him talking loudly to some of our men.

'But Cades did not know what he had coming. He tried to conquer me, true, but he failed dismally! And now look at him—held up in Jasteria's strongest cell!'

Alexia rolled her eyes. Hazaka called her name, and she suddenly became very interested in what Darj had written down so far. 'That's a good start on the arrows. We should have enough by the time they're finished. What do you think?'

Darj played along. 'I think you're right, but I'm still concerned about the greaves and vambraces. I wish no man had to rely on only leather as protection.'

'Yes, but—'

'Alexia! Darj!' Hazaka put a hand on each of their backs. 'Did you not hear me calling? What a great city this is, eh? I knew it was worth fighting for.'

Alexia gave him a look that a more astute man would have taken as a warning to quit while he was ahead, but Hazaka went on as if he had done Targe the favour and forgotten who had saved him from an icy grave. 'Actually, just before you all arrived—'

'You realised you'd forgotten something?' Alexia suggested with a counterfeit smile.

'Ha! Only a little more Jazmardian rum.'

'That's not quite what I meant,' she said under her breath, only keeping her temper in place because Darj was begging her to with a pleading look.

'Oh,' Hazaka said, 'I see what you are alluding to. I know I should have waited for you to get back . . . But there was no real harm done. After all, the city is won! And Cades "the Great" is subdued.' Hazaka laughed and slapped Darj on the back.

Darj managed to hide a scowl, but it was too much for Alexia. 'You had nothing to do with it!' she said. 'And I will never again risk the lives of my men to rescue you—'

'Rescue me?' Hazaka asked with a mixture of shock and anger.

Darj sighed. I went to find Elhian the Diplomat.

When I reached him, he was passing a tavern that had also been re-started as a matter of course. Outside was Naclen, his tall, youthful but waning body leaning against a hitching post near some horses. He stared at Elhian with folded arms.

'You didn't go with Ival to Kest?' Elhian asked Naclen as I arrived by his side.

'Evidently.'

Elhian said nothing. Instead, he patted one of the horse's necks.

'What do you suppose will happen to Brenna?' Naclen asked me.

I considered the question with pressed lips. 'At worst, death.'

'At best?'

'Eternal banishment,' Elhian said. 'Possibly prison in an allied kingdom.'

Naclen grimaced and stared past the prince.

'Even that would be merciful,' Elhian said. 'Naclen, Brenna betrayed the Queen of Targe. And because of that, Cades has Her

Majesty's sword and the power that goes with it. It's how he started this war. Not only that, but Brenna betrayed Queen Alexia again at Egra, and if it wasn't for Darj it's quite possible that the queen and even Lady Adaliah could have died there. These are not crimes to take lightly.'

'I know what she did!' Naclen said without moving, though his face was now Jazmardian red. 'But she's my sister.'

Elhian stepped towards him. 'Yes, but you are your own man and you alone must decide where your allegiance lies.'

'That man is . . . is . . .'

Darj was watching the flustered queen with reserved amusement when I returned with Elhian. Hazaka was out of sight.

'Yes?' Darj asked.

'He is a fly and I am the horse's eye!' She turned to Elhian with her hands on her hips. 'Hazaka is impossible!'

Elhian nodded with a knowing smile. 'He is pompous and short-sighted, yes.'

Alexia seemed to feel another small kick within. She smoothed her dress over her stomach. 'Then what is he doing here?' she asked, attempting to sound calm.

'However he may come across, Xander tells me he was remorseful when they brought him into Jasteria. He knows he's done wrong but doesn't want to admit it, especially . . .'

'Yes?' Alexia asked.

'Especially to a woman, let alone to a woman who has more power than he does.'

'Ah,' Alexia said, 'he is one of those men. I should have known.'

'Don't judge us men too harshly,' Elhian said with a grin. 'It's not easy keeping up with you and Adaliah.'

Darj let out a humph of agreement.

'Besides,' Elhian said, 'he will still fight for you. As soon as the worst of winter is over, he will still go wherever you direct.'

'So long as I let him think it was his idea?' Alexia asked.

'Something like that,' Elhian said with a laugh.

Cades was sitting with his legs folded beneath him in the prison when we went to visit. Two soldiers guarded the cell door and one had the keys. Cades was watching the keys move back and forth, back and forth as the soldier paced.

Darj and Elhian followed me in. Alexia came in after them, wearing the blue dress Darj had provided her. It gracefully accentuated her sapphire eyes as well as her pregnancy.

She stopped a few steps back from the bars that confined Cades.

'So, the queen herself has stooped to come and see an old friend,' Cades said.

Alexia said nothing but narrowed her eyes at him.

'You can stare at me how you will, Alexia Elryane, but I know this isn't the end of it. These bars will not contain me for long.'

'Where is my sword?' she asked with an even tone. 'You know that unless the swords are returned to their rightful owners, there cannot be peace. Where is it?'

Cades' vile laugh filled the room. I cringed. 'Where is the promise your father made?'

Alexia took a small step forward. 'My father made you no promise.'

'You believe that, if it helps you sleep.'

'Even if he did,' Darj said, 'it would have been under duress.'

'Did life with me as an empress really sound so bad?'

'No,' Alexia said, 'sickening. Besides, everyone knows you murdered Elhian's mother, your own wife.'

Cades stood and walked towards the bars. 'There's no way anyone could prove it.' He sniggered at Elhian. 'And throwing me into this pit will not stop me.'

'We destroyed your home in Semanez,' I said.

'Yes.' Cades folded his arms. 'I ordered Parrian's death for letting you in, and I punished Jag for being so easily fooled by your distraction.' He shrugged like it was meaningless. 'Of course, you can't see where I left the scar.'

Alexia held his gaze, then turned on her heel.

'Come Ally, what did Lord Ethaniel Lowelan have that I do not?'

Alexia paused in her step. 'Compassion,' she said, turning back to him. 'Love. Courage. Youth. Integrity. Everything you do not have.'

'Yes, but at least I will not die a martyr for a lost cause.'

Alexia took a quick step towards the bars. 'Ethaniel was murdered, by you, because he wanted to save our people. And when you die, it will be for the same cause.'

'Ethaniel died because of you,' he whispered.

Darj moved towards the bars with a murderous look. I thought he was going to strangle the king then and there, but we had decided to keep him alive beforehand.

The queen's impassive expression hid any grief or anger in her heart. 'Darj?' she called with calm firmness.

Darj stepped back but he kept his eyes on the king. 'Yes, Your Majesty?'

'Begin making plans to push the Casmodians back to Liane, where we will face and defeat them in battle.' She glared at Cades again. 'Their dark shepherd is thrown down.'

Alexia turned to leave for a second time. Darj and I followed her, and Elhian came close behind, looking back at his father one last time before closing the door.

33
KADRAM

The queen and Darj asked me to help train some of the men in sword fighting and, while I agreed, I found it difficult at first. I hardly knew what I did myself. My body still seemed to respond instinctively, in a way I couldn't describe. It wasn't until I slowed down my movements that I was able to show the men some skills, and they practised with me in the yard below the keep. 'No, don't leave yourself open like that,' I called out to one of them. 'I could easily take you out.' In one move, I proved my point and then helped the soldier back to his feet. 'You over there, the only reason you are losing is because you are afraid of the enemy. Take him front on!'

I was proud to see the gradual improvement in them and left them to practise while I went to visit Alexia and Elhian, who were watching me from one of the keep's balconies. I climbed the stairs and hurried around the corner. I heard them talking, and they spoke my name. I stopped and listened.

'She's remarkable,' Elhian said. I felt my face redden.

'Yes, she's very gifted. But I worry, Elhian. When her memory is returned . . . Who knows what they did to her while she was in prison? Or when she escaped, and they found her at Kest River? What if it is all too much for her?'

I hadn't thought of that. Would I be able to cope with the truth?

'What could be too much for her?'

'Fighting is one thing, the past another. Adaliah nearly died trying to save us. The loss of Jeri, Ethaniel and especially her father will suddenly hit her, as well as everything else. While sometimes I wish I had my old Adaliah back, I think the fact she doesn't have the pain of the past might be a blessing through all this.'

They fell silent, and I was about to go and join them, but Elhian asked, 'Do you think she'll blame me?'

It took a long time for Alexia to answer, and I gathered she wanted her response to match the weight of his question. I listened intently. 'She will only denounce Jag and Cades,' Alexia said, and added with a smile in her voice, 'and then they'll be in trouble.'

I warmed at the confidence she had in me, but feared I'd let her down.

I walked to them, and they stopped talking when they saw me. Elhian looked away with an embarrassed downturn of his eyes but, before I could speak, a soldier came running up the stairs behind me.

He gave a rushed bow and tried to catch his breath. 'My lady, the south-eastern wall . . . A message from Cades' general . . . Come!'

At the gate, a group of soldiers were huddling around someone. They saw me approaching and parted so I could reach the man holding a package. The soldier handed the damp bag to me with a crinkled nose. 'It doesn't smell good, my lady.'

I opened it, but it took me a bit to comprehend what I was seeing: a piece of flesh, fingers . . .

A severed hand.

I quickly closed the bag. I gave it back to the soldier and ordered him to dispose of it.

I kept the note that came with it however and, turning away from the gate, opened it. '"Next time it will be a heart",' I read aloud. '"So the queen, who carries Cades' child, knows that her heart will not beat forever".'

It took me a moment to realise what he meant.

Jag is claiming her child as Cades'?

Alexia snatched the note off me to read for herself. 'Where is Darj?' she asked. I could see the anger rising in her face. 'Elhian, find him and send him to me at the keep. It's time we showed these people just whose kingdom this is and whose child!'

By the time Ival Fort and his men returned to us from Kest, Jasteria was busy. Men were being outfitted with armour and weapons of choice, horses were being reshod, and practice targets obliterated with arrows under Darj's instruction. Walking through the streets, it was obvious that battle was paramount.

Ival requested an audience with us, not that he could have avoided one even if he wanted to. Hazaka, Elhian, Darj, Alexia and I met him in one of the keep's larger rooms. He looked much as he had when we'd freed him from prison—somewhat wild and in need of a bath, but muscular and fit.

Behind him stood another man who made my heart stop. 'Lezan?' I stared at the old Jazmardian leaning on his tall staff and paled like I was looking into a window of the past. I hoped it was Lezan, even though I had helped to bury him in Egra and knew that logically it was impossible.

The man smiled at me in a knowing way. 'I am Kadram,' he said. 'Lezan's brother.'

I continued to study him—his resemblance to Lezan was unsettling. He had the same eyes, the same way of carrying himself, the same smile. He was taller and healthier, and his hair wasn't as grey, but in every other way he was Lezan. 'What brings you to Jasteria?' I asked, slowly taking a seat.

'It is not a trip I would choose willingly at my age, that is the truth,' he said. 'But I came firstly to tell you, King Hazaka, that your wife has given birth to a healthy boy and named him Mirza as you previously agreed.'

Hazaka sat up straight. 'What? A boy? I have a son! Did you hear that? Jazmarda has an heir and prince!' He nudged Elhian, who was sitting between him and Alexia.

The room filled with congratulations, some genuine, some merely polite.

'I also came to tell you that your kingdom will once again be united.'

'How is that possible? We are truly cursed.'

Kadram shook his head. 'You are cursed because you say you are cursed. Targe is victorious because they believe they are victorious. Still, the curse will be ended, and your people will unite, but not because of you.'

Hazaka tucked his hands into his armpits and sank back into the chair. Alexia looked down with a small smile, struggling not to enjoy Hazaka's discomfort. 'There are many prophecies,' she said.

'Yes,' Kadram said, leaning forward, 'and many interpretations, not all of them pleasant.'

'Which is why Lezan was forced out of Jazmarda,' Elhian said.

'Yes,' Kadram said. 'He interpreted the Cazinian Papers a certain way and was exiled for it.'

'Not by me,' Hazaka said, raising his palms.

'No, not by you. He knew that Jazmarda's time of power had ended. Even so, he fought to keep the people of Jazmarda together, but they were entranced by the power of the swords. He died before he could finish his work, but he was successful in that he met you, prince.'

Elhian shrugged his shoulders like he wasn't so sure. Every show of low self-confidence surprised me. In my eyes, he'd achieved so much in such difficult circumstances. Couldn't he see that?

Kadram turned to me. 'But the power we know of cannot last.'

I felt his eyes looking straight through mine and shifted uneasily in my seat.

'Now we know why you and Lezan were called the witnesses,' Hazaka said, breaking into the conversation with a laugh. 'Always seeming so wise . . .' When no one responded he coughed and looked out the nearby window.

'Queen Alexia,' Kadram said, turning to her. 'I have heard much of what the Targian army has achieved, and I want you to know that your father was a glorious light amongst the history of all kings and would be very proud of you.'

Alexia gave him a tense and doubtful smile. I knew she feared dishonouring her father and the inheritance he had given her more than anything. Kadram must have known, too, because he reached over and touched her hand to make it clear he meant what he said.

'Now tell me,' he said, 'you are planning battle?'

'Yes,' Alexia said. 'I will stay here, but the men will go to reclaim the rest of Targe. I believe they are ready to leave tomorrow. Is that right, Darj?'

Darj seemed to be lost in thought, but he started when he heard his name. His eyes weren't as bright as when I'd last looked at them. His dark hair was unruly, too, and he had a shadow of weariness over his face. He'd hardly spoken during the meeting. Had he been distracted the whole time? I glanced at Alexia and knew she was noticing the same things.

He cleared his throat. 'We are always ready to do your will, my queen,' he said.

Alexia peered at him as if hoping for something more, but Darj averted his gaze and returned to silence.

'I shall stay with Her Majesty until you return,' Kadram said.

When Alexia decided to see Cades in the keep's prison once more, Kadram and I went with her.

'Well, hello Ally,' Cades said upon our entry. He stood up and stretched his back. 'I haven't seen you for some time. Look at you, ripe with child and almost ready for plucking.'

Alexia put a protective hand on her stomach. 'It is Ethaniel's child, which you will do well to remember.'

'Oh, I see. Jag must have started to spread the word that the child is mine.' He grinned. 'How pleasing.'

'It was delivered with a severed hand,' Alexia said.

'Yes, well, Jag can't resist playing with womanly emotions. Who can blame him? You are at your most beautiful when you're angry.'

Alexia opened her mouth to speak but no words came out. He was infuriating to me let alone her, and I couldn't even remember the pain he'd caused beforehand.

Cades gave a satisfied sigh. 'These bars will not hold me long.'

'Your son has made sure they will,' Alexia said.

'Son?' Cades sneered and shook his head. 'If you speak of Elhian, he is my enemy, not my son.' He pressed his head between the bars.

'He will die, alone and powerless. So will you, Adaliah. And I will tell you something else Ally—your child will not live either. I will let my people think I have had you already, but then I will personally kill the child and you will bear me a son before a year has passed.'

Kadram walked out of the shadows and struck at Cades with his staff, driving him back with a heave of pain. 'Save your words. Soon you will not have even them.'

When we left the prison, Kadram took my arm and pulled me aside. 'Come with me,' he said. 'There's something you need to know.'

'Adaliah?' the prince called later, tapping on my bedroom door.

'Come in.' I turned as the door opened. 'It's time to leave, isn't it?'

He nodded, stepped towards me and took my hand. 'I just . . . I want you to know I'll be thinking of you.'

I squeezed his hand. 'And I of you.'

He looked once again like he wanted to say more but didn't know where to start. He touched my cheek. I looked up at him with a smile, my breath quickening a little. I wasn't sure how I felt about him, but I felt so safe in his presence. When he tilted my chin up with his finger, I didn't object. He leant towards me, and I wouldn't have stopped him, but I saw something hanging around his neck and pulled back.

'What's that?' I asked, pointing.

'The keys to Cades' cell.' He pulled them out of his shirt.

'Why do you have them?'

'To make sure they don't get into the wrong hands. Why? What's wrong?'

I searched his face. 'Does Alexia know you have them?'

'She gave them to me. Why? Don't you trust me?'

'No . . . it's not that. I'm just surprised Alexia gave them to you, that's all. They're important. I thought she'd want to have them herself.'

'What do you think I'm going to do? Let Cades out when no one's looking? She trusts me. Whose side do you think I'm on?'

My head started to hurt. 'That's just it, isn't it? There's so much I don't really know.'

Elhian stepped away from me. 'What do I have to do to prove myself?'

As always, I was frustrated that they couldn't understand what it was like. How could I be sure of anything when I couldn't remember? What if everything I believed was a lie? What if they were all just using me to their advantage? I knew that wasn't fair, but it didn't stop me thinking it. 'It's just hard not to doubt where you're coming from in all this.'

'Why? Because I'm Cades' son?'

I opened my mouth but didn't know what to say. I knew he had worked hard to separate himself from his father and had personally seen him fight with such vigour against him. And yet, the only family they had was in each other, like Alexia and me. I couldn't help but think that meant something.

'You have no idea how much your doubt hurts.'

'Wouldn't you doubt if you were in my position?' I asked, affronted.

'I would value you for what I've seen you do.'

'But how would you know my true motives? How do you expect me to know yours?'

He gave me a desperate look. 'You don't see it, do you? Assuming I don't die in battle, if we lose this war I will be executed by my own father. Nor will I be the only one: Darj, Xander, Raggin—even Queen Alexia will face death once Cades has finished exploiting her. We will all be killed without a second thought.' He shook his head at me. 'You are not the only one who has the right to be afraid.'

He didn't speak to me again, and not to Alexia either. After leaving my room, he went down to Raggin, Xander, and the men he was riding with to the south-east of Targe. They were going to liberate the towns there from the Casmodians as part of a huge campaign. Darj and I were travelling with men to the east, Hunt in particular. Hazaka was taking men to Chettona, and Ival and his battalion were riding to Fenellar. Between the five of us, we would reclaim the Casmodian strongholds of Targe and force them back to Liane. Contained, they would be an easier target, or at least that's the idea that motivated Alexia and Darj.

Alexia, who by then was about six and a half months pregnant, watched as Elhian rode out of the gates with his battalion. 'What did you say to him?' she asked me.

'Does it matter?' I didn't want her to chide me for saying the wrong thing—having seen his anger and avoidance, I was fully aware of it myself. Her disapproval on top of that would have undone me.

I could feel her reading my expression. 'If you don't want to tell me, you don't have to,' she said. We watched as Darj led Bagred and Guntar over to us. 'I wish I could ask you to stay,' she said, 'but I know the A'zyon Warrior must fight.'

'I will be with you soon,' I said.

'Don't forget, they have the swords.'

'Yes,' Darj said, reaching us, 'but if Adaliah is right they're not so powerful in the hands of the faithless anyway.'

'I'm always right,' I said with a grin. 'Despite the fact I have no idea what I'm doing.'

Darj laughed. 'Spoken like a true royal.'

Alexia rolled her eyes at him and embraced me one last time. She handed me a stained note and a small gold chain. 'To put on the grave you made for Jeri,' she whispered.

I looked at them in her hand—small tokens of a childless mother. It was a stark reminder of her pain. I promised to deliver them but wished I could promise healing as well.

Darj moved towards his horse but Alexia touched his arm as he passed. 'Darj . . .' she said, and he stopped. She met his eyes. 'Come back safely, please.'

Warmth filled his eyes again. I don't know where his mind had been over the past day, but it hadn't been with us. I'd been worried that he'd given in or lost hope. It seemed so unlike him, but then he was a hard man to read. Still, Alexia's words seemed to give his life some worth again. He took her hand and kissed it, and then rode with me towards the east.

34
PUSHING BACK THE ENEMY

For over a month, our Targian men and Jazmardian allies fought the Casmodians from the northern borders to the southern mountains. Egra was the first to be freed by the men Darj and I led—it had since been emptied of the many soldiers who had been there when we last visited, so our victory was easy and cost few men. We heard news that Hazaka had reclaimed Chettona—again, not as many men as expected had been there, and Darj soon concluded that Jag must have already drawn back a lot of their soldiers to Liane. I knew the thought of so many Casmodian men crawling over the Targian capital irritated Darj and that he was anxious to see it freed, but we had no choice other than to continue our reclamation of the countryside as planned. We were not yet ready to face the core of Cades' men.

When we came to Hunt, it was raining. The town looked like a forlorn child and it was difficult for me to be there again, especially knowing Alexia personally now and the pain she harboured for Prince Jeri.

Almost all that was left of the town's houses were black skeletons. They looked eerie against a sky that was as grey as Darj's face—I could see he found it doubly painful to return to the town. He'd lost the prince in Hunt, but he also believed he'd lost the trust and love of a queen he adored. I hoped for his sake we wouldn't have to linger long.

Only a hundred Casmodian soldiers were camped there, and we fought them in the rain. I slipped in the mud at one point, and a soldier took the opportunity to strike at me. I moved in time to save my life, but his blade split my left calf open, causing a long and bloody wound. I rolled over and thrust my sword into his side. He collapsed beside me. Unable to get up, I lay there in the rain.

Darj came and pulled me up only after the battle was finished and won. He helped me sit on a broken wall and cleared the mud and blood from my leg before sealing it with a crude bandage.

From there, I limped into the town centre until I came to Jeri's grave. I bent down on one knee and scowled as my wound stretched. I placed the chain on the grave with his mother's note.

'Adaliah, Adaliah, come!'

I looked up even though I knew I had heard the voice in my spirit.

'Adaliah!'

The voice was young and sweet. I closed my eyes, wanting to see Jeri for myself, if only in my mind. A picture did form. A palace corridor, a glimpse of a small child darting around a corner. I was chasing him. Around a few more bends, and then into a great light. Jeri was lifted by a tall, thick-set man, but the light was so intense I could only see their silhouettes.

'Look Adaliah, Father was watching out for me like he promised! I knew he would Adaliah!'

I suddenly saw a clear picture of the small boy. His face was not curved-shaped like Alexia's, but he undoubtedly had her eyes and smile. He grinned at me with dimples in his cheeks. He wore a delicate gold chain around his neck and passed his father a note.

Then, they both began to fade.

I opened my eyes. I touched my forehead and grimaced as I tried to pin down the images, but they seemed to flitter even more. Memories that wouldn't be recalled, thoughts that wouldn't form. I let out my frustration in an angry yell, and only then did I notice the men standing about in all corners of the township, watching me. I studied their faces amidst a solemn silence, wondering which ones I had fought beside before, which ones had lost their family, what their stories were and why I couldn't remember mine.

The note and chain were still on Jeri's grave. I tried to stand, but my wounded leg hurt too much, and I fell. Darj helped me to my feet for a second time.

'Darj, why can't I remember? Why?'

'I don't know.'

'You are the queen's primary advisor!'

'Yes, but not "Darj the Wise"!'

'I don't want to spend the rest of my life not knowing.'

'I don't believe you will. But until your memory is restored, you have no choice but to go on without it.'

We heard from a messenger that Ival had not been able to reclaim Fenellar and that Elhian and his men had gone to reinforce them. They requested our help as well, so Darj and I turned south too, happily leaving Hunt behind us. Unable to tighten the skin near my wound, I rode with my left leg hanging out of the stirrup for much of the way.

It took us almost a week to reach the plains before Fenellar. We arrived in the early morning and found the men, including Elhian, waiting for us to the east of the green town.

I rode by Elhian, but he said nothing to me. I felt both annoyed that he was so unforgiving and worried that I had hurt him beyond repair. I dreaded to think I'd lost his friendship. I needed him just as much as I needed Alexia and Darj. Why hadn't I realised that before?

We could see that Ival had lost a lot of his men, but they were ready to attack as soon as we were. By then, my wound had healed enough for me to ride properly, but I knew that a lot of my fighting would have to take place from Bagred's back. I was afraid that if I dismounted, I wouldn't be able to get up again.

'I hear there are enough women here to turn even your miserable life around, Xander,' Raggin said as the men prepared for our attack. He wriggled an eyebrow and gave a cocky smile.

'Raggin,' Xander said in a grave tone, 'perhaps you should think that there are women here whose miserable lives we could turn around.'

Raggin frowned, but I didn't hear his response. Darj called for us to move towards the gate, and the Targians rode forward, Naclen in front. I imagined he was determined to redeem his hometown.

We heard shouts from the city as we approached the green walls. Darj raised his arm to halt the army. We stopped out of range of any archers and watched as the gate opened.

The first thing we saw was a flash of white, followed by four hundred men or so. I blinked as I realised the white was a flag of truce held by a Casmodian. Elhian and Darj reached for their swords.

'Don't attack us!' one of them called. 'Wait!'

The soldiers dropped to their knees before Elhian. 'Your Highness,' the flag bearer continued in between puffs, 'we pledge our allegiance to you and will fight with you now as you retake Fenellar for Targe.

Please let us join you. The Casmodian army of Fenellar is about to come out and meet you and if we die, it will be by your side.'

Elhian shifted in his saddle as he regarded the men with suspicion.

'I know you have no reason to trust us, but know we are condemned by our army because of our loyalty to you.'

Elhian's gaze moved from them back to the gate. The other Casmodians were coming out and there was little time to argue.

The flag bearer lifted his eyes with apparent sincerity and, before Elhian, Darj or I could speak, he and the others became the first to charge back at their own men.

Elhian dug his heels into Leuk, and the Targian army followed.

As Raggin and Xander toasted to our victory later that night, I walked through the streets of the wounded. We had found the women Raggin spoke of—the ones I had seen on my last visit—but Elhian and Darj organised accommodation and food for them away from the army. Sleet began to fall from the night sky, decorating my torn apparel. I touched my sticky face and looked at my hand. It was covered in dark red blood. I wiped it off and walked on until I found Elhian. He was kneeling beside a wounded enemy soldier.

'No, you don't know me,' the soldier was saying, 'but Adaliah does.' He saw me and chuckled and choked at the same time. Elhian glanced over his shoulder but quickly returned his attention to the soldier. 'Yup, I've been kissed by the A'zyon Warrior. She tried to pull one past me, but I knew who she was . . . Just like her cousin carrying the child of her enemy, just like Jag's wife—'

'Jag's wife?' Elhian asked.

'The one who stole Alexia's sword. He found her in Kest and took her to be with him.'

My mind reeled.

Brenna Caylith?

Brenna married Jag?

The following evening, I paced through the simple camp we had made for the night. Hazaka and his men had joined us in the afternoon, and we were getting ready to go back to Jasteria. Again, I looked for Elhian and, when I couldn't find him, climbed a tree to get a better view over the camp. I was keen to begin the return to Alexia the next day or even that night, but I wanted to talk to Elhian, too. I felt more and more ashamed whenever I thought of the things I'd said to him. How could I question him like that? Had he been angry with me all this time? Judging by the fact he hadn't spoken more than two words to me since, I felt sure he was and that saddened me. I had too few friends to risk losing one.

'My lady?' a soldier called up the tree.

'Yes?'

'Darj has been looking for you.'

'Oh.' I let go of the branch and landed on my feet. The tree shook itself back into place. 'Take me to him.'

'Adaliah,' the general said before I could speak. 'Elhian told me about Brenna. I fear Alexia may be in danger if Jag and Cades are using Brenna. Brenna despises her. Will you ride with Elhian and me tonight? Ival and Hazaka can begin leading the army there in the morning.'

'We're a week's ride away. What can the three of us do if you're right?'

'Protect the queen, if nothing else.'

We reached the gate of Jasteria just before dawn seven days later.

We were too late. The city gates were open and smouldering and Alexia was standing in the streets. She was holding her bow and I could see her quiver strapped over her shoulder, empty.

I ran to her and hugged her. She slumped against me. I examined Jasteria over her shoulder. The buildings were smoking, and some men were attending to the wounded. Others were covering the dead.

Alexia stood back, and I asked her what happened.

'It was Brenna.'

'But how?'

'She seduced one of the guards into letting her into the city and then Cades' cell.'

I stepped back and looked at Elhian. 'I thought you had the keys,' I said.

He pulled out the chain from around his neck. The keys were still hanging on it.

I've failed to trust him again. I avoided eye contact. I didn't want to see the hurt in his eyes a second time.

'She didn't use a key,' Alexia said. 'Jag lent her the swords, and she gave them back to Cades. He escaped, killed the guard, and they let in the Casmodians. Now, he's gone. He was right after all—we didn't hold him long.'

'At least they didn't take you,' Darj said.

'They tried, but with Ru'ach as my guide I fought as hard as I could. We all did, but they still got Cades. They still killed many of our men.'

'I wonder if he knew in advance he'd be captured and was able to plan for it?' Elhian asked.

'What does it matter?' Darj asked. 'What's important is that he was locked away long enough for us to retake most of Targe and subdue the Casmodians. They didn't harm Alexia or her child. It could have been worse.'

'I should have brought her to justice when we had the chance,' Alexia said, her eyes flicking guiltily towards Darj.

'Even if you had,' Darj said, 'Jag would have just found someone else to use.'

Alexia gave him a small smile. 'Cades will be gathering his army at Liane,' she said. 'He's called for every Casmodian left to stand against us. Even men are coming from Semanez and other more northern towns, common men who have now been trained to fight. They will be nigh unstoppable.'

'Unstoppable?' Darj asked. 'We have just retaken Targe after we were almost wiped out. We have survived their persecution. We will meet Cades out on the battlefield and finish this once and for all.'

35
ONCE AND FOR ALL

I pointed my toe down and turned to examine my calf. It had almost healed over but Alexia wasn't convinced.

'Are you sure you're all right to go into battle again?' she asked. 'You don't have to do any—'

'Alexia, it's fine, really.'

Darj walked in the room, talking to Kadram, Ival, Xander, and Raggin as he did so. The men followed him, carrying multiple papers. They spread them out over a table, and I realised they were maps.

'Alexia, we have a plan,' Darj said, pausing to glance at her. 'We need your approval.'

Ival pulled a chair out for her.

'The idea is to separate Cades from his army with a decoy,' Kadram said.

'And Jag, too,' Ival said.

'Wait,' I said. 'Where's Elhian?'

'Oh, I almost forgot,' Darj said, looking up. 'He asked for you to meet him down at the stables. Something about your horse.'

While Darj continued explaining his tactics, I slipped from the room, relieved to think that Elhian was finally ready to talk to me. I went to the stables in a restrained run, my cherry red dress flowing out behind me.

When I reached the stables, I saw the prince leaning against Bagred's stall with one foot on a rail and his back to the door. His tall frame was hunched slightly as he bent down to feed Bagred an apple. I felt my heart quicken at the sight of him. He turned a little as if sensing my presence, and he looked serious, or so I thought. But when he saw me, his face lightened with a smile that I carefully returned.

'My lady,' he said, and then paused. 'You seem so different when you're not holding a sword.'

'I am,' I said. 'Darj said something was wrong with Bagred?'

'Wrong? No, he's fine. Ready for another fight, I think.'

'Are you?'

Elhian stroked Bagred's neck and didn't answer straight away. 'This battle will not only decide the fate of Targe but of Casmodia as well. At least, the Casmodia I believe in.'

'It must be a comfort to know there are other Casmodians out there who believe in the same place, who are willing to fight with you. They will help make you king.'

'Yes. But of what?'

'Of the kingdom you have fought for.'

Elhian studied me and I wondered what it was he saw. 'You always have strength in your eyes, like Ru'ach himself is within you,' he said. 'Unshakeable certainty, even though you are living in one of the most uncertain times and circumstances of all.' He looked away. 'Adaliah, there's something I need to tell you, about before—'

'Wait, let me go first. I'm so sorry I questioned your trust—'

'Why wouldn't you? I have betrayed my own kingdom—'

'Only to save it!'

'And if you had your memory, you'd probably question my integrity even more.'

I took a step towards him. 'Elhian, I know you're concerned about before, that I might judge you for something you did or didn't do, something I know nothing about, but before you say anything, let me say this. You were right. Not having a memory reminds me every day that I can only judge people by what I see of them now. If I can live without a past, what use is it anyway? I see the pain the past causes Alexia every day, Darj as well. I don't remember what they were like, but I know it's impacted them harshly. Elhian, what I have seen of you is enough to make any past insignificant because I see you as who you are now, and that's really all that matters.'

Elhian gazed at me with a tight smile. 'Why do women never let you finish a sentence?'

I laughed. 'Because we know what you're going to say anyway.'

Elhian's smile widened. 'You are a superb warrior.' He took my hand. 'And a beautiful woman.' He brushed my hair back with affection. When he leant towards me, I didn't move away. He left a soft and tentative kiss on my lips, but he suddenly pulled back, and I think he was afraid he'd gone too far.

I smiled shyly up at him. I realised I'd wanted this but had been too scared to let him close to me, too scared of discovering a dark truth I now no longer believed existed. I felt warmed by his presence, safe. How could I have doubted him?

'You are a good man,' I said, cupping his face with my hand and feeling a sudden intensity towards him. He kissed me again, and this time it left me breathless.

Later, I went to talk to Alexia—I wanted to tell her what had happened—but I found that she and Darj were still sitting at the same table I had left them at. I opened the door a little to make sure I wasn't interrupting anything.

The others had left them to their thoughts.

'Alexia . . . ' Darj said. I leant forward, admittedly eavesdropping once more. 'I know you have always blamed me for Jeri's death.'

Alexia's mouth dropped. I engaged in a moral battle with myself, questioning whether I should stay or not. The battle didn't last long, and I leant forward to hear what they were saying. For whatever reason, I longed for peace between the queen and her general.

'And while I understand why,' Darj said, 'I hope one day you can forgive me.'

'Darj—'

'Just so you know, it's Ethaniel's death that weighs most heavily on me.'

'Ethaniel's?'

'Yes. When we got back from the Yellow Forest after retreating, he told me to go straight to the stables, to prepare horses for us all while he went to get you and Jeri. I saw the Casmodians follow him in, led by Cades, and I thought that between Adaliah and Ethaniel you'd all be all right. So I ran on to the stables, knowing the danger, and . . . ' He took a deep breath, fighting hard against his emotions. 'And he was killed. Adaliah, too, or so we thought.'

Alexia seemed taken aback by the glistening eyes hiding behind the hair that fell over his forehead. 'Darj, I've never blamed you for Ethaniel's death,' she said. Tears rolled down her cheeks. 'Yes, I have been angry with you over Jeri's, but it is Cades and Jag I hold in the deepest contempt, not you. I'm sorry for blaming you, for letting you carry this burden alone.'

I know I don't say it enough, but I do appreciate you and all you have done. Ethaniel did, too, right to the end, and even if you had been there, nothing would have been different. There was no fight. Cades impaled him right through the back before any of us even knew what was happening. And as for Adaliah, I thank Ru'ach every day that Adaliah is alive.'

'Not all of her.'

I hadn't realised he blamed himself for my condition as well, and I knew then why he sometimes looked at me with sorrow.

'Darj, you take too much upon yourself. You must promise me to let this go.'

'I would if you would join me in such a promise.'

'That is another thing entirely.'

Darj straightened. 'Alexia, there's something I must say, as your advisor. Ru'ach is our protector, your protector. When you became queen, you promised you would rule this kingdom under his guidance. You are the spiritual leader of your people. If we are to have victory in this battle, then you must make peace and connect to him.'

'I've . . . I've tried . . . It's just that . . . He *is* supposed to be our protector . . . but Ethaniel and Jeri . . . '

'That was evil's doing, not his. I know it's hard, but the other road will only invite death. We're not just fighting against soldiers in a field. We need him.'

She nodded but couldn't look at him.

'Alexia, if I don't make it back off the battlefield, I . . . I want to die knowing you won't spend the rest of your life hating me.'

Alexia's eyes flashed. 'Darj, do not speak of such things! Do you think I don't worry about this? That I'm not anxious every day that I'll receive news that you or Adaliah or even Elhian have been killed?

Of course I don't hate you, but nor do I want to be reminded of the risks we take.'

Darj leant back into his chair. 'I'm sorry.'

I watched as Alexia calmed herself and reached her hand out to him. 'No, I'm sorry.' He took her hand and kissed it, and she squeezed his in turn. 'All is forgiven, my dear friend.'

That afternoon, Darj and I stood either side of the door leading to the small chapel Alexia had spent two hours in alone.

'Do you think she can do it?' I asked.

'I think she's wanted to for a long time, deep down.'

A few more minutes passed, and then the door creaked open. Alexia came out and shut the door behind her. Her face was free of tears.

'Well?' Darj asked.

'I have made my peace,' she said with a small nod.

'What shall we do?' I asked.

'I believe Ru'ach wants us to make sure the Casmodians fighting for us each have a white stone, like our men and our Jazmardian allies.'

'Why?' I asked.

She shrugged with a calm smile. 'I don't know. I just know it'll help.'

Two weeks later, I was walking with Naclen and Xander along the walls of Jasteria and looking out over the snowy plains. Patches of green were starting to show, a reminder that winter was fading. The wind was cold though, and I pulled my cloak in around myself. Below us, on the inside of the wall, Ival was talking to the very pregnant queen. Elhian and Darj were sharpening their sword skills against each other. Naclen watched Elhian until Xander called us both.

'Look.' Xander pointed to a figure on the horizon.

There were two people on a horse, riding closer. They stopped out of range of our archers, but they were close enough to be recognised.

'It's Jag,' Xander said, looking at the bald, tattooed man. He called down to Darj, who hurried to join us with the others.

'With . . . a woman?' I asked.

Naclen grimaced. The woman was dressed in a beautiful, long purple dress with red trimmings. The gold of her excessive jewellery glimmered in the sun as she held onto Jag.

Darj arrived and took in the sight. 'It's Brenna,' he said.

Elhian and Ival stood beside him and followed his line of sight while Alexia still made her way up the slippery stone stairs. She arrived just in time to see Jag and Brenna turn and ride away.

'Yes,' she said, 'and with the royal jewels. Father gave me that dress.'

I saw Naclen grimace again, trying to hide his shame from the queen.

'Naclen,' she said, 'I suppose this means the Casmodian army is encamped just over that hill. Ride out with Adaliah and Elhian tonight and report to me how many.'

We approached the camp on foot, having dismounted our horses when we heard the sound of men's voices. Some were singing in a foreign tongue—the Jazmardians that remained loyal to Cades—others were fighting, and still others were just talking. I could already sense there were many more soldiers than could easily be defeated and, when the three of us crawled over a small ridge, the sight confirmed it.

Thousands upon thousands of men were camped across and beyond the undulating hills.

'No wonder our reclamation was easier than we anticipated,' I said.

Elhian's eyes widened. 'Casmodia must be empty. Cades must have men from Delya fighting with him as well, the Rivermen. And even more men from Jazmarda have joined him—look at them all!'

'How does he do it?' Naclen asked.

'I think he has more help from darker powers than we realise,' Elhian said.

'How many men will we have?' I asked.

Elhian raised a finger and pressed it to his lips. I wondered what I had said but then heard footsteps. They were close. Elhian turned, grabbed at something and brought a person down. He covered their mouth before they could say anything, unsheathed his sword and pressed it into their neck.

It was a young girl.

'Brenna!' Naclen exclaimed in a whisper. 'What are you doing?'

Brenna struggled to get free. Her movements pricked the skin on her neck against the sword. She stopped fighting and only then did Elhian remove his hand from her mouth. She spat on the blade that threatened her life. 'Well, brother, since you're not defending me—'

'Defending you? You're not the sister I once knew, Brenna Caylith. You have been poisoned with jealousy.' I wasn't sure what he meant until I remembered what I'd heard her lover say in Egra: *Even your queen must have been jealous of you.* Apparently Naclen thought the reverse was true.

Naclen gave Elhian something of a nod, as if accepting she would have to die. 'For the queen,' he said.

Brenna resumed her struggle against Elhian. 'Kill me then,' she said. 'Kill me and be a defenceless woman-slayer just like your father.'

Elhian flipped her onto her front, crossed her hands over each other on her back, and held them there. 'Naclen, get the rope out of my saddlebag.'

'You're taking her prisoner?' Naclen asked, confused.

'Everyone deserves one last day to repent,' Elhian said. 'She will face the consequences of her actions soon enough.'

Upon our report the following morning and Darj's subsequent advice, Alexia ordered for the army to ready themselves for what we all hoped would be our last battle.

Men soon began to pour out of the southern gates of Jasteria, splitting into twelve battalions. Hazaka's men made up two battalions. Ival, Xander and Raggin had been chosen to oversee two Targian battalions each. They all rode out into the morning sunshine, their horses sloshing through the melting snow.

I stood with Darj as he talked with Alexia about what to do should Jasteria be taken. 'For you, the only real enemy you need to be concerned with is death. Your child comes first—it is the future of Targe. You must flee as fast and as far as you can should death seem near.'

'Until then, I shall be shooting arrows as fast and as far as I can.'

'Alexia, you are more than eight months pregnant!' He looked at me for support, but while I agreed with him, I knew better than to think she would change her mind. 'When we return to Liane, I want to lead a victory march, not a funeral procession!'

'Please don't argue with me Darj.' She strapped a full quiver over her white dress. 'I'll be safe on the wall, I promise.'

Back in my room, I viewed myself in the mirror. A part of me didn't want to replace the beautiful dress I was wearing with the leathers that lay on the bed. I studied my sword and, not for the first time, imagined what my father would have been like when he held it. Was he as powerful as King Amaz was said to be? Did he teach me to fight so I would be here now, fighting for Targe? Had he been loving and strong like Alexia, tough and quiet like Darj, or something else altogether? Would he have approved of Elhian? What did he think of me now? Would I soon meet him and, if so, would I remember him when I saw him? 'What if it's all a lie?' I asked myself aloud.

I took a deep breath and started changing into my armour. I tugged at my high, thick boots, added a long, thin dagger inside my left one, and adjusted my breastplate. I picked up my sword, and the amethyst stone glowed. I faced the mirror again and considered the difference. How could I feel both calm and nervous at the same time?

Almost ready, I walked out of the keep and down to a well to fill up my goatskin water bottle.

'Adaliah?' the prince called from behind me. 'Are you ready?'

'Yes,' I said. 'Are you?'

'Yes.'

He touched my cheek gently with the back of his hand, and then wrapped his arms around me. I rose up on my toes to steal a few last kisses. For the first time, I was acutely afraid of losing him.

Alexia was waiting for us at the main southern gate. Elhian knew she would want a private word with me so presented himself first.

He bowed before her and kissed her hand. 'By the end of this battle, Targe will be wholly yours again,' he said.

'By the end of this battle, you shall be king.'

Elhian hesitated at the thought. 'No matter what happens, I'm glad I fought for you.'

Alexia's eyes flickered with the teasing spirit Darj had told me about. 'You and I both know it wasn't just me you fought for.' Her smile reached me, and I felt my cheeks flush.

Elhian gave her a hug, mounted Leuk and rode towards the gate. Another rider arrived by his side: Naclen Caylith.

'I thought you were riding with Darj,' we heard Elhian say.

'I would rather . . . ' The youth glanced at the prince, the man he'd hated for simply being a Casmodian. 'I'd rather ride by you.'

I didn't move straight away and for a moment Alexia and I were in a world of our own. Her ebony hair was blowing back from her shoulders and her fine blue eyes were steady and purposeful. She was a beautiful woman but burdened by the death she'd seen. I recognised the latter in myself.

'I'm tired of this,' I said. 'I'm not sure how much more I can endure.'

Alexia placed her hands on my shoulders. 'I know. Just be safe, Adaliah. Be safe. Promise me.' She moved a hand to her back and frowned.

'Are you unwell?' I asked, furrowing my brows at her.

'No, I feel fine.' She forced a smile. 'But I want this over and done with, too.'

'I guess it is nearly over, one way or another.'

'Then go, A'zyon Warrior. Let there be justice had for Ethaniel, Jeri, and your father. Let it all be finished.'

36
FACE TO FACE AT THE END

Through the gate I could see Cades Edangard himself on his pale horse, behind his army and on a small rise that lay in the distance. He was holding the Casmodian sword in one hand, but I had no idea where the other two were.

Jag Warhin was at the head of the army. Seeing him, I thought about how he had wrenched me from Bagred's back and dragged me to the dungeons in Liane. I had been so afraid. I barely felt different now. I chastised myself for not being braver—surely after all we had done, I could face him now. He was just one man after all, and I had defeated many.

He was rallying his soldiers, shouting with them and riding up and down the frontline with a vivacity Cades could only wish for. Their army chanted what I guessed to be a patriotic song, but our Targians stood still and silent.

I dug my heels into my black horse and rode out of the south-western gate of Jasteria. The Life Sword was shining so bright in my hand that it was almost impossible to look at directly.

I cantered through the men. Reaching the head of the army near Elhian and Darj, I paused and held my sword high. The Targians erupted with chants of 'Arjla divala!'

I was encouraged but then realised the full force of numbers that lay before us. Somewhere deep down I knew the truth.

We could not win.

Great Spirit . . . what do we do?

Cades had had the right to be smug—he'd known we'd push his men back and had been prepared to relinquish Targe's countryside in order to defeat us here. We had played into his hands. We were about to sacrifice ourselves on Cades' altar, to throw away all we had achieved so far. Surely the general knew this. How did he and Elhian think we could ride to victory here? What if I died without ever remembering? What if Alexia was killed, or her child?

What if I fail?

I didn't want to waste any time and knew the men were waiting for me. I lowered my sword until it pointed forward.

I will not be afraid.

I will not be afraid!

I kicked Bagred and charged. Some of the soldiers on Jasteria's walls behind me sounded the call to battle, and soon the battlefield swarmed with patriots.

I sought Jag out, flinging soldiers to the ground as I rode through the mesh of men. I held the Life Sword in my right hand and the tree-blade in my left, gripping Bagred with my legs.

A mounted soldier swooped at me from my right. I ducked just in time, impaling him with my sword. He was the first to fall on my blade. Before I could fight another, Jag appeared on my left. He knocked me off Bagred with an unexpected, forceful blow.

I lost consciousness as I hit the ground. I blinked and slowly pulled myself to my feet. Jag had ridden off, turned, and was now charging back at me. I evaded him with a sidestep but almost lost my footing.

The light in my sword lessened with my uncertainty but, when he charged at me again, I sliced his girth strap and the saddle came loose. He fell to the ground and rolled in the dirt.

He didn't get up at first. I used the moment to seek Elhian and Darj on the field. Darj was fighting two men, and a second later one fell down with an arrow protruding from his chest.

Both Darj and I glanced up at the wall where the queen stood, protecting us. It was the first arrow she had shot. It would also be her last.

Jag ran towards me, pounced, and pushed me to the ground with more force than I was expecting. He pinned my shoulders down. I kneed him hard in the stomach and forced him off me. Blood ran down my arm as I propped myself up. I tried to catch my breath. Luckily, Jag was also struggling to get up.

'Come on men!' I heard Hazaka say somewhere to my left. 'We're winning by far!'

One look around would have contradicted him.

I stood, but before I could face Jag again, the Casmodian king rode right past me to Hazaka. He stopped before him with a casual air.

The Jazmardian king took a few steps back on foot. I lifted my sword, preparing to rescue him. Jag rose to his knees. I pointed my other sword at him in case he became a concern.

'Don't worry,' Cades said to Hazaka with a wiry grin. 'I'm not going to kill you yet.'

Hazaka charged. He ducked Cades' overhead swipe and ran his sword into the pale horse. It reared and neighed before slamming into the snowy ground, Cades falling with him.

A circle formed around the fallen king as the soldiers backed up. Cades bent over his dead horse and then straightened with a sword in each hand and another sheathed by his thigh. He looked about for Hazaka, but the craven king had disappeared.

Jag used two hands to bring his sword down against me as if he were about to cut firewood. He was quick, and I barely got out of the way. The fast movement put pressure on my old leg wound, and my focus wavered.

I can't do this.

Yes, I can.

He struck at me again. I pushed him back into the dirt. I didn't follow this with a second attack but rather caught my breath and checked on the queen. I searched the walls of Jasteria once, twice, and then again. I couldn't see her. I waited for a second, hoping she would reappear. Perhaps she was just getting more arrows.

But she didn't come back.

My heart seemed to stop.

Where is she?

'It's all right,' Jag said. 'Brenna will be there to assist her.'

'Assist her?' I didn't know what he meant. Elhian had imprisoned Brenna in a cell when we brought her back to Jasteria . . . but with the battle taking up all of our attention, one of the Casmodians could have easily broken her out without us knowing. And if Brenna was anywhere near the queen, then I had to help. Jag lunged at me, and I sidestepped him. I took the chance to run through the soldiers to find Bagred and rode back towards Jasteria, Jag yelling after me.

Darj met me at the gate. He'd noticed the queen's disappearance as well. 'Elhian's holding the line,' he said as we rode into the city. There, the streets were busy with wounded soldiers, runners restocking archers, and one or two panic-stricken horses.

Darj and I searched the streets for Alexia but couldn't see any sign of her. We ran up the stairs to the wall and stopped almost every soldier to find out where she was until we were finally pointed in the right direction.

She'd moved around the wall away from the battlefront. We saw her white clothing behind four archers, who had formed a protective circle around her. She was slumped against the inner edge of the wall.

Darj pushed the archers out of the way. 'Alexia! Where are you injured?' He knelt beside her and checked her body for the wound he thought had felled her. I looked at her face and knew there was no wound.

Her eyes were full of pain as she groaned softly. 'It's my child,' she said. I grabbed her hand.

'What?' Darj asked.

'It's coming.'

'Coming? Now?'

'Yes, now!' She leant back into the wall with a less restrained groan.

Darj stuttered trying to get his words out. 'But it's early! We're in the middle of a battle! Can't you . . . can't you hang on or something?'

There was no mistaking her glare. 'Find Kadram,' she said. 'We must begin the decoy now.'

We sent a runner to Kadram and helped Alexia down to a small, hidden room at the bottom of Jasteria's keep, Darj supporting most of her weight as we walked. We came to a bed—he lifted her into his arms and gently lowered her onto it.

'This is not how royalty should be born,' he said, listening to the sounds of battle still storming outside the damp and dark room. The day was already drawing to an end and still no ground had been made or lost. I hoped Elhian could hold the frontline by himself.

Alexia gripped the side of the bed, and her quiet groans became more of a painful cry. She leant forward, all her muscles taut.

Darj paled at the sight. He ripped a piece of cloth off the bed linen, saturated it in the basin Alexia had asked us to bring, and went to her side. He plumped up the only pillow we had. With one hand on her shoulder, he coaxed her to lie down again. I continued to hold her hand. Darj dabbed her forehead with the cloth, trying to calm and cool her. A few minutes later, she grabbed his forearm and dug her nails in so hard Darj flinched.

'What do we do?' he asked me.

'What? I'm no more a midwife than you!'

The horrified look he gave me told me that was not the reassuring answer he had hoped for. 'But you're a woman!'

Alexia let out an agonising cry that made Darj shiver. 'Why is it that men get out of everything so easily?' she asked.

'Alexia—' Darj said as if he were about to give her a lecture.

'Ethaniel just gives me this and leaves!'

'I don't think he meant—'

'Shut up!'

I heard shouting outside and went to the single window to have a look. I could see the carriage Kadram was now driving out of the city. He careered out of the gate. A man on horseback sped after him, and then another.

'It's worked,' I said. 'Jag and Cades have gone after him. They think it's you, Alexia.'

She groaned as another wave of pain passed. I knew I was going to have to make a hard decision.

'Darj,' I said, pulling him aside. 'I have to go. Kadram told me . . . I have to be the one to end this.'

Darj gestured towards the queen. 'You can't leave me.'

'The baby won't come for a while yet—'

'I've known women to birth a child in two hours!'

'In which case it'll be over soon enough. Either way I'll get back as fast as I can.' Before he could argue any more, I said the same to Alexia, although I didn't tell her where I was going.

'Don't be long,' she said, 'please.'

I squeezed her hand and kissed her hot forehead, not telling her how I feared I might not make it back at all.

Bagred cut through the woods with primitive skill. I trusted his steps and kept my eyes on the two men just ahead of me until I decided to take a detour in the hopes of getting ahead of them. I had been riding for an hour and had only just come within range of them.

I heard the river before I saw it and was surprised to think we'd made it into the Valley of Kest so quickly. We were at a bend that came further east than the rest of the river. I turned Bagred back to the main path just as I came out of the woods and saw the carriage begin a risky crossing over the river. Jag and Cades were following.

Something was digging into my leg. I looked in my saddlebag and pulled out the small but sharp white stone I had collected all that time ago. I tucked it in behind my breastplate, the thoughts of Zavad's small face and Alexia's belief that Ru'ach would somehow use the stones giving me courage.

'The river takes sides,' I called out to the Casmodians once I was near. 'Are you sure it has taken yours?' I dismounted Bagred and walked into the cold water.

'Adaliah . . . ' Jag said, and then he sighed like I was nothing more than an inconvenience. 'Let's get it over with, then. Put down the Life Sword and fight me as an equal.'

'Put down your sword and you won't have to fight me at all,' I said.

'I've defeated you once before.'

I hesitated. 'I will put down the sword if Cades puts down the other three and promises not to interfere.'

Cades and Jag shared a knowing glance and they both dismounted. For whatever reason, Cades complied. I thrust the Life Sword into the ground beneath the rushing water and gripped the tree-blade, ready to fight.

I waited.

Cades copied me by jamming the other three swords into the river, too, forming a rough square. None of the stones glowed. After the carriage made it to the other side, there was only the sound of rushing water. Dusk was settling in and the quietness seemed strange, especially when I knew a battle was being fought not so far away.

I was ready when Jag ran at me. Our swords clashed once more in a series of quick movements as we lunged, parried, and tried to disarm each other. I nipped Jag's left upper arm and then his right, but he kept darting around me. I knew he was trying to wedge me in between himself and the Casmodian king. I kept pushing him upstream, hoping the torrent of water rushing against the back of his legs would make him lose balance. The water was deeper there as well, and Jag did slip backwards, but he kicked up as he fell, hitting my tender calf and causing me to fall, too. I went under the water and lost my sense of direction. I flailed my arms, trying to get a breath, but I couldn't get up.

Cades and Jag were holding me under.

I panicked and struggled. I felt a boot on my skull and a sharp stab on the edge of my thigh. I cried out in agony, but the water muffled it. Water began to slip inside my lungs. A rib cracked as they beat me and held me down, and soon I was faint with pain and lack of air.

Ru'ach . . .

This was not how I wanted it to end. I hadn't followed them to drown in the river. Even then I felt so disappointed. *I'm sorry Alexia.*

But Cades pulled me out of the water and held me suspended in the air. It flooded my lungs, giving some relief, but mostly I was heaving up blood and water. I could feel thick liquid running off me at numerous places and my body felt more broken than I thought possible.

I was convulsing when Cades dragged me to the shore and threw me down against a tree. Blood began to pool around me, and I couldn't move the way I wanted to. Cades raised the sword I'd carried and was about to bring it down on my neck.

I no longer cared. I was done.

It's over.

I can't do this.

'No!'

The voice across the river distracted the king.

Kadram had abandoned the carriage and was rushing back through the water. 'You have already killed her!' he called out. 'Have mercy!'

Both Cades and Jag scoffed at the old man. Jag put a boot across my shoulder blades, his weight crushing me. Cades strode towards Kadram and kneed him in the stomach. Kadram fell to his knees in the river, winded.

No . . .

'Your death and Adaliah's will merely serve as the beginning of the end for Targe,' Cades said. 'Only the queen will be remembered, and even then, only as one of my mistresses. The Targians will be a forgotten race.'

Cades pressed a knife into Kadram's throat.

No!

Suddenly, it was no longer about revenging my father, Ethaniel, or even Jeri, or helping Elhian and Alexia to their thrones. It was no longer about me regaining my memory. It wasn't about what we wanted—if it were, I would have given up then and there, or I wouldn't have followed the Casmodians there in the first place or fought in the battles I had.

It was about fighting back when evil reared its head. That was the only choice I had to make. The others were fighting a losing battle, and they would only survive if I succeeded in my task.

Covered in my own blood, I forced Jag off me and struggled to my feet. I used all I had left to retrieve my sword and stumble back into the river.

Kadram had told me what would need to happen long before. Now it was time.

'Stop her Jag!' I could hear the panic in Cades' voice and knew he'd realised what I was doing. 'Hurry! Stop her!'

Jag raised his sword and threw it.

I thrust my body towards the other swords. As I came down in the water, Jag's blade pierced me through my left shoulder.

I fell into the river between the four swords, still clinging to the tree-blade. The silver arrow that had opened the door to the tunnels fell away from the sword and sunk to the bottom, followed by the white stone that had slipped out of my breastplate. The engraving of my father's name in the tree-blade flashed and faded.

Each of the four stones in the swords glowed so brightly they filled the night sky with light. Then, it was as if the light burst, shaking the very ground and causing a great earthquake that rippled right across the land. Trees fell and dirt shifted as the earth rumbled like thunder.

Jag and Cades were knocked to the ground, unconscious.

The stones dropped from the swords.

The last flames of Hazaka's stone flickered, burning off the word *Despair*.

The Casmodian beam flashed upwards, *Fear* disappearing.

The final drops of elixir dripped down Alexia's blade, erasing the word *Hate*.

The Armoured Butterfly emerged and hovered while the four stones slowly fell towards the river.

As they touched the water, they turned into ordinary stones, smooth and beautiful.

And my body floated above them, the word *Death* finally melting away.

37
LIFE AND DEATH

Kadram would later tell me what happened next.

He waded through the water and withdrew the sword that pierced my shoulder, finding it more cumbersome than he'd anticipated. He said he never resented his age so much as when he tried to turn me face-up and drag me to the shore. He only managed to get my head out of the water and onto the bank. Then, he ran to Bagred. He searched through my saddlebags and threw various objects to the ground, digging deeper when he couldn't find what he wanted.

Finally, his fingertips scraped against something made of glass. He gripped the object with his frail fingers and brought out the vial with the strange green liquid Lezan had concocted all those months ago. *It's for you,* he'd said to me. I'd thought of that often but had never understood what he meant.

It lacks the last ingredient . . .

Kadram ran back into the river, to Alexia's sword, and captured the final drops of elixir that had yet to wash away. He shook it into the tonic and struggled to my side. I had no breath and the warmth in my body was fading, but he said he could tell something was different. The wound on my thigh . . . it was gone. He tilted my chin backwards and parted my bruised and cut lips. He tipped the vial up and poured the completed mixture into my mouth before closing my lips again.

Nothing.

Ru'ach, you are the king of life. Breathe life back into her, I beg you.

A cold breeze shifted through the trees. Kadram said Cades had woken and ridden away, presumably thinking his general was dead, but Jag was now stirring on the bank. On the other side of the river a stag came down to drink. It raised its heavy head and watched us intently while the breeze grew.

Kadram's attention was drawn back to the Armoured Butterfly, still hovering but beginning to fade. He said it landed on my chest. There, its wings opened and closed once or twice, and then it shattered into white dust.

Kadram held my hand and sat by me. He closed his eyes and continued to pray.

I thought I was in the afterlife when I first woke. There was no more pain—just a beautiful night sky full of stars. I felt relieved. I was sure it was all over. We might have lost, but at least I had done everything I could. I had tried. I had loved. I had sacrificed. There were no regrets, and I didn't have to fight any more.

Get up.

It was like someone had spoken in my mind.

Get up and live.

A gentle wind encircled me. I felt a warmth spread through my body. It was courage. It was love. It was life. My hand gripped Kadram's. I turned my head, trying to remember where I was.

I'm alive.

I looked at my friend and rescuer.

'The Great Spirit is certainly on your side,' he said with a nervous laugh.

My wounds had healed, leaving nothing but a small trace of blood and dirt on my skin.

I didn't speak—I couldn't. Something else was happening. My mind . . . I fell to the ground, gripping my head. My mind raced with a rush of fragmented memories. They whirled around and around. I cried out. I could feel myself going mad but, before I did, Kadram grabbed my forearm and pulled me into a sitting position.

'He killed my father!' I said, hot tears filling my eyes as the memories came rushing back. 'Jag stabbed him again and again! And poor little Jeri . . . Ethaniel! Cades, he . . . And prison . . . They locked me in a tiny black cell, for weeks . . . There was no light . . . I couldn't even stretch out my legs! I turned wild and broke the door and escaped to Kest River, but they followed me!' I let out a yell that bordered on the hysterical. 'I remember! I remember it all!'

Further up, I saw Jag struggling to his feet and focusing on me.

I was filled with such anger there was no longer any room for fear.

He took a step backwards, away from me. I had no sword, but I began to run at him.

Never before had I seen the fear in his face that I was now witnessing. He was trembling before me. He had always run away in tight situations, but now he was fastened to the ground. I was no longer afraid of him. My feet thudded on the dirt as I closed the gap between us. I reached down to my boot and pulled out my dagger.

'You killed them!' I yelled.

He shook his head like he didn't understand. A wild and dreadful sound shot out of his mouth, like a deer about to die. He pulled a small knife out of his shirt and tried to raise it, but it slipped from his hands and he fumbled after it.

He bent down, and his fingers brushed against his knife just as I reached him and kicked his hand away.

He straightened and looked up at me with hatred. I didn't hesitate. I thrust my dagger into his chest.

His whole body stiffened from the impact. He blinked at me, and fell forward.

He was dead before he hit the ground.

I rolled him over and withdrew the dagger. I walked back to the tree I had been thrown against and impelled the dagger into its trunk. There it would stay for years to come. I shivered, and my eyes filled with tears. I felt one weight lifting off and another falling on me at the same time. It overwhelmed me, and I slipped to my knees.

Kadram ran over and bent down in front of me. He touched my cheek. 'Now is not the time to grieve the ones you have lost,' he said. 'Now is not the time to try and make sense of it all.'

I was shaking, but I struggled to my feet.

I left Kadram and rode back towards Jasteria, hunting Cades. Jag was dead, and Cades would soon follow. I was determined to get back to Alexia. I feared Cades would beat me to it and that even now we would suffer great loss. I remembered what she'd read from the Cazinian Papers: *The dragon, who will deceive the world, will find the woman with the twelve stars in the dark. There, his anger will be quenched.* I dreaded to think what that could mean.

The night was beginning to feel like an endless blanket of darkness but, before long, I found myself back at the battlefield of Jasteria.

But there was no more fighting. The battle had stopped.

'What happened?' I asked one of the soldiers.

'We were victorious,' he said. There was no joy in his voice though, only shock. 'Every man who did not have a white stone fell down in the earthquake and died.'

My mouth dropped as I looked across the battlefield again—Cades' entire army, including the Jazmardians who had fought for him, were lying in the grass like they were asleep. I couldn't even comprehend how it had happened.

It's a miracle, I thought, giving a thankful glance upwards. *The white stones were our protection. Ru'ach blessed them when Alexia asked him for help.*

'Where is the prince?' I asked.

'Inside the keep.'

I rode into the city for a second time—stones and other debris littered the road—and ran towards the room where I had left Alexia.

I could hear a lot of yelling before I even got to the room and knew Cades had found my cousin. Alexia still sounded like she was in pain, her labour clearly ongoing.

I tried to get into the room, but something was keeping the door shut.

'I only came to help!' I heard a girl's voice say inside. It was Brenna.

'Stay away from her.' Darj's voice was dangerous. Desperate.

I pushed against the door with all my strength. I did it again, but someone opened it, and I went crashing to the ground at the foot of Alexia's bed.

I turned and froze—Cades had a sword at my throat. 'Stay down,' he said. 'I don't care!' That was directed at Brenna. 'You weren't supposed to come until much later!'

'I was doing your bidding, Your Majesty. You know how much I hate her, how much I want revenge for her hardheartedness!'

'I do my own bidding.' He moved the blade from me and flicked it. Brenna fell to the ground and died not an arm's length from me.

I heard Alexia's breathing quicken but, before I could move, Cades' bloodied sword point was back at my throat. I didn't dare challenge him from such a position. With one flick, I, too, could be dead, and there were no living waters nearby to save me now.

'What are you going to do now?' Darj yelled at the king. He sounded like he was at the end of his strength. Alexia let out a tired but fretful cry that made both Darj and Cades return their attention to her. 'It's coming,' Darj said. 'It's crowning.'

Cades seemed to forget about me—he walked hungrily to Alexia and waited for the child to be born.

One of the windows opened and a breeze filtered through the room.

Alexia gave one final, groan-filled push, and the room filled with the sound of a newborn's cry. She let out a sob as Darj cut the cord and wrapped the crying child in what used to be bed linen.

Cades stepped towards them. Alexia cried out in distress.

I grabbed desperately at his foot, but he kicked me away. I crawled onto my knees and tried again but received a blow to the face and fell back.

Darj shielded the baby in his arms but was backed into a corner without a weapon. Cades moved closer with a vile grin. 'Come, my child, let me make an example out of you for your mother.' He outstretched his hands to take it.

But then, his body heaved forward. His old, fading eyes widened as he gulped. I saw the glimmer of metal poking out under his rib cage.

His body shook again, and the glimmer became a distinct point of a sword. Then the sword was withdrawn, and Cades fell down to the ground. His head rolled to one side and his eyes settled on me before they froze in death.

Behind him stood his son, Elhian.

I don't know how long the four of us were silent. For an eternity there was only our short breaths, our sobs, our heartbeats.

Elhian's face was white as he stared down at his father's body. 'It's over,' he said, like he could hardly comprehend what the words meant. He dropped his sword and sunk to his knees. 'It's finished.' Tears ran down his face. I put my hand on his arm. I felt such admiration for him, and such pity.

'Thank you,' Darj said, meeting his eyes.

Unable to keep propping herself, Alexia fell back on the bed in an exhausted heap. I hurried to her side and pulled a blanket up over her, wishing we had another to keep her warm. I put my shaking hand over hers. Her skin was cold and clammy. 'Are you all right?'

'No,' she said softly, tears dampening her cheeks.

'Your child is safe,' Elhian said, sounding more like himself.

'And healthy and lovely,' Darj said. He placed the small babe in her arms. 'You're a mother again.'

Alexia peered down at the little face and stroked the dark downy hair with a finger. 'My child . . . ' She looked up at Darj expectantly.

Even his eyes were red with tears now. 'You have a daughter, Alexia,' he said. 'You have a beautiful daughter.'

38
REMEMBERING

With mother and child soon sleeping and Darj watching over them, I went to find Elhian. He had carried Cades' and Brenna's bodies out of the room but hadn't returned.

Although it was night time, the moon was so full and bright it was hiding some of the stars near it. The battlefield ahead of me was drenched in a milky light and looked like it was covered with fireflies. In reality it was filled with men carrying torches.

I borrowed one and found Elhian on the field kneeling next to someone. Xander and Raggin stood either side of him with solemn expressions as they, too, looked down on the fallen soldier.

It was Naclen Caylith, and he had a gaping wound in the middle of his torso.

The youth gripped Elhian's hand. 'Targe . . . Targe is ours?' he asked. He looked cold to touch.

Elhian forced a smile. 'The queen will be very proud of you.'

'Are . . . are you?'

'Yes, I am,' Elhian said. 'You will be remembered with honour.'

Naclen's body shuddered. I think he was trying to say something else, but his grip slackened, his breathing slowed, and he died on the battlefield as so many others had.

Elhian reached over and closed the youth's eyes. He folded Naclen's hands over each other and we stayed by him for a few minutes more. 'He was fifteen,' Elhian whispered.

I could see the Jazmardians picking up their dead and piling them up to the side. They were even collecting the ones who had fought for Cades. Hazaka was standing near them, watching on with an uncharacteristic sombreness.

'You can take him,' Elhian said to Xander and Raggin. The two of them carefully lifted Naclen up and carried him away.

Elhian watched them go and then gripped his stomach. He doubled over as he tried to keep his stomach contents inside and groaned like he was in pain, but the wave of sickness seemed to pass this time, and he straightened again. His face was ashen when he turned back to me. 'I thought . . . Cades told me you were dead.'

I shook my head with a faint smile. 'He was wrong before, and he's wrong again.'

Elhian was shivering with shock and exhaustion and still looked like he could vomit at any second.

'Jag is dead,' I said. 'The river cleansed the swords.'

'Ru'ach did, I think. They say he came from the river and gave it life, remember. But tell me what happened.'

'You and Alexia both mentioned that the swords could be used for good or evil. Someone could misuse the sword of faith for fear, hope for despair, and so on. Remember?'

'Yes . . . '

'That evil had to be washed away. After visiting Cades in prison, before we left to reclaim the Targian countryside, Kadram asked to speak to me alone. He told me my father melted down the Medallion of Courage—the one with the butterfly engraved in it and the power to cleanse the four swords. Kadram said my father had made something less conspicuous out of it and hidden it somewhere, but no one, not even Kadram, knew where. Then, I figured it out. It was the silver arrow in the tree-blade, Elhian, the piece that got us into the tunnels. And when reunited with the river at the same time as the swords . . . they were cleansed. The swords can no longer be used for evil. They can only respond to good now.'

Elhian shook his head as he tried to take it in, but I had more to tell him.

'I remember.'

He knew what I meant straight away. 'What? H-how?'

'Kadram told me that the river healed my wounds, but it was the tonic Lezan made for me before he died that freed my mind, though only because Kadram saved the last drops of the elixir from Alexia's sword and gave it to me before it washed away . . . And then, the Armoured Butterfly sacrificed itself to bring me back to life . . . Kadram had said before that the final message it would carry was that when all is lost, there is still hope. Even though there is death, there is life. Always life.'

'And?' He obviously knew I had more to say and was bracing himself for it.

'I remember, Elhian. I remember us. I remember your marriage proposal at Alexia's birthday ball in Liane. I remember saying yes and never feeling happier!'

'And then you will also remember us keeping it a secret from everyone except Alexia and Ethaniel, and then me telling my father with the hope of him calling off his attack on Targe, and then him being disgusted and tracking you down and beating you and imprisoning you and killing you like he did my mother . . . '

I placed a finger on his lips. 'Alexia said I would laugh to think I had ever doubted you, and she was right. Despite everything, I began to love you all over again, even though I remembered nothing of what we had before. I am still yours, Elhian. Only yours.'

He stared at me with tired red eyes as if waiting for a darker reality to face him. I knew now he had spent months loving me on his own and had probably not even allowed himself to believe this moment would come.

'Why didn't you tell me?' I asked.

He stroked back my hair. 'You were already so confused—how do you think you would have reacted? It would have put even more pressure on you, and I didn't want you to feel you owed me or had to love me. I told the others to keep it a secret, too. I knew that if you did care . . . you would remember it.'

'Well, not for the first time, you were right.'

He finally smiled. 'I bet those are words I won't hear very often.'

I laughed. 'Then you better enjoy it while you can.'

His smile widened as he leant down and pressed his lips against mine.

39
REWARDED

The sun was shining in Kest when Darj thrust the green Targian banner into the ground, and Xander blew a horn. The exiles ahead of us stopped what they were doing, like they could hardly believe what they were hearing.

Xander blew the horn again. The Targian call of victory.

They turned and saw us—the small group of warriors returned to call them home.

A little boy ran out from the people. 'Adaliah!' he called. 'Adaliah!' He dropped the bucket of water he was carrying and ran towards me at full speed.

'Zavad.' I dismounted Bagred and held my arms out to him. He rushed into them. 'I'm so glad you're safe,' I said, holding him close. 'And I think you're taller.'

'Soon I'll be as tall as you.' He gave me a grin and ran over to Darj, who leant down and pulled him up into the saddle with him. Xander blew the horn for a third and last time. The people were gathering around us and there was an excited hum in the air. 'Have we won?' Zavad asked.

Darj smiled and turned to address the people. 'Targe has been victorious!'

A cheer rose among the people. Some ran to their shelters to get ready to leave. Others stood stunned, unable to comprehend it.

'And you, my boy,' Darj said to Zavad, 'Ru'ach used your white stones to save our men. I am very, very proud of you.'

Zavad beamed. 'My father always said that great castles are made out of many little stones, but that together they can withstand all the forces of evil.'

'Your father was a wise man,' Darj said.

'Are you ready to come home?' I asked.

Zavad nodded eagerly and got down to help his family pack.

Back in Jasteria, I held the little princess as her mother slept, now in the more comfortable chambers she'd had in the top of the keep. I gazed out the window. 'Look, some of the people are coming home already.' The small girl in my arms blinked. 'Don't worry, we'll get you to your palace soon.'

'Has the queen risen yet?' Darj asked, peeking around the door.

I shook my head but gestured for him to come in.

'How is our little princess?' He touched her tiny cheek with his finger.

'Very well, though I think she'll be hungry again soon.' We turned and looked at Alexia, who had barely moved since falling asleep.

'You know,' Darj said, 'of all the battles I've fought and problems I've faced, getting this girl born was the most traumatic. And yet, the most wonderful as well.'

The little girl began to cry. She clenched her hands. I shifted her over my shoulder and tried to comfort her, wanting to give Alexia as much time to sleep as possible. But it was too late—she woke and opened her arms for her daughter.

'Come here, darling,' she said with a yawn. 'I had a dream about you and your father.'

'What did he say?' I asked, handing her daughter to her.

'How beautiful she is, how proud he was. I told him I've decided to call her after his mother.'

'Eva,' I said approvingly, relishing my ability to remember again.

'That's perfect,' Darj said.

Eva started crying again, and Alexia began to unbutton her clothes to suckle her.

'Well . . . ' Darj said. 'I'd better . . . ' He pointed over his shoulder and stepped back until he reached the door. He opened his mouth to say something, but then just gave a quick bow and left.

Alexia and I shared a smile. 'It's nice to know there are still some things that can shy even a hardened general,' she said, winking at me.

I later found him walking towards Raggin and Xander. Men surrounded them. I pushed my way through the crowd and followed Darj to Xander, who was leaning over some parchment. Raggin was arguing with someone.

Darj interrupted by holding his hand out to him. 'Well Raggin, I believe I won the bet.'

'You and half this kingdom.' He thrust two coins into Darj's hand. 'What? Is that it?'

'It's more than what you had to start with.'

'What's the matter with him?' I asked Xander.

'He has to give his commission to the poor after all, by order of the queen, who called him out on his little enterprise.'

Darj laughed but stopped at Raggin's glare.

Over the next few weeks, the Targian people returned to their hometowns. Many families were reunited; others never would be. Some went home to find their houses burnt, broken, collapsed, or all three. Some found everything in order as if there had never been a war.

In Jasteria, Darj organised a division of men under Kadram's leadership to fix Liane and its palace as much as possible before the queen's return, something we talked about daily. Part of his instructions was to make sure Targians filled the city once again and that the windows were flung open to the warming spring air. He told the men to polish the throne, take down the blue flags and replace them with Targian ensigns.

He later received a letter from Kadram describing how the royal jewels and artefacts had been strewn through the palace, but made it clear they were now returned to their proper place. He said they had restored the royal cot and placed it ready in Alexia's chambers. They had also burnt the sheets Cades had slept between.

Most importantly, the royal carriage had been sent for us.

It was time to go home.

Alexia had warned me that the streets would be filled with people, but I still wasn't prepared for the honour they showed us when we rode victorious through the city gate.

Trumpets were sounding but even they were drowned out by the crowd's cheer. Ahead of us was a sea of green banners and flags—the people waving them against the sky.

Darj was riding first, looking handsome and proud in his full general's uniform. An ornate sword was sheathed by his side and he wore a green sash around his waist. Elhian and I rode behind him, the prince dressed in Casmodian blue while I wore a lavish mauve dress with a cloak that draped right over Bagred's back. On my head was the Kestian circlet once more, which Elhian had taken with him from the Keep. I tried to remind myself that I was not just returning as their A'zyon Warrior, but as Lady Adaliah Elryane as well. Sheathed on Bagred was the Life Sword, which had been collected from the river along with the others.

Behind us was the queen's carriage, and following her were our soldiers and Jazmardian allies, King Hazaka included. He was once again greeting the people with boyish waves.

It took us an hour to reach the palace. The people followed us there and crowded into the forecourt. Kadram was waiting for us on the palace steps where the carriage came to a halt. Elhian, Darj, and I dismounted. The crowd had been singing and cheering, but they fell silent as twelve long golden trumpets sounded.

A herald moved to the carriage door. 'Her Most Glorious Majesty Queen Alexia of Targe, and Her Royal Highness the Crown Princess Eva!'

The crowd erupted with cheers that grew louder as the door opened. The queen, holding her daughter close, stepped outside.

Her Majesty wore a white gown with a long and magnificent green cloak pouring out behind her, fastened with a diamond brooch on her right shoulder. White gloves stretched up above her elbows. Her dark hair was curled and pinned back over her cloak with a shimmering clasp that accented her jewellery.

'She is captivating.' It was Darj's words and my sentiment.

Kadram approached her with the Targian crown and sceptre on a pillow edged with gold cord. He bowed before her.

Alexia passed Eva to one of the five maids who had come to wait on her. She faced Kadram again and bent down.

He placed the crown on her head. Its green emeralds and diamonds shone on gold strands that were interwoven as thick, glimmering threads. With twelve gold stars raised on points, I knew it was heavy but also magnificent. The sceptre that lay beside it was solid gold and also decorated with priceless gems. Words were engraved around the tip in ancient Targian: 'Remember those who died, but fight for those who live'. Alexia had told me it was something King Amaz often quoted to her, and that that was what my father had engraved above his tunnel doors.

She straightened and Kadram handed her the sceptre. 'Blessings upon the queen!' he shouted.

'Blessings upon the queen!' the people echoed.

Kadram stepped to the side, and Alexia began her walk up the carpet like the stately monarch she was. The others and I followed her in procession. When we reached the top of the stairs just outside the great door, we turned to wave to the people once more. Above us, the royal ensign was raised. The queen was in residence once more.

Full of emotion, I watched as Her Majesty took her rightful place on the throne in a hall full of people. Darj, Elhian, and I were now the only ones standing directly before her, while the maid who held Eva remained nearby.

'Your Majesty,' Darj said, moving forward to begin the formal and most important part of our return. 'The war is ended and won.'

'Then I will make all things new so that everyone in and beyond my realm can live a life of peace,' Alexia said.

'Casmodia has been defeated and is now under your rule,' Darj said, 'unless you choose another to rule over it in your stead.'

'I choose His Royal Highness Prince Elhian Jacob Edangard, the rightful King of Casmodia. Please step forward, your highness.'

Elhian glanced at me with an expression that conveyed mixed emotions. I knew it was what he wanted, but he hadn't expected to have to kill his father to get it. It troubled him; I could see it in his face. I gave him what I hoped was an encouraging look and watched as he walked up the steps. He knelt before the queen while Kadram came forward with the Casmodian crown, which had been salvaged from Cades' body. On the pillow with it was a small bowl.

Alexia stood, took the crown and held it above Elhian's head. Then, she spoke in a commanding voice. 'Do you promise to uphold the ideals of a world free from the bondage of death and pain, to direct your kingdom under the gentle guidance of Ru'ach, the Great Spirit that gives life to all, to protect those who cannot protect themselves, and to build your kingdom as with the loving care of a father?'

'I do so promise.'

Alexia placed the crown on his head. She dipped her finger into the oil that was in the bowl and drew a line with it on his forehead. 'Then rise, King Elhian of Casmodia. May you be held to your oath by Ru'ach himself, the Great Spirit that connects us all.'

Elhian bowed and kissed her hand. Then, he turned back to the crowd.

'Blessings upon the king!' Raggin called.

'Blessings upon the king!' I echoed with the people.

Elhian swallowed and met my eyes. Neither of us could smile, but we understood each other and that was enough. He descended the stairs and came and stood by me once more.

'There are those of us here who are honoured and blessed to be the monarchs of the kingdoms of the Rhea Lands,' Alexia said to us all, still standing. 'King Elhian's name is now amongst those. Yet, it is the defenders of the people who remind us all of what matters most—fighting not for glory or gain, but to ensure that love, life and all that is good prevails. That is the creed of Targe.' She paused. 'General Darj Naythan Ryder,' she called. The man in question looked up at her, surprised like the rest of us. This was not part of the original plan. 'Come forward.'

Darj walked up the steps before her and bowed.

'For your services to my kingdom, my family, and me, I honour you with the Order of Amathea.' Kadram passed her a gold star brooch embedded with jewels, which she pinned on Darj's chest. He stood and could hardly look at her.

I was so touched that she had chosen to surprise him with this. Darj had saved our lives more than once. I would never forget it, and I knew Alexia would not either.

She nodded her head as an indication for him to descend.

'Lady Adaliah Clair Elryane,' Alexia now called.

I blinked at her. Surely she was not expecting to honour me in the same way. Elhian's expression told me he knew nothing.

I walked to the throne and curtsied before her.

'Your ladyship,' she said, 'for your heroism on the battlefield, your fearlessness in the midst of confusion, and for giving us all the gift of faith, hope, love, and life, I honour you with the Order of Jovan.' She placed a necklace of gold stars around my neck, the diamond star pendant in the middle similarly styled to her own brooch. 'Targe thanks you.' I stood, feeling humbled and wondering if she had forgotten the fear and doubt that had marked my experience more than any valour she spoke of now. She reached forward and took my hand, as if reading my thoughts. 'And so do I,' she added in a whisper.

40
A STEP FORWARD

I sat alone on a stone bench under a large oak tree and gazed at what stars I could see between the branches above. I could hear the music and laughter coming from the palace forecourt where the celebrations were taking place. I had danced for most of the night but now needed a minute alone. Having my memory returned meant the nightmares, fear, and confusion had all stopped but, even now, it was a lot to piece to together, a lot to try and take in.

It was my turn to grieve now.

I missed my father the most and longed for his counsel. But at least I could see him in my mind's eye again, teaching me, training me, and playing games with me as well. He taught me not only to survive but also to live well. Now that the war was over, that was all I wanted to do. But so many had died, including those I loved. I felt an intense guilt at the thought of enjoying my life without them.

I wiped away a few stray tears and realised that all this time I had been afraid of becoming something I wasn't, or of never remembering who I truly was. But the person I had been throughout the war was just the same as the person I was now. My true identity had never left me just as Darj had told me all those months ago. I had learnt to love and trust the same people I had before. I'd kept my faith. Cades had stolen my mind, but not my heart.

And yet, it didn't make me feel any better. No matter who I was, the harm was just as real.

I could hear Alexia humming nearby. I saw her walking along the path, holding Eva against her heart and gazing at her like she was the most beautiful thing she'd ever seen.

'What will you do when she's too old to cuddle?' I called out to her.

Alexia looked around and smiled when she saw me. 'She will never be too old for that, I hope.' She took a seat beside me. 'She is the loveliest baby I've ever known.'

'She seems to have a calming effect on you.'

'I guess she does, yes. When I'm holding her, I feel like the rest of my family is with me, too.' Eva slept in her mother's arms with an open mouth.

'You do me great honour,' I said, 'in giving her my name to bear along with other such women.'

Alexia had formally named her daughter Eva Jenethea Adaliah Elryane. 'It seemed only natural for your name to be with her grandmothers'. They were strong women, elegant and steadfast, just as you are.'

'You knew I'd have to cleanse the evil in the swords, didn't you? When you were first telling me about the Ordained, and how the Keeper of Kest had the medallion that could alter the swords . . .'

She nodded slowly. 'I knew that Lezan was right—the evil had to be destroyed. I sensed you were the one to do it, but you'd already gone through so much. I didn't want to burden you with such a responsibility. I'm sorry if my silence let you down.'

I reached for her hand and opened my mouth to reply but was interrupted.

'Is it custom for Targian royalty to hide from their own celebrations?' Elhian asked as he appeared up the path.

Alexia and I laughed. 'Only when there are outspoken kings present,' Alexia said.

'Are you referring to myself or Hazaka?'

Alexia smiled mysteriously. 'I suppose I should get back,' she said. She stood and moved Eva from the cradle of her left arm to her right. 'Don't be too long. I will announce your engagement soon.'

Elhian sat next to me in her place. 'The greatest trial that child will face will be too much love,' he said as we watched the queen walk away.

'Yes. I fear Alexia will never let her go. She still mourns for Ethaniel and Jeri you know—at night, when she thinks we're asleep. I can hear her tears through my own.'

Elhian put an arm around me, and we sat in silence for a few minutes.

'You shall be a good king,' I said. 'I'm very proud of you.'

He kissed me, and I felt like the young girl I was again, though not yet washed clean of war. 'So long as I can enjoy just being myself with you.'

'There's a long way to go before Jazmarda will be united again,' Kadram was saying to Hazaka the next day when I joined them in the palace courtyard.

'Those who fought for Cades are coming home with me.'

'Yes, they can see clearly again.'

Hazaka turned to me. 'How were you able to save us?'

I didn't know how to explain it. For me, it had simply been a task to complete, but how and why it had worked I couldn't say. 'Ru'ach was on our side,' I said in the end, with a smile. 'He always was, I think. Darj was right. I felt it in my heart.'

'Yes, and she was willing to give her life for it, to fight for good,' Kadram said. 'The Jazmardians back then, and Cades now—they wanted the swords for power and to conquer. They forfeited the Great Spirit's blessing in their greed. They used the swords for all the wrong reasons. A sacrifice had to be made for it all to be set back in order.'

'I suppose the old wives will now say that Cazine is appeased, and the valley no longer haunted,' Hazaka said, rolling his eyes.

'Who knows what they will say,' Kadram said.

The three of us walked down to Hazaka's army, which was waiting for him just outside the palace with Alexia, Darj, and Elhian.

'Time for me to go home,' Hazaka said to them. He mounted his horse and tugged at his cloak to ensure it fell correctly. 'But Alexia— what do you think? My son . . . your daughter . . . ?'

Alexia humoured him with a smile. 'My daughter shall marry a man of her own choosing.'

'Hmmm . . . Well, any time you need me to come and rescue your kingdom again—'

'Hazaka,' I said, seeing the instant irritation in Alexia's face, 'your services have been invaluable. Have a safe trip home.'

Hazaka rode away, and Elhian held Kadram's horse for him while he mounted.

'I will never forget your services to Casmodia,' Elhian said, 'nor that of your brother. He was truly an honourable man.'

'He saw something in you—a good man, something I think you are only just beginning to see yourself.' Kadram winked at him. 'Darj?' The general looked up. 'Elhian mentioned that Cades spoke of the

Zalems. You know about them, don't you?' Darj gave a small nod, his expression a little concerned. Kadram, seeing that he understood, gave a nod as well. 'Be vigilant, always.'

Elhian and I began to talk of our plans for Casmodia as we wandered the gallery of Liane Palace, staring up at the portraits of the Targian kings and queens of old. Some were well known; others would have been forgotten if it were not for the tenacity of old legends.

Would we be remembered? For Elhian, many of his men still saw him as a traitor, not a saviour. I watched as he stopped and looked at the portrait of King Amaz. Now that I could remember, I knew that such a king would remain in people's hearts for all eternity.

To add to Elhian's troubles, news had come to us that Semanez had been destroyed beyond repair. It had collapsed under an avalanche caused by the great earthquake I had caused at Kest River. The main line of ruin had roughly followed the Casmodian border all the way to its capital. Elhian's home city and the seat of the Casmodian monarchy were gone.

'Where will you reside now?' I asked.

'I've been thinking about that,' he said. 'There is a castle in Tiathi—I think I'll take that as my home. It'll remind me of the battle that took place nearby, the first victory we had against Cades. It is also close to the border of Targe, and therefore close to my allies.'

He kept walking, but I stopped and looked out a window. I leant out the arch and into the warm, clean air. Down in the garden, Darj was teaching Zavad to fight. The boy held a wooden sword that was almost as tall as him, but he eagerly obeyed every instruction. Not too far off, Raggin and Xander were arguing over something and a brawl would have ensued had Alexia not just come out of the palace with Eva. Raggin and Xander suddenly became polite and civil.

'Elhian?' I called, and he walked back to me. 'I do love you, and I do want to marry you, but I don't think I'm ready to move to Casmodia just yet.'

'Is it because of Alexia?'

'I don't want her to be alone, not after everything she's been through. But it's more than that . . . There's my grief as well as yours. I have so much to process, so much to work through. So do you. We're still so young, and we've lost our childhoods to war and death. I think we both need time to heal before we start our lives together.'

He took my hand, and I knew by the way he looked down, he was disappointed. 'I need you, too, you know.' I opened my mouth, but he put a finger on my lips. 'Sorry. It's just that none of this is how I wanted our lives to go. I'm scared, Adaliah. I never thought this is how I would become king. But you are right. I will focus on rebuilding Casmodia, and we will have our wedding when we're both ready.'

I kissed his cheek. 'I love you.'

Away from the plains of Targe, the mysterious Valley of Kest became peaceful and beautiful once more. I returned to visit what was now my Keep, and stopped Bagred by the river on the way. After a few days of rain, it was noisy, fast, and rippling white. I cupped the water in my hand and drank, cherishing each mouthful. I walked through the same shallows I'd first woken in and paused to feel the weight of change. It still hurt to remember the agony of the last nine months. I wasn't ready to relive it yet, even in my memories. Instead, I looked at the tree where I'd found the sword engraved with my father's name. I'd put it there myself, just before my hunters had reached and attacked me. In leaving it there, I'd saved more than I'd realised.

Yet, I felt no glory, not even pride. Jeri, Ethaniel, my father . . . The price of war had been far too high.

I watched the river flowing where the four stones had fallen, now plain rocks with no more purpose than those around them. Over the years, with rain and drought, the river's path would alter and turn, and the stag that walked towards me now would find its home changed like the rest of us.

A flash of purple light flittered behind a tree. I blinked and stared at the tree, waiting for it to reappear. When it didn't, I decided with a smile that it must have been my imagination. I turned to Bagred, slipped my boot into the stirrup and lifted myself up. Taking one last look at the river, I rode on.

Enjoy this sneak peek of

THE ZALEM CRISIS
BY TRUDY ADAMS

THE ARMOURED BUTTERFLY
BOOK TWO

PROLOGUE

Dead will the boy be if the lady does not abstain.

Dead will the lady be if her dear king does not pay.

Dead will the ghosts be if the general does not recall.

Dead will one and all be if Queen Targe does not obey.

The paper in my hands was old, and the words were fading. The edges had crumbled over time, and it smelt like leather. That was all I noticed at first when I found the note lying on the King of Casmodia's throne in Tiathi. It had been tied with a black ribbon, and someone must have delivered it in the night.

I read the words again.

Dead ... Dead ... Dead ... Dead ...

'Elhian? Elhian!'

1
RETURN TO LIANE

If you reach the small hill to the north of Liane before midday, before the shadows are stretched by a falling sun, you can see the city glistening ahead of you like a pearl. In the spring, the first things you notice are the sweeping meadows, luscious farms, and vast King River, all teeming with life and rejoicing at the end of winter. The meadows dress themselves in tiny flowers that afford a purple lustre known as the Royal Carpet, which invites you to the Targian capital like you're a long-lost friend.

Liane itself spreads out in an easy manner. It rests below its hilltop palace in the same way a youngster burrows into its mother. There's something about it that invites you closer, that offers you peace and safety within its walls.

'Adaliah?'

I turned at the sound of my name and watched as the King of Casmodia rode towards me on his white horse, Leuk.

'I thought you said you could keep up!'

Elhian Edangard smiled. 'The carriage is ahead of us. That last diversion cost us more time than you said it would.'

'Well, it's been a while since I've travelled through this countryside.' I leant down to stroke my horse's neck. Bagred was turning his ears, listening to the woods. 'I want to see as much of it as I can.'

Elhian peered at Liane. It compared to our home, Tiathi, like gold to copper. 'Do you miss it?'

'A little, but my real home is Kest, not Liane; and even though I lived there, it's not the city I miss so much as my cousin. The cousin I had before Ethaniel's and Jeri's deaths, that is.'

'You don't think she's still grieving, do you?'

'No, it's just that her letters to me are always void of emotion, like she's forgotten how to feel. Now we need her counsel, and I'm worried.'

'Worried about her—or the note?' Elhian asked.

I didn't answer. Leaves were moving on the trees, but there was no wind.

A man jumped out of one and pushed Elhian from his saddle. He tried to pin Elhian to the ground, but Elhian reached for a rock, struck it against the side of the man's head, and pulled out a dagger from his boot. I dismounted Bagred, sword in hand, but Elhian thrust his dagger into the man's stomach first. He shoved the man off him. Bleeding, the man pulled himself to his knees and screeched at Elhian like a wild animal. I cringed and stepped back, taking in his black armour and the patch of blood on the side of his head. He looked hungry and thin, but it was something in his eyes that convinced me he was mad.

'The traitor must die!' he yelled. His voice was husky and tense, like his throat was half the size it needed to be. 'The High Zalem will prevail!' He pulled Elhian's dagger out of his stomach and attempted to stand. He shrieked again, so piercingly I felt compelled to cover my ears. I kicked him backward. He collapsed into the dirt, turned to Elhian with a snarl, and died with it set on his face.

Elhian looked at me. I opened my mouth but didn't know what to say. Elhian poked the man, testing for a response. Assured that he was in fact lifeless, Elhian proceeded to search the man's pockets.

'Do you think it was one of his kind that left the note?' I asked.

'Perhaps.' He pulled out some coins from the man's front pocket and turned them over between his fingers. 'I don't recognise these . . . but they look ancient.' He held one up. There was a symbol pressed into the gold—a crescent moon overlaid with an eye. I wasn't sure about the eye, but the crescent moon was the symbol of Anash, the great dark spirit that was said to linger in the night and bring torment to mankind. He was known as the invisible Prince of Death; those who worshipped him were usually in pursuit of great power. Elhian kept the coin and left the others scattered over the man's chest.

I looked out at Liane again. The view no longer seemed as beautiful, nor the sun as warm.

We arrived at Liane Palace a few hours later. The Casmodian carriage brought us into the courtyard while a servant took our horses to the queen's stables by a private route. People had gathered to welcome us. They cheered when Elhian stepped out of the carriage door. I mused with a smile that although he was the King of Casmodia, he was more appreciated in Targe than at home. In Targe, he was the slayer of Cades, the kingdom's foremost enemy. To many in Casmodia, he was still just the murderer of their former king.

I heard the people's cheers rise as Elhian reached back towards me with an open hand. Taking it, I stepped out to a warm reception and waved to the sea of smiles as the Queen of Casmodia for the first time.

Casmodia was an uneasy kingdom for some time after Cades' death. Elhian had to deal with several men in high positions who openly disputed his right to the throne. I supported him as much as I could, but my time was stretched between him in Casmodia, Alexia in Targe, and the Keep in Kest.

Still officially the Keeper of Kest, I had to play my part in maintaining peace between Jazmarda, Casmodia, and Targe. I was no longer able to reside at the Keep, though, so Alexia and I installed a contingent of men and a trusted captain there to act as steward—Darack Symes. Without the Armoured Butterfly, messages were sent to Liane Palace the traditional way—on horseback. I committed to travelling to the Keep every three months to keep a check on things. The commitment continued after I married Elhian and made my home in Tiathi and would last until Alexia had a second child and they were of age.

In the meantime, Elhian persevered in his reign with a few supporters and managed to reform his court, but even now held little trust for the people around him. We had, of course, planned to delay our wedding after The Northern Invasion but not for the entire year and a half it took. When it did finally occur, Casmodia secured stronger relations with its Targian neighbour, but I knew some in Targe judged Queen Alexia Elryane for her quick forgiveness of a kingdom that had brought Targe to its knees and murdered her husband and child. They did not know what was going on inside, though, for she was, as her General Darj Ryder described to me in a letter, 'a master of hiding her heart behind her duty.'

Still, having not spent time with her since our wedding six months earlier, I longed to see her now and was disappointed when Lord Fenton of Egra, one of the men of her court, came down the palace stairs to greet us in her place.

'Her Majesty sends her deepest apologies,' he said, bowing to us. 'She is still holding court.'

'Of course,' Elhian said. 'We are two days earlier than we said we would be.'

'Yes, but come—I will take you to her.'

The criminal who knelt before the throne with a royal guard on either side of him seemed more afraid of her majesty's presence than his punishment. Lord Fenton told me the man had never seen her before, and even now he was only staring at the ground. The tall, warm throne room was filled with priests, nobles, councillors and courtiers, all judging him. A breeze shifted the long, green banners that hung from the ceiling with nobility, reminding us all that we were in the presence of royalty.

The criminal shook as a chancellor introduced his matter to the queen in a loud voice that echoed around the room. He bit his lip and lifted his gaze to the steps that were just ahead of him.

I saw the queen through his eyes. There was the long, burgundy gown that draped over the stairs, lavishly embroidered with gold thread. Resting on her knee was the jewelled sceptre she held as a symbol of her authority. The diamond necklace on her chest sparkled in the light with every breath. Long earrings embraced her beautiful but serious face, and her ebony hair fell over her shoulders, curling at the ends. The famous Targian crown with its twelve points was set on her head, heavy but grand. Finally, her startling blue eyes, full of calm confidence, were focused on him.

As he began to plead his case, speaking too fast to be coherent, Her Most Glorious Majesty Queen Alexia the First, my cousin, leaned to her right with an inherent coolness. She stared at the man with boredom and, with her spare hand, tapped her jewelled fingers over the armrest. I could see the criminal watching her nails arch and fall on the gold surface.

Elhian and I listened to the proceedings until we were distracted by something to our left. Two maids had appeared and seemed to be chasing something. That something was forcing the councillors to move out of the way, some of them uttering loud protests as they did so.

'I have heard it all before,' the queen said, interrupting the criminal's plea. 'The point is you have been found engaging in treasonous acts yet again, for which I can no longer show mercy. You will contemplate your actions in prison, so you may have some explanation to offer Ru'ach when you meet him.' She indicated with a wave for the guards to take him away.

It was only then that she, too, heard the commotion to her right. She turned to see some of the men near her in a fluster, stepping back. A small child ran between them.

'Mother!' the little girl called when she saw Alexia. 'Mother!'

I had to put a hand over my mouth to stop myself from laughing as the princess stumbled up the steps towards the queen. If Alexia was embarrassed, she was hiding it well, but I knew the maids responsible for the girl would be spoken to later. Princess Eva tripped on the stairs, but the queen gathered her up into her arms before she fell.

Eva snuggled into her neck. 'I found you, Mother.'

Alexia suppressed a smile, as I'm sure many others did, but before she could decide what to do with her daughter, the main door to the throne room opened, and we all turned.

General Darj stood in the doorway, clutching his arm. His shirt was covered in blood, and a group of men were behind him, looking back over their shoulders.

For more information about
Trudy Adams
&
The A'zyon Warrior
please visit:

www.trudyadams.squarespace.com
www.facebook.com/trudyadamsauthor

For more information about
AMBASSADOR INTERNATIONAL
please visit:

www.ambassador-international.com
@AmbassadorIntl
www.facebook.com/AmbassadorIntl

If you enjoyed this book, please consider leaving us a review on
Amazon, Goodreads, or our website.

More from Ambassador International

Dreaming of attending art school in London, gifted artist Beth Wilson paints masterpieces in the studio-attic of her home—but she's stuck in a rut. She paints the same theme over and over. If she doesn't come up with something new her art teacher will drop her. Solution: work for her Mimi and help her research the life of her fourth great-grandfather, Allen Hamilton.
Once Upon an Irish Summer
by Wendy Wilson Spooner

Abandoned as infants, Tovi and her twin brother were raised by an eclectic tribe of warm, kind people in a treehouse village in the valley. After her brother's sudden disappearance Tovi questions her life and her faith in an invisible King. Ignoring her best friend Silas' advice, she decides to search for her brother in the kingdom on top of the mountain.
Kingdom Above the Cloud
by Maggie Platt

Fred Thorne must keep his family together and surviving. After numerous tragedies, their only hope remains in the faraway land of Orden. So many perils lie in their path, along with so many surprises . . .
The Journey
by Verity A. Buchanan